GETAWAY

Out in the street with the helmet on her head, which was enough to induce claustrophobia itself, Polly experienced a sensation of complex fear unlike anything she'd ever really experienced before. When it came to it, she was frankly terrified at the thought of being on Ellen's motorcycle, and the feeling was not unlike the one she'd gone through moments before a minor operation she'd once had, that had entailed a general anaesthetic. It was a complete unknown. She simply could not imagine what it would be like to streak along the road, her safety and her very balance in the hands of a woman she hardly knew, and yet already held in awe.

And yet there was exhilaration about the prospect too. It was dangerous, but the pump of her heart made her feel high. High, and somehow desperately excited too. There was a sexual aspect to it, definitely, but also an intellectual peril ahead that only added to the sheen of eroticism.

As she buckled the helmet straps, under the supervision of Ellen, Polly finally and fully recognised the blend of feelings.

She'd felt like this just before she'd burnt her boats, handed in her notice and quit F&X to make her getaway.

GETAWAY

SUZANNE BLAYLOCK

First published in 1999 by
Sapphire
an imprint of Virgin Publishing Ltd
Thames Wharf Studios,
Rainville Road, London W6 9HA

ISBN 0 352 33443 6

Cover photograph by Laurence Jaugey-Paget

Typeset by SetSystems Ltd, Saffron Walden, Essex
Printed and bound in Great Britain by Mackays of Chatham PLC

CONTENTS

With heartfelt thanks to Redvane . . .
Behind every nethead there's a great computer guru!

ONE

Doing a Runner

'Doing a runner, isn't that what they call it? Running away from people and the consequences of one's actions . . .' Polly Sayers clicked the pause button on her Dictaphone, thought a moment, then let it record again: 'It's not like me, I know that. I'm not a wimp and I'm not a coward . . . But then again, I've never stolen anything before, have I? Even if it isn't really stealing . . . This is a whole new ball game, and I'm entitled to get a bit uptight, aren't I?' Pause . . . 'Oh God, this is all too heavy! I don't want to think about it . . . And I'm bloody well not going to!' Pause . . . 'Maybe in a little while. When I've got some perspective . . . Then I'll make a plan.'

The motorway stretched ahead like a black ribbon, scattered with jewels, and as she tossed the tiny recording device into the bucket seat beside her, all Polly really wanted in her head at that moment was some music. Switching on her stereo, she flinched at the immediate blast of sound, and the car twitched and swerved slightly in its lane. The music was cranked up far too loud for safety, really, but who cared? It was an escape, it took up mind-space, and she needed it. Safe behind her audio wall, she could temporarily banish her jabbering demons.

All except one, that was. That old devil hunger. It was hours

1

and hours since she'd eaten, and if she didn't take in some calories and some sugars soon she would faint, she could feel it coming. And if there ever was a good time to have a car crash, this wasn't it!

Muting the relentless but mannered voice of Mr Bryan Ferry, Polly decelerated off the motorway and prepared to face the world again – which to her was now a decidedly uncertain place.

Ah, the guilt of it, she thought, acknowledging the sticky truth that she'd been so steadfastly trying to avoid. Beginning the rationalisation process all over again, she cruised the pools of light in the car park, looking for a space. Why did she have to be so conventional in some ways, so old-fashioned? If it hadn't been for the guilt, this entire situation would have been a total blast.

But they ripped me off first, she told herself, feeling her jaw begin to ache with a familiar tension as she peered out amongst lines of hulking, sulking cars. Grinding her teeth when she was wound up was a terrible habit. They were the ones who never paid me what I'm worth, and never rated me . . . or gave me full credit for things. Spotting a possible space, she steered her small black car towards it. It was easy enough to talk herself on to the moral high ground where F&X Developments, her former employers, were concerned, she thought as she switched off the engine, and sat for a moment. But it was someone else, an individual, that she so wished she hadn't had to lie to.

She picked up the Dictaphone again.

'Which, of course, leads me to yet another home truth I'm trying not to analyse,' she muttered into the machine. 'Oh Jesus, this is making my head ache!' Clicking off the little gizmo, she flung it down. Sometimes she wondered why on earth she bothered with her personal journal, with all its angst-ridden meanderings, but whenever she tried to give up she always found herself missing it.

She looked around, taking stock of where she'd ended up. Her parking spot was in a shadowed area, some distance from a light source, therefore far from ideal, but there was nowhere else nearer to civilisation. At least she had a good car alarm system. If she hadn't had that, she would just have had to move on again. She'd screwed up far too much already to take risks with her precious equipment and her potentially valuable software.

The hardstanding underfoot was damp and it glistened beneath her soles as she walked round and round the car, double-checking everything before zapping the alarm on. There was a sort of skewness to the night itself somehow, which didn't do anything for her strung-out nerves, except exacerbate them. What was she going to do? She had no bloody idea, but at least her growling stomach was a distraction.

As she approached the service area, Polly caught sight of a woman beyond the glass doors and her heart did a flip and seemed to leap into her throat. The cropped blonde hair and tight dark clothing looked so familiar that she increased her pace, almost running on the shallow concrete ramp that led to the entrance. But then, almost as she reached the doors themselves, she did a double-think and skidded to a dead stop in her tracks.

What if it was *her*? Did Polly really dare see her again in the circumstances? Patricia Keyser was probably the very last person she ought to be talking to right now. Much less doing anything *else* with. High emotion had a dangerous way of making her babble.

Yet she owed Pat so much. Without Pat, she would probably have still been walking about with blinkers on, and she might have worn those miserable blinkers for a long, long time, if not for the rest of her life. It was Pat who'd really begun to make things happen.

And yet again, a question . . .

What *had* happened?

One morning, Polly had walked into the office – late, just when she didn't want to be – and found a bold, blonde, athletic-looking woman waiting for her at her desk, casually sipping a cup of coffee. Polly knew theoretically who the stranger was – the dreaded troubleshooter from the F&X mothership, across in America – but even that knowledge couldn't account for her reaction. She'd felt at a total loss for something to say, or to do, or even to feel, but in the final analysis, she'd simply and silently whispered, 'Wow!'

Wow?

Over a woman?

Acknowledging that 'wow' had been one of the most frightening things Polly had ever experienced – but not in a bad way, just an exciting and rather outlandish one. Shock of the new and all that, she supposed. Forward motion after what felt like centuries of inertia. It was no wonder she'd had the collywobbles, that weak, girlish feeling of butterflies in her stomach.

As if echoing those abdominal disturbances, Polly's gut growled and reminded her yet again that she was hungry. She'd been so desperately set on the idea of making this journey, once she'd decided to do it, that thoughts of simple day-to-day ordinary things like eating sensible meals had seemed irrelevant. In a self-induced state of exhilaration, she'd just piled everything of importance into the car and set the whole crazy cycle of events in motion. It had been mad, and it still was, but what did that matter now she'd gone over the precipice? She couldn't go back; she'd cut all her ties. Well, not quite, but that was just another variable, one of many, and not quite crucial enough to worry about yet.

Standing outside the service complex, still debating, Polly peered through the glass doors again, and saw that the blonde woman had turned, and was now clearly not Pat. Which was both a relief and a jag of disappointment. Polly was on her own again, facing everything alone like Ripley against the Aliens, until she achieved the dubious refuge of Chandler's Haven, her nominal destination unless she changed her mind again.

Suddenly a man jostled Polly, and she swung round and glared at him. He backed off, muttering an apology. Surprised by his almost cowed expression, Polly hurried on through the sliding doors, wondering just how fierce she'd looked to him. She'd never thought of herself as an Amazon warrior, but clearly the changes she was going through had had a visible effect on her. She couldn't remember ever making men cringe before.

Once inside, she paused surreptitiously in front of one of the many mirrored panels, so favoured by modern planners, and slyly studied herself. She didn't want to seem vain, but somehow she had to assess the image she now presented. It was brand new and sometimes she wasn't sure she liked it . . .

The leather jacket created most of the look. The black, butter-soft beauty that she couldn't really afford until her plans came to fruition, but which she'd bought anyway, what the hell!

It was a cool coat, a stylish coat. It made her look impressive in a way that bore no relation to the comparatively quiet persona she'd always projected at F&X Developments. There had been no dress code there, so theoretically she could have turned up in leather whenever she'd wanted – as Pat had done, that first day – but she'd never felt any desire to make an impact. Until now. Now, she loved this coat to bits and had hardly had it off her back since she'd devastated her credit card to get it.

Is this a symptom? Pondering, she touched her fingers to the surface of the leather as she stared at it in the glass. Is it a sign? Who chose this, the old me or the new me? Formerly she would have chosen something more innocuous, a soft blouson, maybe, with a bit of tooling and a trick collar. A curvy shape.

But this jacket wasn't a bit like that, and she was inordinately glad of it. This jacket was square-cut, designed like a crombie, strong and hard and workmanlike.

And it's so mannish, my dear, murmured a sly voice inside her, and she frowned.

Mannish? Dear God, is that what I've become? She paused, then strode to the ladies' room to look more closely at herself in a proper mirror.

Yes, the coat was architectural and tough – but the rest of her was still relatively tender. Her sweater was angora, powder pink and fluffy, and her jeans were a designer brand, cut to flatter. Her shoes, she supposed, were neutral. Simple black slip-ons, not particularly delicate, but not lumpish either. Certainly not a mission statement.

Pushing her fingers through her freshly trimmed hair, she

wondered if that was an indicator. OK, so she'd had it cut, but if she'd really been going to declare herself big-time, shouldn't she have had a crop? A razor cut? A number one? In reality this short, layered style made her appear even more female than she'd done with her previous look, a cutesy bob. Her dark red hair had a slight, natural wave, and that made the cut cling softly to her head like a glossy, gamin cap. Something like an early Audrey Hepburn, exquisitely womanly, but also an urchin-tomboy.

For crying out loud, stop analysing everything, will you, Poll, she told herself, returning to the washbasin to wash her hands after her pee, her inner debate still raging.

You look *good*, you idiot! You don't have to be in a category. The time for that comes when you know which one you want to be in. For now, just enjoy yourself. You deserve it, what with everything else you've got to contend with!

In the cafeteria, her new spirit of rule-breaking prompted her to select a foamy, choc-sprinkled cappuccino and a disgustingly enormous piece of fruit pie. It probably wouldn't taste nearly as good as it looked, but who cared! It was the principle of the thing. From now on she was going to follow her instincts, bad *and* good.

'One raspberry and apple pie. One cappuccino. That'll be –'

Oh, God! Oh shit!

Instantly sucked in by yet another, far stronger instinct, Polly didn't really listen to the price of her junk food. Blindly trawling through her pocket for money, she could only concentrate on the melodious sound of the words and the pale, shrimp-pink lips that had framed them.

The girl, the waitress tending the till, looked like a young Brigitte Bardot, but without the extreme, pneumatic pout. Something she was all the prettier for. As Polly fumbled with a ten-pound note, she reflected that the girl probably smiled that gutter-angel smile at every customer she served, barely even thinking about it. But to Polly's newly descaled eyes the other woman's expression appeared genuine and enticing. Full of delicious messages, and secret, coded promise.

'Keep the change!' Hard up as she temporarily was, Polly felt a renewed rush of exhilaration. How many more totally insane things was she going to do today?

The exhilaration changed in texture when the blonde murmured a low, sultry 'thanks' and placed the over-generous tip into a box marked 'gratuities'. She clearly wasn't French, but perhaps one didn't have to be to lay claim to the great Brigitte's allure?

Polly felt her knees go wobbly as she walked away towards the mundane refuge of a Formica-topped table and an over-stuffed corner banquette furnished in a lurid orange leatherette. As she sat down, only slopping a small amount of coffee into the saucer, she marvelled at her own intuition, at her own newly activated radar. Without even thinking about it she'd chosen an ideal vantage point for discreetly observing the object of her obsessions. The latest object . . .

'Brigitte's' uniform wasn't designed to do anyone any favours, but somehow the girl seemed to have the capability to turn an orange polyester overall – actually, the same goddamn colour as the upholstery! – into the very *ne plus ultra* of sleazy alternative chic. The horrid fabric skimmed over her trim figure with all the panache of something in silk by Galliano, and even the little white catering hat she wore looked as if it had been chosen by some clever, witty stylist. Polly wished that either the girl would rise from the stool on which she was sitting, or that she herself could stand up again and stare without attracting attention. Either way she longed to see what Brigitte's legs were like.

Long and slim, probably, the lucky bitch, ruminated Polly, observing the slenderness and grace of the blonde girl's hands and arms. If she were entirely in proportion, as Polly fervently believed she was, Brigitte would have fabulous pins that led to the heaven beneath her skirt.

With a wrench, Polly tore her eyes away from the direction of the till and applied herself to her sugary chunk of pie. Just recently, in between bouts of general paranoia, it had become quite a task to stop herself from fantasising all the time; having thoughts and dreams that were so delicious and dirty that she astonished herself with her own perfect 20/20 inner vision. It had never been like this in the old days. Before Pat. Back then she had occasionally daydreamed about sex, but it had always been a fuzzy and vaguely unsatisfactory experience. She'd had to force herself to paint the pictures somehow, and that had often defeated the object.

But now, with hindsight as flawless as her imagination's eye, she could see what the problem had been. What it'd always been. And now that she'd permitted herself to just go with it, and let her psyche do the directing – instead of her sense of what she thought she *ought* to be dreaming of – the fantasy process was effortless and arousing.

How easy it was to look up and see that Brigitte was smiling at her. To discover that, as if by magic, she and the young woman were on the same wavelength, and that there would be no need to go through the difficult dance of winkling her true feelings out of her.

Chewing a forkful of pie, Polly grimaced. It was just as gruesome as she'd expected it to be: cloyingly sweet and artificial-tasting. So much so that she felt an overwhelming urge to be rid of it, to spit it out. To reject it like so many things that no longer tasted quite right to her. Abandoning her plate, she left the cafeteria and returned to the sanctuary of the cloakroom, aware of her own motivation on a variety of different levels, and at the same time hoping and praying for the diversion that she now craved.

In front of the sink, she splashed cold water on to her wrists, to tamp down the fever that suddenly burned in her, then looked up into her own face again. Astonishingly she was pale, not blushing. Calm, not frazzled. Enigmatically appealing, not a total, transparently horny wreck. She touched her own eyebrows, and her lips, wondering for a moment if she were actually real. Then, glancing downwards, she sought a reference point of normality in the washbasin's water-slicked surface.

'Are you all right?' a voice asked, the simple syllables entirely

English, yet still infinitely exotic in their softness and intimacy. 'I saw you dash out of the cafeteria and I wondered if something was wrong. It wouldn't be the first time the rubbish we serve here had made someone ill.'

How in Christ's name had she managed to slink in here so soundlessly? So invisibly? Polly looked up again and saw that 'Brigitte' had materialised, at her side, and in her reflection.

'I'm fine,' she replied, mustering a smile but afraid that it wouldn't look right. 'There was nothing wrong with the food, it was just that I wasn't really all that hungry . . . I hadn't realised.' She licked her lips, tasting the syrupy sweetness that was no substitute for certain other flavours, then almost laughed out loud at how clichéd that little mannerism must seem. It might not even work with women . . . 'Well, not for raspberry and apple pie,' she finished, thinking, in for a penny, in for a pound.

'It *is* a bit sickly,' conceded Brigitte, touching the centre of her own, softly shaped lower lip with a tongue as brilliantly pink as the pie's fruit filling. 'It's not to my taste either . . .'

Polly's heart leapt. A sign from above! It must be! Her fingers prickled with indecision, as if the effort of choosing between reaching out and staying still were doing something to her minor blood vessels. She tried to imagine what Pat might have done in the same circumstances, but her brain seemed to have turned to mush. To sweet, raspberry and apple mush. She felt as if she were going to burst if she didn't do something soon; to faint; to pull a high camp, Edwardian swoon and expire. But it was just at that moment that Brigitte reached out. And saved her.

The blonde waitress said nothing, but her fingers, as they clasped Polly's, seemed to impart a very clear and unequivocal message. As they tightened, and began to pull, Polly followed.

In a moment more dreamlike than even the previous ones, she found herself inside one of the toilet cubicles with Brigitte, the small space, and the size of the pedestal, forcing them into closeness.

Brigitte didn't speak, and Polly didn't feel able to. But it didn't matter. The fluorescent lights smiled down from above them and

9

everything happened with a beguiling naturalness. Like a houri shedding a spangled shot silk robe, Brigitte the waitress unbuttoned her tangerine-coloured overall and let it slide to the floor. It seemed more natural than ever that she was naked beneath the work-dress, sporting no underwear to impede a lover's vision. Or to obstruct said lover's explorations. Knowing it was exactly what she wanted to do, Polly sank gratefully, but awkwardly, to the floor while Brigitte kicked off her shoes, put one slender foot up on to the loo seat – and revealed her sex.

Polly salivated as she had never done for her ersatz fruit pie and her creamy cup of coffee. A far choicer delicacy lay open to her now, something far juicier, far more succulent and more sought-after. About to plunge forward, she felt herself checked by Brigitte's hand on the crown of her head. She remained immobile; frozen; her eyes, nostrils and lips all enchanted and enthralled by the sounds and sights that assailed them.

Yet still the spirit of Bardot did not speak to her. Instead, she released Polly's head, then reached down between her own legs and began to manipulate herself. Burrowing through the lush hair – that was most definitely not the blonde of that on her head! – she opened herself out with the very tips of her fingers, so that Polly could have a perfect view of her quim.

Polly's jaw dropped. The pit of her stomach ached. The top of her head seemed about to explode. Brigitte was all liquid, all scarlet, all throbbing; a vision of blood-engorged fecundity. All life lay there between those thighs, those two lithe white columns that spread yet wider, and flexed, as Polly gaped in wonderment.

This is what you want, Poll. What you *are*. The elegant symmetry of her yearnings took her breath away. The sense of coming home to a place that had always been there, existing alongside her lifetime world, like Alice's looking-glass realm, chock-full of marvels.

Brigitte began to moan, but it didn't seem as if she was inciting Polly to act. The waitress, naked now, and glorious, seemed content to just be herself. Exhibited and aroused, she waved her slim hips, moving her sex from side to side, and gasping as she did so; as if the tautening and relaxing of the tendons in her thighs were creating a motion and a tension that caressed her.

It certainly had an effect on Polly. She could feel her own cunt engorging and growing heavy, a dribbling wetness gathering in tribute to that of Brigitte. She wanted to reach down and hold her crotch, to grip herself through the tough fabric of her jeans and rub the stitched seam against the swollen tip of her clitoris. She wanted to match Brigitte's rhythm with a swaying lust-dance of her own.

But she couldn't move. Her sex goddess had her paralysed. Worshipping. Yet completely happy. Her knees were aching from the hardness of the linoleum beneath her, and her quim was in an agony of desire. But she was, really and truly, happy.

Brigitte, her eyes closed, smiled too – as if she'd sensed the euphoria in Polly's helpless grin. Then a second later, she thrust forward her pelvis, bringing her nakedness and her sex into even greater prominence. Digging again between her thighs, she peeled back her labia like the folds of some rare aquatic creature, and revealed her slick and swollen clitoris to Polly's eyes.

With so few similar sights to call up memories of, Polly found it hard to make comparisons. Yet she knew that Brigitte's body was a superior creation. A living casket of flesh containing a precious gem of sensitivity and transcendence. Her clit, big, fat, luscious and velvety, was a pearl, a precious jewel to be savoured and slavered over.

'Let me taste you,' Polly murmured, astonished to hear her own voice. The confined space seemed to distort it somehow, and she sounded huskier, and older. A clothed Dietrich to the naked Bardot before her. It was a moment when she sensed that she should assert herself, but she didn't feel able to. It came as no surprise when Brigitte shook her head, her eyes still closed.

Polly could only watch as Brigitte flaunted her hips still further forward and, still holding herself open with one hand, began to stroke herself with the other. Her fingertips looked very white against the vermilion tints of her pudenda, and their movements were precise, yet swift and hungry. Half in a daze, Polly noticed that Brigitte sported an immaculately executed but brutally short French manicure – and the telling significance of such meticulousness made her laugh, despite her aching lust. She remembered words of wisdom that Pat had imparted to her, tales of activities that had made her eyes pop, just to think about them . . .

Still writhing, still stroking, her eyes still tight shut, Brigitte chuckled too, her voice soft with a delicious blend of joy and pleasure, her gorgeous body perfectly expressing those happy emotions. Her rounded breasts jiggled, a trickle of fresh sweat running between them, and the entire surface of her pale, faultless skin seemed to gleam with a soft aura of exultation. In that moment, Polly almost believed she could have died for her.

But then the moment was gone, and other baser, yet no less valid emotions took over. Impatient at being just the watcher, Polly shuffled around where she knelt, scrabbled at her jeans' fly and zipped it open. With a gasp of both relief and hunger she thrust her hand inside.

At the very instant that Polly's forefinger found its target, Brigitte's eyes snapped open. Their gazes locked and jousted, and Polly felt a rush of complicity. It was as if some unseen, but most decidedly female commandant had rapped out 'synchronise your watches, ladies!' and with a concerted will and an unrestrained enthusiasm, they both rushed towards orgasm.

One-handed, Brigitte clung to the toilet cistern, and Polly clung to Brigitte. In both of their slits, their fingers worked, moving swiftly and roughly. Polly had never had sex – any kind of sex – as urgently as this. It was instant. Animal. Sordid, almost. Yet even as she snarled and bucked and frigged herself, she was conscious of beauty. A conjunction of disparate elements had come together and produced a miracle. And even as she half-collapsed, her vagina clenching, she sent up a prayer of thanks. She heard Brigitte begin to whimper, and recognising the sound as her own feelings echoed, she looked up into those burning, stranger's eyes and saw the sweetest affirmation.

This was right. This was true. This was as wonderful and meaningful a sex act as the slowest and most reverent of conjugatons in bed were. With a groan of completion, Polly slumped backwards against the wall of the cubicle, her clitoris still pulsing. The last thing she remembered clearly was Brigitte's bare body folding gracefully over her.

'Are you all right?' a voice asked, the simple syllables alarmingly East London, yet still not unpleasant in their note of genuine concern.

Sitting at her table, Polly jerked awake. She realised to her horror that she'd been so lost in her little fantasy of 'Brigitte' in that ladies' room, that she'd closed her eyes, thrown back her head, and slumped against the back of the seat. To see the object of her obsessive little mind-theatre standing before her now, a worried look on the face that only seconds ago had been ecstatic, was a wrench in the fabric of reality. Polly felt disorientated.

'Yes . . . yes, thanks, I'm fine,' she muttered, unable to look 'Brigitte' in the eye now, as if what they'd just shared in her mind had actually happened. 'Just a bit tired. I think I'll go for a wander round outside before I hit the road again. I need some air.' Flashing the girl an edgy smile, she slithered out from the banquette and prepared to leave before she did anything else even more incriminating. She could only thank her lucky stars that she hadn't been caught with her hand between her legs too – she'd been so out of it that it wouldn't have surprised her at all if she'd unconsciously begun to rub herself.

Yet as she reached the door of the cafeteria, Polly felt compelled to turn around and see if 'Brigitte' was watching her.

Sure enough, just as Polly's gaze panned the till area, the girl glanced up from where she was punching in a price and their eyes engaged. An expression of collusion seemed to form on the waitress's face, although from the distance of the doorway, Polly found it hard to be certain whether this was anything more than just a simple trick of the imagination. Even so, it was enough to rekindle a jolt of stunning pleasure.

What the hell are you doing, Sayers, you idiot? You're a total stranger to her.

She must see a thousand women a day in here, Polly thought, so how can I be anything special? But even so she couldn't prevent herself from smiling when the blonde girl nodded, then also smiled, before returning to her task.

On the point of turning back to claim her trophy for real, Polly stopped, appalled by her own foolhardiness, and mentally shook herself. You've got enough complications on the go already, Poll. You've got to leave this.

Pushing open the cafeteria door, she felt the cool, welcome rush of the open air and, at the same time, she saw that a thin sliver of a moon had come out. Its baleful light was making the dark, greasy tops of the parked cars gleam in a way that was strangely reminiscent of the leather that clothed her.

She muttered, '*Au revoir*, Brigitte. *A bientôt!*' then shrugged and set off towards her car.

There seemed no diminution in the range of hazards and anxieties that lay before her, but somehow, as she walked, Polly felt a shuddering lift of her spirits. Maybe if she got the sex sorted, all the rest would follow too and the glittering prizes she so wanted would just tumble into her lap like the face of a beautiful sex-starved woman.

Zapping her alarm off she suddenly realised she was still aroused.

TWO

The Company of Women

In the curtained room the two women were naked. Ostensibly equals, they both presented bare bodies with the same degree of vulnerability, but as the interaction developed, it became nothing like equality.

'And how will you feel when she arrives?' asked the mistress, revelling in the reticent, almost shuttered, look in the eyes of the woman who was temporarily her slave. 'Will you desire her? Make advances to her? Attempt to corrupt her?'

'I will welcome her,' murmured the slave, pulling down the shutters entirely and fixing her gaze upon the wall beyond her.

The mistress smiled now the slave wasn't looking. Her companion had evasive skills that had not previously been apparent. Did the woman think she was being clever? Did she even think she was allowed to be clever? The mistress's rosy mouth thinned, but it was for form's sake only. Inside she continued to smile – and to anticipate.

'I ask again,' she said sharply. 'Will you attempt to make advances to our new friend? To touch her and discover her preferences?' Rising on to her knees, on the bed, she leant over and took the slave firmly by the chin, forcing their gazes to meet.

'Answer me honestly . . . You're already in quite enough trouble as it is.'

'Yes . . . yes, I w– will . . .' the slave stuttered, her spirits visibly quailing, even though a slight, aroused flush was beginning to rise in her. 'She's very pretty. Very sexy. I don't think I'll be able to stop myself coming on to her.'

'Ah, yes . . . The photographs,' said the mistress, her voice vague and musing, as if she were more concerned for the moment with the growing agitation in the woman who lay before her, than the promising possibilities in the images she referred to. 'I must admit that she does appear very appetising . . . But don't you think that it's presumptuous of you to lust after her?' She inclined over her prey, taking one of the other woman's nipples between her fingertips and rolling its revealing stiffness in a slow, contemplative action. 'Choice new morsels should, after all, be reserved for your betters, don't you think?' She pinched then, and the woman writhed. 'All that you're worthy of are the scraps from the tables of others.'

The mistress continued to nip, and to manipulate, aware of a reciprocal phantom sensation in the tips of her own breasts, but making certain she didn't show even a trace of reaction. It wouldn't do to reveal how easily her cool could be disturbed.

'You haven't answered,' she said quietly, tightening her grip and drawing out her victim's breasts like two cones of elongated flesh. They were fine titties too, lush and shapely, the best of all clays to mould with. 'You must answer, my dear . . . I require it of you. I demand it of you.' The words were strong, but her delivery was restrained. Cool. Cool. Cool. Think cool!

'Yes, I was wrong,' the slave replied, fighting audibly for control. The mistress knew that her companion relished this discomfort, even though it would never be her place – within this scene – to admit to that. 'I don't deserve her. I don't deserve the best. I should be punished . . . I should be denied . . . what I want.'

The tricky little minx, thought the mistress, having trouble suppressing her smile again. The slave was playing her own game here, trying to wangle herself a reason to be punished by saying she should be *denied* punishment. True retribution would be to abandon the scheming creature now, without the punitive action she obviously wanted so much.

To hell with it! Why deny *myself*, the mistress mused. Slinging a leg astride her slave's shapely thigh, she sank down, and at the same time drew the other woman's tits yet further up and out from her body. Circling them, she made her victim groan long and plaintively. Telling evidence that the agonising fun was shared . . .

'Now, tell me what you think you'd like to do to our beautiful new friend? Your filthiest fantasies . . . All the things you know you'll never be allowed to do.' Lowering her face, she let her teeth close momentarily over the hard stub on one tortured nipple, whilst rolling and twisting the other with fresh ferocity, 'And don't hold back!' she instructed, licking the place she'd hurt, then nipping it again. 'You know I can always tell when you're keeping things from me.'

And as the other woman began to talk and gasp and whimper, the mistress who cherished her began to nibble and pinch – and rock.

Polly pulled the car into the lay-by, on the little promontory that overlooked the bay, then flung open the door and almost threw herself out on to the grass verge. Her head was buzzing with images, just as it had been all along the motorway since she'd left the last services and 'Brigitte' . . .

It wasn't so much her fantasy of the blonde waitress that obsessed her though, as much as the greater whole – of which the one, hot scenario was just a facet.

I'm a lesbian, she thought, staring out to sea and finding the vastness of water a source of tranquillity. I'm a lesbian and there's no reason now not to admit it.

Watching two distant figures – female figures? – taking a walk on the small beach far below her, she wondered if it was owning up to the word itself that was the problem. 'I'm a lesbian,' she said quietly, but found the word neat and round and unalarming. Comfortable on the tongue as if it'd always been meant to be there.

And it wasn't as if it was something that was carved in stone either, she realised, looking out over the bay, and imagining the ever-changing nature of sea. The great mass of water might look immutable but, in a way, it had a lot in common with her sexuality. It was a limitless concept, constantly shifting and prone to currents.

She didn't hate men. She felt no real animosity towards them as a sex, in spite of the ages-old crimes committed in the name of patriarchy. Over the years, some of her best friends had been men, and she assumed that that would still continue to be the case. It was just that now, as a woman of thirty, it was women she wanted to be in love with. And to have sex with. If she could find some women who wanted to be in love with and have sex with her, that was.

She'd found Patricia, of course. Or been found by her. Pat was vivid, blonde and feisty and had seemed to see, in one glance, exactly what it was that Polly wanted. Before Polly herself had even known she wanted it. Oh God, what a shock it'd been that night when they'd been working late and Pat had come on to her!

There had been a sense of danger around already, of course. Pat had represented a major, palpable threat to Polly's plans; not only because the American woman was as sharp and clever with computers, in her own right, as Polly herself was, but also because Pat's very function within the company appeared to be to root out deception and employee fraud. There had been a lot of it about – I won't be the first, and I won't be the last, Polly thought – and every time Pat Keyser's eagle eye had fallen upon her, she'd felt so scared, and so nervous, that she'd almost wanted to wet herself! It was only on that night, when she and Pat had suddenly been alone together in the workroom, that Polly's fears had taken on a new and more urgent colour.

18

It'd been another 'wow' moment. And this time she'd understood why.

They'd been close, poring over a screen together, and suddenly, in a wave of some sharp, clean perfume that seemed as fresh and potent as if it had just been applied, Pat had leaned in towards her, kissed her on the cheek, and said, 'Let's take a break now.'

She kissed me! Polly had thought. She kissed me, and goddamnit I liked it!

And she *had* liked it. Especially when Pat had taken her face between her two long hands and kissed her again, this time making it a real, more comprehensive kiss.

The sensation of a tongue entering her mouth had been as pleasurable as it always was – but knowing it was a woman's tongue had added a whole new dimension. Made the act of kissing into a different activity altogether. The warm moist dart of Pat's tongue felt like a tiny living creature in Polly's mouth. Something menacing, yet tentative – and entirely irresistible. The temptation to suck on that tongue was irresistible too and Polly gave in to it, slobbering and suctioning messily. She moaned in her throat when Pat reached round and held her buttocks. A burning heat seemed to sear her through layers of fabric.

'I've been wanting to do that since I first set eyes on you,' said Pat, drawing her upper body away from Polly's yet still retaining her rude grip on Polly's bottom. 'But I didn't know whether you'd want me to . . .'

Polly wasn't quite sure how to answer. She hadn't known exactly what she'd wanted when she'd first seen Pat, but she'd certainly wanted something. Now it turned out that she'd wanted this kiss – and more. Gazing into the other woman's eyes, she found that not even the sight of her own lipstick smeared across Pat's face perturbed her. In fact, it seemed to add an animal sense of charm to features that already had a power. Pat herself wore no make-up at all, but neither did she need any. Her face was as beautiful and strong as an icon's; enhancement would only be superfluous.

'Oh, I did . . . I do,' said Polly, lifting a hand to rub at her own mouth and wipe away the offending lipstick.

Pat laughed, then released Polly's bottom and mirrored the action, drawing the back of her hand across her face like a cowboy wiping away the foam of a well-earned beer. It was a casual gesture, yet full of a bravado so unstudied that Polly felt quite faint with lust. Everything about Pat was sure and confident. She knew exactly who she was and what she wanted, and she made Polly feel like a nervous little girl who simpered and giggled because she couldn't keep a hold on her hormones.

'Shall we do something about it then?' Pat went on, smiling.

Polly glanced around the office.

'Not here, you ninny!' Pat's laughter was rich with amusement, but still kind. 'Let's go to my hotel. It's not too far away.'

Polly remembered little of the taxi ride, the only clear feeling being a sense of wickedness and fear of discovery when Pat held her hand and occasionally goosed her upper thigh. And when they reached the hotel room, she felt just as confused and disorientated.

What did women *do*?

Standing watching Pat, she felt sure the other woman could see her shaking. And it didn't help that Pat was calm, relaxed and smiling.

'Come here, you little idiot,' said the American woman, holding out her hand. Polly realised that she'd been hanging back from Pat, cowering, keeping her distance. 'I won't bite you . . . Unless you want me to, that is?'

'I . . . um . . .' Polly felt herself blushing at the image of Pat nipping her, delicately chewing on her nipples, then nuzzling lower and using her mouth on even more intimate places. 'I don't know what to do!' she blurted.

'Don't worry, girlfriend, I do!' Pat almost growled, closing the distance between them then branding Polly with their hottest kiss thus far.

The other woman's hands were everywhere, making Polly gasp under the onslaught of mashing lips and a marauding tongue. She felt her breasts being squeezed, her bottom fingered and palpated, her cunt being gripped with a graphic, vice-like force. The hold there was so strong that she was forced to rise up on her toes.

'What?' said Pat, her voice smeared by passion. 'Don't you like it?' But the words weren't a question because she continued to grind and massage.

'No! Yes! I . . . I don't know,' wailed Polly, aware that her face was crimson now and that her cunt was dripping wet.

'Of course you like it or you wouldn't be wet,' said Pat, removing her hand from its niche and lifting it to Polly's face. There was no visible moisture on her fingers but the smell that enveloped them was pungent. And Polly could feel the dampness in the crotch of her knickers and her trousers. She'd have to have this suit cleaned, she thought absently, before she ever wore it out in public again. She tried to turn away, sorely embarrassed by her own rampant yearnings.

'No, no, no, don't be shy, my little slut,' murmured Pat, coming close again, then – to Polly's astonishment – licking her own odoriferous fingers. 'You want it, don't you? Even if you don't quite know what it is yet.'

'Oh, I do! I do!' said Polly gratefully. She felt weak and swayed against Pat, wanting her strength as much as her sensuality.

'Let's get you stripped, then,' said Pat, her voice brisk, her body flirting away to deny Polly the support she so needed.

Confused, Polly made as if to shrug off her jacket in preparation. If she was keen and obedient, Pat would be pleased with her. She'd let her stay. It suddenly seemed of life or death importance that everything should go right. If tonight went wrong, the implications, in a million ways, were unthinkable. God alone knew how the wrath of an insulted or disappointed lover might be channelled. I might end up in court, or even in prison, thought Polly, shaking as the outside world of what she intended to do broke through into the inner sexual zone . . .

Pat took hold of Polly's wrist and held it tight. Any minute now, she'll say 'gotcha!' thought Polly, and the game will be up.

But all the other woman said was, 'Keep still. You're my little present. It's my job to do the unwrapping.'

Polly stood still. Continued to shake. Watched the expression on Pat's face move through phases. Delighted. Almost gloating. Then softer . . . Compassionate. Affectionate. Loving.

With meticulousness and grace, Pat began to undress Polly. First she took off the sharp-cut jacket and laid it over an adjacent chair, then she followed it with Polly's formerly crisp, but now crumpled and sweaty blouse. Looking down and seeing her plain and serviceable white chain-store bra, Polly wished she'd had the wit, or the prescience, to wear something more alluring. The brassière was so uninspiring – not ugly, but just a garment that served a purpose rather than informed a fantasy. She felt an intense desire to put her hand up and cover not her own flesh, but the fabric slung around it.

'Yes, it is a bit ordinary, isn't it?' observed Pat as if she'd heard Polly's inner maundering. 'Shall we get rid of it? I mean *really* get rid of it?' She smiled again, the wicked, wicked grin that Polly was becoming more and more enslaved to. 'You don't need it anyway . . . Your titties are fabulous!' To prove her point, she took hold of Polly's breasts again and handled them in a vigorous circling motion through the plain, unworthy brassière.

For a few moments, completely out of it, Polly forgot about what she'd done, and what she was wearing and just flew on the sensation of being mauled and massaged. Ley lines of pleasure seemed to be singing throughout her body, connecting every critical point. Her nipples, her navel, her clit – even her anus. Forgetting her every preconception about sexual response and so-called ladylike behaviour, she writhed where she stood, running her hands over her still-clothed thighs, bottom and crotch. Her hands moved in counterpoint to Pat's, stroking and squeezing her flesh as Pat woman-handled her breasts. Frustrated, Polly wished that she was already completely stripped, and that there were yet more hands available to her. She wanted her every erotic place probed and fingered all at once.

'Jesus, you're a hot little thing,' whispered Pat, sliding closer, releasing Polly's tits and pressing their pelvises together. For a moment or two they gyrated in sync, then Pat, clearly increasingly impatient, stepped back and as good as tore at Polly's charcoal grey, tailored trousers.

'Yes! Little slut!' the American growled, not allowing Polly to shed her shoes and step out of her slacks, but just letting the dark cloth pool around her ankles. 'Oh yes! I was so right about you!'

Through a daze of lust that seemed so thick and mind-warping she could hardly breathe, Polly watched as her companion slipped a hand into the pocket of her own leather trousers, then brought out – oh dear God! – a small, silver penknife.

As Pat snapped open the knife, its slim blade glittered. Light seemed to rebound off it, even though the room was dim. Polly felt her jaw drop; she experienced real fear. Yet even as a cool hand gripped her heart, a red hot one seemed to slide between her legs and slick at her. No, it wasn't a hand! It was a warm, silky tongue lapping at her clitoris. The sensation was so tangible that she groaned and edged ever nearer to orgasm.

'Stand still, sweetheart,' said Pat, raising her tiny weapon. Then, with neat, economical strokes, she began to slice away Polly's white bra and pants.

Lozenges of cotton–lycra blend fluttered to the carpet, little flags of total surrender. In a few moments, she was naked, save for the hobble of her trousers round her ankles, and as Pat stepped back and studied her, she tried again to free herself of that.

'Oh no you don't!' said Pat, darting forward again, flinging aside the knife as she did so. Taking Polly's chin between her fingers, she steered their mouths together and inflicted another stringent kiss, her tongue digging deep and jabbing repeatedly.

Oh Jesus Christ, she's fucking me, thought Polly faintly, experiencing the thrust of Pat's tongue as it was evidently, so patently, intended. Is this how she'll do it . . . down there? Is this what lesbians do? Or will she use her fingers on me? Or . . . or a thing?

Polly swayed again, realising that her body was sagging, almost hanging from the other woman's finger and thumb grip on her chin. Her knees were gaping, and her cunt was opening. She could actually feel the trickle of her own juices beginning to crawl down her bare inner thigh.

And still her lover's tongue was raping her. She could feel her jaw begin to ache as her mouth was forced wide open. She was being sucked on, consumed, laid open by the simple expedient of a kiss. It made her nipples harden to stones of need, and her sex begin to drool, lubricating more heavily than it had ever done for the male of the species.

Oh God, I must have it! I must have it now! Whatever it is, I've got to do it and I've got to come!

'Please,' she rasped, her voice hoarse, as Pat released her lips at last. 'Please, I –'

'Please what?' demanded Pat, her face harsh yet smiling as, quick as a wink, she caught both Polly's wrists in one of her hands, and held them behind Polly's back.

Polly felt as if her tongue was glued to her palate. She could not speak. Sweat was trickling now too, pungent hormonal sweat that she knew Pat would easily be able to smell. She knew she could not articulate the words for some reason, not ask – specifically – for an orgasm.

'You have to ask for it, you know,' purred Pat, the great Marvo, the mind-reader. 'You have to say the word – or you won't get it.'

'I can't!' Polly said, the words tiny. Tinny.

'You must!' replied Pat, the fingertips of her free hand moving just centimetres from Polly's aching nipples. The American woman was a magician now, and a dark one, making arcane passes over the body of her acolyte.

A sound issued from Polly's throat. A raw, feral groan. She thrust forward her pelvis again, shimmying her hips like a belly dancer, pleading with her naked crotch for what she still couldn't beg for in words.

'Ask!' commanded Pat again.

'Please! I – I need to come,' croaked Polly, feeling crimson blood rushing into her face and neck again, the shame an aphrodisiac that made her cunt ache with a real, hard pain.

'That's better!' cried Pat with a genuine sound of delight.

With a swift, rough movement the American half pushed, half lowered Polly to the carpet, making her naked, hindered body sprawl on the carpet, still hog-tied by her crumpled trousers. With a growl of irritation, Pat wrenched away the offending items of clothing and left Polly bare of everything save her black suede high heels.

'Now, slut, hold yourself open for me,' the older woman said, her strong face triumphant. 'Show me what you've got, baby . . . Go on, girl! Show me all of it!'

Again, Polly hesitated. The room was still partially lit, and she was exposed enough already.

'Show me your cunt now, Polly, or get your clothes and go.' Pat's voice was low and controlled, almost icy, even though her eyes were still filled with sparks and fire.

Trying not to whimper, Polly complied. She reached down, put the flat of her palms on her inner thighs, and drew them apart. As she did so, it seemed natural to tilt her pelvis, to lift herself and make her most intimate parts more accessible.

'Good girl,' encouraged Pat, coming down on to her haunches, close up against Polly's exhibited crotch. 'But I want more . . . Hold your cunt-lips open. I want to see everything . . . Your clit. Your holes. The entire shooting match.' She almost seemed to smack her lips with relish. 'Come on, baby. Give it up for Mama!'

'Oh yes!' cried Polly, her voice echoing into the clear night with a volume that sent it flying out across the vastness of the bay. She dropped back into the real, now version of her body as if she were in a lift out of control, and felt the jolt almost physically in her fingers, her toes, her thighs and in her heavy, bloated crotch. Looking around herself frantically, she panned her gaze down to the beach, terrified that the women below had heard her.

But they were long gone now, and as she realised that, Polly felt a sense of loss. Both for her intimacy with Pat, and in a more diffuse way for her contact with the couple who'd been below her, on the sand. They probably hadn't been aware of her presence, but they had shared the night with her. While they'd been down there, strolling on the beach, there had been certain 'possibilities'. The women had been available for inclusion in fantasies, possibly as replacements, if that were conceivable, for Pat Keyser.

Now, however, the idea of the two women was too vague. She had not looked closely enough to distinguish their faces, the colour of their hair, the shape of their bodies and the style of their clothing. Polly felt yet another drift of ennui, and of doubt and fear, and the feeling combined and seemed to suck her into them like an under-swell in the sea below.

'No! Goddamnit! No!' she cried aloud. She would not give in to it. She had risked everything. Love. Future. Freedom. She had to proceed with a purpose. Make a way ahead, all for herself, with her skills and what she'd created with them. And she'd find love too, or whatever the closest viable alternative to that was, either with some individual woman or with the gender en masse.

Squaring her shoulders, and drawing strength from the leather that enclosed them, Polly turned from the sea and strode back to her vehicle.

Ten minutes later, after coasting around the headland and starting her descent towards her destination, Polly was tempted to stop the car again and get out.

Below her, huddled around the inlet, was Chandler's Haven, the secluded coastal resort where her friend Inez Parker lived; intriguing Inez who had offered Polly sanctuary exactly when she needed it.

'What a bloody peculiar place,' murmured Polly, slowing down to try and take in what she was seeing. Bigger than a village, but a bit on the miniature side for a town, Chandler's Haven looked like no English rural hideaway that Polly had ever seen before. It looked like a small, dark city somehow, a displaced environment from another world entirely. Someone's mad idea of building a sort of potted, low-rise, neo-fifties Manhattan on the English south coast, for no other reason than purely their own amusement.

'You weren't kidding, Inez,' Polly went on, subconsciously disquieted that she couldn't seem to stop talking to herself since her flight from London, even when the Dictaphone wasn't handy.

The older woman had spoken of her hometown being a little 'unusual' and Polly could see now that was far from an understatement. Her spirits lifted as she accelerated, eager to arrive.

It didn't take her long to reach the centre of Chandler's Haven, and the more she saw of the place, the weirder and more out of place it seemed to her. The various residences were dour, blocky and decidedly urban, set out like town houses, and mostly made of a weathered brown stone that, with their front steps and porches, only added to their New York City ambience.

This is quite, quite mad, thought Polly as she drew from her memory the precise details of Inez's address, and from baser, more instinctual areas, some more attractive particulars – the older woman's appearance.

As she scanned the house names, looking for the one she was seeking, Polly tried to remember when she'd first been introduced to Inez Parker. It had been at some family bash, maybe for Christmas or a birthday, when Polly had been quite young, but although the image was clear, she couldn't pinpoint the actual date of it. She just seemed to always have known Inez. And always admired her for her poise and sophistication at the various events they'd both attended.

Polly couldn't ever remember actually talking to Inez all that much in those days. Inez was older and had seemed to hang with a far more soigné group than Polly had – but their eyes had often met. I used to watch her, Polly admitted now, realising how much her true colours must already have been showing. To everyone but herself . . .

Had Inez known? Even then? Was that why she had now offered her home to Polly as a refuge? As a haven, Polly thought with a grin, thinking of the off-beat locality she was driving through. If that was the case, it could well mean that Inez was a lesbian herself. Which meant in turn that the days ahead would be interesting to say the very least.

Deep in her musings, Polly almost drove past her goal. Ash House, a good-sized, solidly built home that wouldn't have looked out of place on Park Avenue, had it been scaled up a bit. It stood back from the road, fronted by a handkerchief of neatly tended but unfussy garden, and over the porch an exterior light burned beckoningly and illuminated the steps.

Well, why wouldn't it beckon? She did invite me here, thought Polly as she parked the car beneath a conveniently placed street lamp. Once more, she felt deeply leery about leaving what was locked in her boot – her laptops, her personal organiser, and her portable storage drives and media – but she could hardly pitch up to the front door lugging armfuls of hardware. Inez knew nothing about what Polly notionally thought of as her crimes; the invitation had been purely social.

But had it really? Been social?

Still noodling over the complications of her life, Polly pressed the doorbell, and as she waited she reassessed Inez Parker's invitation.

They'd met in Polly's favourite art gallery, the Tate, where she'd gone one day to escape and think during the last days of her planning. It'd been purely a chance encounter, but when Polly had casually mentioned she wanted to get out of London for a spell, Inez had immediately asked her to come and stay. Which was weird, considering how little they'd ever really said to each other before. But Inez had been insistent and Polly needy, so she'd agreed.

Through the frosted glass panel beside the door, Polly at last saw a sign of movement. A slender figure, dark clad, striding purposefully towards the door. Inez, recognisably, even through the obscuring glass. She had that quick, light way of walking that Polly hadn't really thought about until now, but suddenly found unexpectedly provocative. Half hidden behind a fold of her leather coat, she crossed her fingers, as her heart and certain other organs, seemed to leap.

Then the door swung open to reveal an elegant, familiar figure.

'Hello, Polly,' murmured Inez Parker, her smile warm, yet tantalising and complex.

Game on! Polly thought, framing a smile of her own.

THREE
Miss Parker's House

'Hello, Inez, how are you,' answered Polly, aware of the stilted quality of her words, yet helpless in the grip of feeling flustered. She'd never had this sensation with Inez before, so to experience it now was both alarming and strangely sensual.

It was as if she was seeing the woman through a brand new pair of eyes, Polly thought. Or seeing a brand new woman through the *same* eyes. There was an air about Inez that she couldn't recall ever sensing whenever they'd met before. A discrete excitement that seemed to meet and mate with her own perturbation, something that happened in an instant, with no time lag and no build–up.

'Do come in, Polly,' said Inez and, like a nervous schoolgirl, Polly followed her inside.

Well, not perhaps a schoolgirl . . . Did schoolgirls look at older women and notice the sweet compact roundness of their buttocks beneath their skirts? Inez was wearing a strangely formal suit for the time of night; a fact which made Polly even more uneasy, as it dawned on her it must be after midnight. Quite a bit after midnight in fact.

'I'm – I'm sorry to be so late,' Polly said, as Inez stood back, ever the perfect mannered one, and ushered Polly from the

30

narrow, white-painted hall into a much more spacious room, that was also creamy-white.

New York chic, thought Polly, following on from her notions of Chandler's Haven's transatlanticisms. 'The journey took far longer than I expected. I'd hoped to be here hours ago . . . I hope you didn't prepare a meal or anything? I feel awfully guilty.'

Inez spun around unexpectedly, making Polly's heart bobble again. She caught another flash of that differentness about Inez tonight, a sort of sleek, compressed energy that was well hidden but which seemed to border on mania. The older woman had something on her mind, that was for sure. And it didn't appear to be anything to do with the unexpectedly late arrival of her guest.

'Guilty?' she said, smiling and moving forward to stand disturbingly close. 'Oh, don't worry about that, Polly. I'd prepared cold cuts anyway . . . The motorways are murder. Things happen . . . One has to be prepared for anything around here.' Her smile crinkled, went crooked, and she suddenly looked younger and a little mischievous. 'Sit down. Make yourself at home and all that.' She gestured towards a capacious but stylish sofa upholstered in tobacco-coloured suede. 'Would you like a drink? Tea or coffee? Just give yourself a minute, then we'll see about your luggage.'

'Yes. Um . . . Wine if you have some open,' muttered Polly, taking the offered seat, and feeling more and more wrong-footed with every second that passed. What had Inez meant by 'prepared for anything round here'? Was this a general thing, or was this the overture to a pass already? Good God, she'd only been through the door less than a minute.

Inez nodded, then sashayed smoothly across to the sideboard, where a bottle of white wine stood in a cooler, uncorked, but with only a tiny amount already consumed. As the older woman set up a glass and poured the straw-coloured liquid with a neat, deft economy, Polly took the chance of a few moments to observe her.

Inez had always been beautiful, always elegant, always composed. And as it had done as long as Polly had known her, her hair hung in a silky, almost unnaturally smooth bob, parted in the middle, just flicking her shoulders. It seemed to float, perfectly controlled, over the fine grey cloth of the immaculately tailored jacket she wore, light as thistledown, yet thick and bright with vigour.

And she's wearing full make-up too, thought Polly as Inez approached her. It's well after midnight and she's done up to the nines as if she's going to a high-powered business meeting. Killer lipstick, power suit, fuck-me shoes . . .

Indeed, Inez's turnout was as faultless as it seemed bizarrely ill-timed. It looked as if she had painted her lips that sharp red shade only a few seconds ago, and a sudden instinct told Polly that this was actually the case. She got a lightning, out of the blue, flash of intuition that Inez's perfection was at this moment a reconstituted thing. That not so long ago, she'd been *déshabillé*, abandoned, mussed and lewd.

'Thank you,' she said, taking the drink from Inez and fighting to keep her voice level and normal in the face of such a wild, uncalled-for supposition. 'I need this!' she added with forced cheerfulness as if the welcome cool of the glass she now held could settle her system. Taking a sip, she found the wine to be a lifesaver: strong, lively on the tongue, dry yet fruity, not too challenging.

Inez neither poured herself a drink, nor sat down, and again Polly got a strong impression of agitation beneath her friend's polished exterior. The sense that the cool, immaculate Ms Freeze had very recently been writhing and perspiring in the throes of sex.

And not only that . . .

Any minute now she's going to tell me that she's got to leave, thought Polly, swigging down the good wine a lot faster than she should and only just avoiding making herself cough.

'Look, Polly, I know you'll think this is terrible of me, but would you mind if I went out for a while? It's – it's something I really can't get out of.'

The accuracy of her own premonition was what saved Polly from really spluttering this time. Although she supposed she shouldn't really have been surprised, given Inez's clothing, and the strange expectancy and urgency of her manner.

'Oh no, it's fine! Don't worry about me,' Polly said quickly, taking another long, swift pull at her wine. 'I'm tired anyway. I wouldn't want to keep you up. Well, if you were staying in . . . But you're not, so it doesn't matter . . . Really.'

Inez gave another of her complicated twitchy smiles. 'Are you sure? I'm being a terrible hostess . . .' She let the apology linger a moment. 'You will let me help you bring your stuff in first, won't you?'

At the mention of her belongings, Polly experienced a pang of alarm. Jesus Christ! What am I thinking, she silently berated herself as she leapt to her feet, almost spilling her wine. Here she was, yattering away, lusting – be honest, Poll! – after a woman who had been a respected family friend for more years than she cared to remember, and outside was a collection of the most crucial computer software she'd ever handled, much less written. Not to mention her hardware too. It all amounted to a precious hoard of electronic treasure that would make a computer-savvy felon rub his thieving hands with glee. In a quiet, suburban street under less than adequate lighting, her car was even more likely to be burgled than it had been in the motorway services car park. Not that anyone at F&X knew what she'd made her sudden getaway with . . . Did they? She'd tried to cover her tracks, but in a world of ever-changing variables and fortunes easily made and lost, you never could tell.

'Oh no, please don't trouble yourself,' she continued as she and Inez went out into the hall again. 'It's you who's doing me a huge favour, Inez, by putting me up. I'm really grateful. Just show me where I sleep, then I'll get my things and sort myself out. You just get off to your meeting or whatever it is.'

Despite Polly's protests, Inez did help her though, showing a surprising facility for carrying heavy loads whilst dressed in a corporate-killer suit and high heels. She seemed curious, too, at the amount of computer paraphernalia Polly had brought with her.

I wonder if she isn't asking me questions so I won't ask her any, thought Polly, setting one of her three laptops down on the bed, in the airy and surprisingly large bedroom, while Inez lugged in a digital-tape, back-up module, with two lockable plastic storage boxes full of media balanced on top of it.

That could be it, Polly mused on, watching Inez relinquish her burdens, and inadvertently expose a good deal of glossy finely hosed thigh as she bent down over the bed to arrange the various items. It's downright strange to be going out, dressed like that, at – Polly glanced at the neat, black-faced bedside clock and saw that it was 1.00 a.m. – this hour. I don't know how she can expect me not to be curious.

Exhibiting a remarkable ability to read minds, Inez said, 'You must think it's rather peculiar of me to be going out at this time?' Straightening up, she smoothed the lapels of her jacket, then her abbreviated skirt in a way that made Polly, newly sensitised to such gestures, feel weak and hot.

Trying to offset her discomfiture, Polly said, 'It's your business, Inez . . . and not my place to pry.' She gave a shrug that she hoped looked louche and knowing.

Inez's expression reflected her own. Studiedly unconcerned, but with an edge. Only in Inez's case the edge was of slight amusement.

'We'll talk tomorrow, Polly,' she said, hesitating a second, then immediately and visibly rousing herself for purposeful action. 'But believe me, this's nothing sinister . . .' She ran her fingers lightly over her crisp lapels. 'It's just that people around here tend to keep eccentric hours. At least the ones who're my friends do . . .'

For a long time after Inez had gone, Polly mused on what she'd said, and on these 'friends who kept eccentric hours'.

Inez had given Polly a quick tour of the essentials – bathroom, kitchen, security arrangements – and then encouraged her to make herself completely at home. By the time Polly was in the kitchen, making herself a snack, her imagination was hurtling.

Polly hadn't really thought much about her friend's life since she'd made her decision to come here, but now she found it strange that someone who was an artist should be such a night owl. Shouldn't Inez be a day person, making the most of natural light? But then again, Polly knew even less about Inez's art than she did her day-to-day life. Perhaps there were examples she could study, scattered about the house?

Taking her glass of wine – more of the same she'd consumed earlier – and a plate of crackers smeared with an unctuously creamy full fat cheese, Polly padded through to the sitting room. She'd taken off her coat and her shoes, but that was as far as she'd got before she'd realised she was ravenously hungry again. Somewhere in the back of her mind, she seemed to remember not finishing her pie . . .

Inez's sitting room was as cool and calm and elegant as its owner was. Understated, yet alive with a hidden persona, it was lit by several large, modern table lamps. The pale wooden furniture and the cream-washed walls had a decidedly 'butter wouldn't melt' quality to them, as if they'd looked down on, and been the scene of, a degree of debauchery that was at odds with their mild, pacific aura.

'Or maybe that's just me,' muttered Polly, settling on the sofa and placing her glass and plate on a low glass-topped table before her. There was a pile of magazines lying there too, and she munched her crackers as she studied them, one by one, in the lamplight.

The first few were innocuous enough. One or two of the glossier women's monthlies, an entertainments review, a couple of art journals. But beneath them lay surprises of many colours . . .

Inez had several computer magazines amongst her selection. Most were middlebrow, aimed at the reasonably experienced amateur user, but there was one, *Pro Code*, that was much more of a professional entity. It was a journal to which Polly herself had sometimes contributed, and she couldn't begin to imagine what a person like Inez was doing with it. Feeling suddenly threatened again, Polly flung it aside, as if it might harm her. For the moment, she really didn't relish being reminded of what she'd done.

The last magazine, at the bottom of the pile, was both a surprise and almost exactly what a part of her had expected. It was called *L'Enclave*, and on its cover was a naked woman.

'Gotcha, Inez,' said Polly to herself, abandoning her food and wine in the face of a different form of nourishment. The feeding of an appetite that was becoming more and more consuming even despite her uncertain situation.

L'Enclave was not some scurrilous sex rag. It was clearly a lesbian magazine, but not the kind of prettified, distorted lesbianism that was often paraded purely to titillate men. It was a piece of art and literary magic that women had clearly made for themselves, and themselves alone.

The nude on the cover was a drawing. What looked like a fine colour pencil in a deep burgundy tone, done on a creamy background. It showed a woman posing before a mirror, standing with one foot up on a stool so that her long slim thighs were flexed and parted. She was touching herself, and the echo of 'Brigitte' in Polly's motorway restaurant daydream was astonishing.

Polly swallowed. Studied both the drawing and the inner mental image. Caught the crest of a huge wave rising inside her, the flow of desire that had been swelling since she'd begun her journey here. 'Oh, baby . . .' she whispered dreamily, not sure whether it was the masturbating nymph in the drawing she was addressing, or enigmatic Inez, or even Pat, who she still missed passionately. On the other hand, maybe it was an 'everywoman' she wanted, as the drawing suggested, or perhaps just a fantasy like the archetypal 'Brigitte'? The only certainty was that her cunt was already weeping. And she had not yet even opened the magazine.

Touching her fingertip to the paper, she felt a reluctance to move on from the young woman in the image. She wanted to stay with her, do what she was doing, feel what she was feeling.

Almost without thinking, Polly began to struggle with her button and her zip.

Still studying the positioning of the drawn woman's limbs, fingers and genitalia, Polly pulled down her jeans and panties until they were a tangled bundle of fabric around her ankles. There was something outrageous about sitting exposed in such an elegant room; something quite delicious about pressing her naked bottom against the rough suede surface of the sofa . . .

Oh God, what if I stain it? The sudden thought sparkled like a glass shard in the amorphous haze of Polly's growing desire, but so great was her compulsion that her brain neatly offered a solution. In a couple of seconds she'd whipped her angora top off over her head, bundled it up, and placed it beneath her. Her appearance now, she realised, was even more lewd than before. She was tantamount to naked, wearing nothing more than a thin, soft bra, and she was grateful that the light from the lamps was muted.

Turning again to the image of the woman, which now seemed to look less like Brigitte, and more like some new, but as yet unknown paramour, Polly craned over, momentarily, to see more clearly.

Incredible as it seemed, the artist had managed an amazing degree of verisimilitude with just the medium of a wine-coloured pencil. Though they were only tiny, the curls and crinkles of the woman's inner labia were indicated in loving detail, and even the gleam of copious moisture was apparent, as was the impression of engorgement. The clitoris was like a gemstone set in a complicated setting, a prominent feature which the woman's fingertip was lightly caressing. Polly doubted if she could effect such a degree of precision in her contact with her own body. She was now so horny that all her fingers seemed like thumbs.

But still she tried. Emulating the pictured masturbatrix, she set her forefinger lightly on the very tip of her clit. Then moaned at the shocking intensity of the stimulation. How long had she been waiting for this, and needing it, she wondered, patting the tiny organ with only the most gossamer-like of touches and yet still seeing her bare thighs jerk in a galvanic reaction. She withdrew her hand in order that she might be able to think for a moment.

There had been no sex since Pat, she realised, not even any real self-pleasure, such as she was indulging in now. Her thoughts had been full of the immediate realities of her decision to leave F&X, and serious as those had been they'd been of the mind not the body. She'd subsumed the inevitable loss of Pat to those plans and schemes, and even sidelined the realisation of her sexuality. It was only as the actual journey had begun that the pull of her cunt had reasserted itself.

'Goddamnit!' she hissed, impatient with what she'd realised. She reached down between her legs and almost scared herself so hard did she lash at her clitoris. Pounding the tiny hot bead, she jerked her pelvis, her torso, her shoulders, wriggling and bucking on the makeshift cushion of her jumper, then stiffening, arching and screaming in another almost electrified contortion as the so-longed-for climax ripped through the quick of her. It was like being open-legged, facing an avalanche of stars.

What seemed like an hour later, but in actual fact was probably only a moment or two, Polly lifted her sweating and suddenly aching body from the sofa back, and once again leant over the magazine, and the image that had inspired her recent orgasm.

The drawing looked just as beautiful, but was defused now, merely something to admire in a detached and peaceful way. It was a representation, she saw now, of a blonde woman, quite young and athletically feminine, with high breasts, long legs, and classical features.

Someone I'd rather like to know, thought Polly, dragging her jumper from beneath her, and still looking at the front of the magazine as she reached down to pull up her knickers. As she leant even closer to it, she noticed something about the cover illustration that she'd not seen before.

In the corner were a tiny set of initials. The artist's signature.

'I.P.'

Inez Parker.

Inez had drawn it. She had illustrated this women's sex

magazine. And as Polly flicked through the pages, she saw a lot more of what was clearly her older friend's work. All drawings of women, all of them stunningly good, but clearly executed in a variety of different media.

Returning to the cover, Polly recognised its subject now – but only from other images of the same woman inside the journal. She wondered how many of the other models were also intimate with her hostess.

'All friends of yours, Inez?' she asked, setting the magazine aside and continuing with her dressing. 'I do hope so.'

Her heart seemed to shudder at the prospect of meeting such a gallery of muses.

Probably due to the lateness and the strangeness of her night, it was almost afternoon by the time Polly woke up the next day. Last night it had been gone three when she'd finally managed to drag herself through a quick shower and into bed, and she'd been so tired that for the first time in a long time she hadn't even made an entry in her journal.

Not that it had only been weariness that made her resist recording her thoughts. She'd felt strangely inhibited about making an account of her own masturbation, and even more reluctant to cast the light of analysis across her suspicions regarding *Pro Code*. And as she'd finally drifted off into the hinterland of sleep, she suddenly realised that Inez was still missing . . .

This morning, however, when Polly arrived downstairs and found that the kitchen table had been re-set for two, she knew for certain that her hostess had come back some time within the intervening period – and been mindful of her guest.

Please forgive me again, said the note that had been left for her, propped up against the butter dish, *if I'm not up in time to prepare your breakfast. I'll be sleeping in. Help yourself to anything you like. There are cereals, croissants, all the usual . . . and eggs and bacon in the fridge if you want something cooked. We'll talk properly later. Love, Inez.*

Breakfast?

Polly looked at the clock. Lunch would probably be closer to the mark . . . And yet she suddenly had an almighty craving for scrambled eggs. And for toast and marmalade. And for lashings and lashings of hot, strong tea.

'Something normal,' she said quietly to herself, opening the fridge and finding most of the things she needed there. 'Something mundane. Something that's nice, and self-indulgent, and nothing to do with lesbians or computers or people mysteriously disappearing for hours on end!'

For a while it was possible to achieve normality. Making toast; beating eggs; melting butter . . . But as she looked out of the kitchen window, on to a day that was somehow unsurprisingly cold, grey and slightly drizzly, Polly's new and disruptive cogitations reasserted themselves.

Had she jumped out of the frying pan into the fire here, she thought, wryly eyeing the expensive heavy bottomed Circulon pan she was cooking her eggs in. She'd thought she'd be out of sight here, difficult to find, yet perhaps London would have been a better place to disappear in after all?

Initially, Inez had seemed the perfect person to hide out with, but now it seemed that the older woman offered threats and challenges in herself, ones that only added to Polly's existing preoccupations. Setting aside the question of whether Inez was likely to make a pass at her, Polly considered the reasons why her friend – an artist, and seemingly the last person one would expect to be interested in technology – would have a highly specialised computer journal lying about on her coffee table. One that Polly realised, in retrospect, had a feature article on the very type of software she was currently, and clandestinely, developing.

It's as if she knows *exactly* what I'm up to, thought Polly, taking the eggs off the heat before they became rubbery. And that she also knows it's far more threatening just to imply the fact rather than confront me.

Polly ate her breakfast more quickly than she'd intended to, her mind a mélange of 'whys' and 'hows' and 'what ifs', and when she'd finished and washed her dishes, she quit the kitchen.

She felt oppressed by the need for action, the desire to do something that would at least clear up some of the many questions that were beginning to bug her. The view from the kitchen window, out on to a small, immaculately neat, but now somewhat rain-sodden garden was not inspiring. She wondered if the aspect from the lounge, which by rights should feature the road leading down towards the centre of the town and the bay, would be more enlightening.

As Inez had still not surfaced and total silence ruled in the pale, but somehow also menacingly shadowy sitting room, Polly felt it was safe to investigate the magazines again, and see if there were others amongst them that could offer more clues to the gathering mysteries.

Polly flicked through the pile. Then went through them again. Once. Twice. Three times.

Pro Code had vanished.

'But it was here!' Polly whispered to herself, flicking open the pages of other magazines, to see if the one she sought had accidentally become tucked inside one of them. But there was no sign of it, and she couldn't believe she'd just imagined it.

Now that other one – *L'Enclave* – now that was the sort of thing one might dream up in a horny, slightly inebriated daze . . . but nothing so prosaic and, to most people, boring, as a professional computer journal.

Casting her gaze around the room, Polly wondered if somehow, in the aftermath of her masturbatory shenanigans of the previous night, she might have moved the magazine and not remembered doing so. She noticed a bulging magazine rack standing beside one of the easy chairs, and she was just about to investigate it when another stray thought assailed her. Flicking through the mags on the coffee table she discovered no *L'Enclave* amongst them either . . .

'This is weird,' she muttered, looking again for the risqué publication that had triggered the need, and supplied the inspiration, for her glut of solitary pleasure. But it wasn't there, so she moved across the magazine rack and tipped its contents out on to the carpet.

The magazines had definitely been in this room, on the coffee table last night, but now they were nowhere to be seen. Polly knew that her memory wasn't fooling her. In fact, her recollections were exquisitely clear, the echo of the pleasure she'd given herself, and the beauty that had provoked it, still reverberating through her, strangely strengthened by a kind of extremely short-term nostalgia. Someone had removed those magazines, and that someone could only be Inez.

'Looking for something?'

As if the thought could summon the person, Polly looked up and found her hostess had entered the room and was watching her as she scrabbled amongst the slippery pile of glossy paper.

'I . . . er, yes! Yes, I am,' said Polly, grabbing up the disorder and returning it to the magazine rack. 'I was glancing through a computer magazine last night while I was having a bite of supper . . . and I just wanted to have another look at an article that was in it.' She straightened up, and stepped away from the evidence of her search, trying all the time not to stare too blatantly at Inez.

The older woman was not dressed – even though Polly knew that by now it must be gone three in the afternoon. Inez wore a full, almost modestly cut wrapper of navy-blue silk, which suited her beautifully and made her unpainted face look luminous. Either that, or her bloom had another more earthy source . . .

'I'm sure it's around here somewhere,' she said, advancing towards Polly, the silk swishing around her legs as she approached. 'I bought a computer not long ago. I've been experimenting with graphic design, self-publishing . . . one or two things . . . and not being very technically minded I find magazines very helpful.' As she reached the magazine rack, she sank down gracefully and sat beside it.

'Yes . . . Some of them are very good,' said Polly hesitantly. Somehow she'd assumed Inez would be evasive and deny all knowledge of the magazine, and this simple helpfulness was as perplexing as it was unexpected. And the fact that Inez was clearly naked beneath her long dark gown didn't help matters either.

I never realised how beautiful she was before, thought Polly, feeling distracted as Inez leafed methodically through the contents of the rack. Polly had always considered the older woman good-looking whenever she'd met her, but she'd experienced it in a detached way, not with this sudden, visceral tug.

She could see the long curve of Inez's spine as the other woman bent to her task, the line of bumps, her vertebrae, clearly defined through the heavy, moulding silk. The sight of this was somehow deeply sexual, an image of both strength and vulner-ability, and Polly wanted to run her fingers down those bones, then kiss each one of them tenderly. She was just about to bend over and begin the process, when Inez straightened up.

'Here, maybe one of these is the one you want,' she said pleasantly, holding out a wedge of three magazines.

Polly took them, and said, 'Thanks. Yes . . . I'm sure it'll be amongst them.' She was lying through her teeth, as she'd seen all these and they were much more elementary stuff, even if worthy.

'You have a look,' said Inez pleasantly, giving Polly the impression of being fully aware of the deception. 'I'll make some coffee. Would you like some? Or would you prefer tea?' She was already walking towards the door, every step seeming strangely exultant as if she were enjoying a game – and winning it.

'Coffee would be lovely,' answered Polly. She gripped the magazines excessively tightly; her hands were shaking.

Oh God, on top of everything else, I *do* fancy her! Polly thought, when Inez had left the room in a swish of heavy satin, and a flash of long slim leg. The missing magazines suddenly didn't seem quite as important, as threatening somehow. Inez might well have bought *Pro Code* by mistake, and just thrown it out, when she'd arrived home, because it was no good to her.

That's all bollocks, girl, Polly told herself, and you know it. And it doesn't even account for *L'Enclave* disappearing either. Her explanations were ludicrous, yet somehow she felt unable to latch on to them for analysis. She threw aside the unwanted magazines and began to prowl around the room.

This morning, she noticed more of Inez's artwork on the walls. Small, discreet sketches in unassuming frames were hung in low-key locations, offering no indication of artistic ego. But they were all of women in various stages of undress, and some were conceptual images of classic female icons. Marilyn Monroe. Marlene Dietrich. Catherine Deneuve. The drawings showed these women how Inez, presumably, had always dreamed of encountering them. In attitudes of languor, and of desire, prepared for sex.

Yes, and sex with Inez herself, thought Polly, feeling the stirrings primed by her hostess gain new momentum. The image of Deneuve she found particularly tantalising. The face was cool, and the body like marble, but the eyes were hot. It was lust controlled, yet possessing an added power for it. There was a quality about the drawing that reminded Polly keenly of Pat.

Don't go down that road, she warned herself. Patricia Keyser was a closed book for her now, completely off limits. Pat both knew too much about Polly's sphere of computer expertise, and had wielded too much power over her when the two of them had been together.

'Do you like Deneuve?' enquired Inez from the doorway. Polly was glad it was the older woman who was carrying the coffee tray, and not herself, because the suddenness of Inez's return had made her quite jump out of her skin.

'Yes, I do,' replied Polly, gathering herself as she took a place beside Inez on the sofa. 'She's a subtle actress and, of course, she's extraordinarily beautiful.'

For a moment, Inez did not reply, but simply concentrated on pouring the coffee. Polly noticed that she was not asked how she took it. Inez simply prepared it correctly – with milk, no sugar – without prompting.

When did I tell her that? Polly thought, taking the proffered cup. It must have been at some family thing, but I really can't remember.

'Do you admire beauty in a woman?' enquired Inez, pausing to take a sip of her coffee, then very daintily licking the curve of her lower lip. 'Some women are a bit inhibited about admitting to it. I suppose they're scared that people will think they're strange.'

Was this the question then? Was this the challenge to declare herself, Polly wondered.

But when she looked closer into Inez's eyes, all her doubts were dispelled.

She saw a reflection of all the fire that she'd seen in the drawings . . .

FOUR

Layers of Encryption

This time it was Polly's turn not to answer straight away. She drank some coffee, barely even noticing its heat and its dark, velvety deliciousness, while her head whirled with possible responses to Inez's gambit.

'Yes,' she said at length, aware that though she didn't show it, she'd taken a great mental breath, 'I do admire beauty in a woman. Why shouldn't I? I'm not ashamed of the fact.'

Inez smiled. Not so much the sultry, knowing smirk that Polly had half expected, but more a happy open grin of unmasked pleasure. Polly felt her own heart lighten and suddenly she tasted the coffee's good flavour.

'Excellent,' replied Inez. 'That's a start, at least.' She crossed her long, beautiful legs and the silk panels of her robe slid a little further open. Nothing was revealed, though, apart from more of one pale and slender thigh.

Expecting clarification, Polly was taken aback again, however, when Inez launched suddenly into a description of her current art projects: how she was illustrating a book on relationships; and also engaged in a mass commission to draw all her local friends. She seemed particularly fired up by the latter, and somehow Polly wasn't surprised when not a single man was mentioned. Inez's entire clique was female, it seemed, and from the way she spoke, Polly had no doubt now that some of them were her lovers . . .

'I'm sure you'll meet them all very soon,' said Inez, pouring herself more coffee, then enquiring by gesture whether Polly wanted any.

Polly shook her head.

'That is if you want to, of course,' Inez went on, looking more flirtatious now, but still light-hearted. 'If you prefer to keep yourself to yourself and work, well, that's quite all right by me. I lead a very busy life myself, to be perfectly honest.'

Polly felt herself blushing. She felt painfully gauche, pinned right to the spot, and unable to articulate, or even decide, exactly what she wanted. To hide away here and finish the final refinements to the code on her new program had been her original intention. But suddenly, new vistas were opening ahead, and she wanted to be in them.

'Well, I do have some work to do . . . But I don't want to be antisocial . . . or ungrateful . . .' She thought of all that she owed Inez at the moment, for providing this haven, and realised that there were ways she could thank her hostess that didn't involve money. 'Because I am grateful!' she hurried on, putting down her coffee cup and feeling more confused than ever. She felt herself driven and compelled to act by a deep and rushing force. 'I mean I can pay my keep, or do housework . . . I don't know . . . Maybe I can even help you with your computer or something?'

Inez laughed softly. 'Don't worry, Polly. You don't owe me a thing,' she said, smiling slowly over the rim of her cup. 'It's my pleasure to have you here. I just want you to feel at home and not left out when I'm busy with – with things.'

The little hesitation seemed to say quite a lot, but in a language that Polly had as yet only a pidgin knowledge of. She wasn't at all used to this woman to woman flirtation, and she wasn't even quite sure she could do it right. Her time with Pat had been far too brief and far too focused on interaction between just the two of them. All she really knew right now was that Inez wasn't talking about artistic projects alone.

'Let's just take things gradually, shall we?' Inez went on pleasantly, her voice perfectly assured as if her revealing little verbal bobble had never occurred. 'Just spend a few days settling in and doing what you have to do. Then I'll start introducing you to my friends . . . I just *know* they'll love you!'

'Inez says her friends will love me. I wonder if that means literally?' muttered Polly into the Dictaphone later, when – unsurprisingly – she found herself alone again.

It was evening, and while Inez was in her studio, working on some urgent but unspecified commission, Polly had taken the opportunity to finally get to grips with her own project. Sanspareil, a revolutionary, multifunctional software program that she hoped was going to blow all similar, competing products out of the cyber water – and possibly make her a tidy fortune into the bargain.

The trouble was that even though she had the necessary peace and quiet, and all her carefully assembled resources at her disposal, she simply could not force herself to concentrate. Even an unexpectedly comfortable chair and table at which to work didn't make any difference. The lines of code that were usually almost like friends to her seemed to dance before her eyes and turn into squiggles that made no sense. Every function that had always been so elegant, and made her gloat, almost, at her own phenomenal cleverness, now seemed nonsensical. It was almost as if the mental program that allowed her to do what she did had become corrupted.

Pushing herself away from the screen, Polly rubbed her eyes with the heels of her hand and made a new and more lurid troupe of squiggles dance in her vision. It seemed impossible to focus on the job in hand, feeling as she felt.

Her cerebration was under attack from two quarters, she realised wearily, stretching now, and attempting to ease kinks from her back, torso, and pelvis, which she knew were not entirely due to fatigue. One onslaught was pleasant, but scary, and the other deeply disquieting and potentially disastrous.

The first was sex, of course. The fact that she wanted it; and she wanted it with women; and that she'd decided that she specifically wanted it with Inez – although she still didn't know how to suggest that.

The other was the implications of the project that lay before her, and certain fears, certain heebie-jeebies she was beginning to feel about it. When she'd first conceived what she'd thought of as her grand and daring scheme she'd been completely convinced she could pull it off, and supremely confident of her own skills, both technical and evasive.

But now paranoia was setting in. Some basis of that had been there already, it was in her nature, but the rapid escalation had come about when she'd seen that copy of *Pro Code*. That and other things, like Inez's new computer . . .

Polly had been astonished to see the machine that her hostess claimed to have recently purchased, despite knowing nothing about computing. Inez's PC had the latest chip, far more than the decreed industry standard amount of memory, and a humungous hard disk. What did Inez need such a monster for, if she wasn't a tech-head? Admittedly, if she intended to do complicated graphics, she did need a considerable degree of processing power, but even so, it seemed an enormous outlay for someone who was only a beginner. And she'd been so vague, too, about its actual purchase.

Someone in the town had advised her . . . She'd seen it in a catalogue . . . The salesperson had persuaded her . . .

When Polly had taken a closer look at the machine, she'd discovered its general configuration was extraordinarily sophisticated. Whoever had set this up had been an accomplished, long-time computer geek. Polly would have liked a closer look, but Inez had been in a hurry to shut it down.

'And this stupid place doesn't help, either,' added Polly into the miniature tape recorder. 'It's either a misplaced film set or the town planner was a loony!'

While Inez had made dinner, Polly had taken a stroll around

the town and found that the atmosphere of Chandler's Haven itself made her uneasy.

It was a downright peculiar little place, moody and artificial-seeming, its sense of oppression heightened by the gloomy, glowering weather. The gleam of the rain on the pavements, and on the mainly sombre, self-contained dark-hued buildings seemed to eat the light rather than increase its luminescence. Not many people were on the streets. Presumably everyone was inside, watching television or preparing meals – or perhaps engaged in rather less mundane pursuits, Polly thought wryly – and though those that were about smiled at her, the strongest impression she received was one of suspicion and watchfulness.

When a middle-aged man had bade her a pleasant good evening, her mind seemed to substitute an accusation of perfidy.

Oh, yes, we know what you've done . . . You're a thief . . . You're a criminal . . . You wrote that program in your company's time. *They* own it.

In the end, Polly had been glad when she could return and sit down to eat.

Dinner was innocuous enough. Inez had cooked a light but tasty chicken casserole, and as Polly was hungry, she enjoyed the flavours and tried to forget her qualms and quibbles. The television burbling quietly in the corner of the room was helpful, and for once there seemed no undercurrents, no shadowplay.

But now, alone with her laptop, Polly felt the full return of all her doubts and fears.

You'll never get away with this. You *have* done something wrong. You're under surveillance.

And . . .

You're a raving lesbian. No woman will want you. You'll never meet Pat again.

'Oh fuck this!' she cursed, having scrolled back and noticed a painfully obvious error in her work. A slip up in her code that would mean the whole shooting match – her precious 'baby' that she'd designed to do the work of several different programs at once in a way that nobody else seemed to have thought of before

– was doomed to crash. 'Time to pack it in for the night,' she muttered to herself, then began the careful process of saving, encrypting and backing up her work, making doubly sure that no one, not even the most canny of computer nerds, could understand what she was doing. She would have liked to test the program tonight, try some of its search capabilities on the Web, but she knew that in this state, she'd make some stupid security error, and the program's integrity might be compromised.

Yet she felt regret as she locked away the laptop she'd been working on, and the high capacity disks, in the bottom drawer of the sturdy dresser in the corner of her room. Inez had no strong box, so Polly had decided that this would have to do as a primitive form of safe. Asking her hostess pointed questions about secure storage in the house would only arouse suspicion, and Polly already felt that Inez would soon become curious.

'Now then, to log on or not to log on, that is the question,' said Polly, taking up the Dictaphone again to help her make her mind up. 'Am I really going to drive myself crazy trying to surf on a mobile connection, or am I just going to be reasonably sensible and see if there's anything interesting on the mailing lists?' She snapped the off button and laid the little machine aside.

Polly hated not being in touch with the Web, and all its various temptations, but she knew she had to be careful at the moment. So, flipping open the other laptop she had with her, she logged on via her mobile phone and one of the several free Internet accounts she'd set up for herself. These were all anonymous connections made using the usual crafty tricks involved to conceal one's electronic location, along with a few special twists of her own for added good measure.

First of all, Polly attempted to access some of her favourite industry information sites, to scan for any late-breaking news in her own area of software expertise, but pretty soon she was cursing with frustration at the pathetic download speed. After checking out what she considered the most crucial source, and finding nothing there to worry her – not even the tiniest breath of wind that anyone else was working on anything remotely like

Sanspareil – she reluctantly abandoned her surf and wondered if she dare open her e-mail and news program instead.

Clicking, she supposed there was no harm in checking out one or two newsgroups and downloading from the small selection of mailing lists she'd clandestinely subscribed to as an additional means of keeping abreast of critical developments. With her safety precautions, there was no way anyone could trace her.

Again, there was nothing in any way alarming, but nothing that particularly excited her either. She was just about to log off, when she decided to try one last 'send and receive' . . . and though she hadn't expected it an additional message began to download.

Polly blinked. And blinked again. There was nothing in the 'from' window but a string of gobbledegook – which was unusual, but probably just somebody else's way of retaining anonymity – yet the subject line instantly leapt out at her and made her shiver. It was just a single, yet now very strangely familiar word.

Enclave.

'What the b–' whispered Polly as she read the rudimentary message beneath.

'To subscribe, type "subscribe Enclave" in the body of the message and hit "return".'

Don't do this, Poll, she instructed herself, wise in the ways of the Internet and knowing this was probably just one of a zillion scams and spams and get-rich-quick schemes. And yet surely the cryptic name 'Enclave' couldn't be just a coincidence?

Almost as if she were acting on a compulsion that had bypassed her higher reasoning functions, she had typed 'subscribe' before she knew it, and had the pointer over the button, her forefinger poised.

'Don't do it, Poll!' she pleaded, vocally this time, already feeling the weight of the possible consequences dancing heavily on her fingertip.

Then, all of a sudden, a loud scuffling sound, coming from outside, through the open window, made her hand jerk and the mouse-button depress, as if of its own volition. The 'sending' flashed, but was gone before Polly could wake up and click to cancel . . .

Oh fuck! she mimed, quickly logging off as soon as the send had cleared, then moving to the window.

Some sixth or seventh sense made Polly hang back and conceal herself behind the curtain as she looked out. An instinct she was immediately grateful for, because what she saw outside was intriguing and mysterious . . .

There was a young woman out there, shinning up one of the drainpipes, like a trapeze artist up a rope. Even as Polly watched, the climber reached one of the other open upstairs windows, then leant across, clinging on by what looked the most precarious of holds, and boosted herself inside.

For the second time in the space of a few minutes, Polly wondered if she was imagining things. First the e-mail message, and now this! Who on earth was that agile, acrobatic creature and, more to the point, what was she doing climbing into what Polly now realised was Inez's bedroom window?

But then again, if Inez were indeed a lesbian, why wouldn't she have gorgeous women flinging themselves in through her bedroom window? Especially if she had 'company' and she was still trying to keep her preferences a secret?

Polly came away from the window and went to her door, straining every ounce of concentration in her efforts to try and hear something. After a second, she eased the door open, relieved that its hinges were well oiled. Out on the landing she could detect the faintest sound of voices and, feeling guilty, she padded forwards. The door to Inez's room was standing slightly but tantalisingly ajar . . .

As she approached the gap, engaging her nearest approximation of a cat burglar, Polly re-ran the extraordinary inner film clip, the rapid sequence of the athletic woman's climb.

Inez's visitor was blonde, slim and, as far as Polly had been able to tell in the relative darkness, extremely beautiful. She was also slightly familiar, and though at first Polly couldn't place her, after a second or two she knew where she'd seen her before.

Bloody 'Enclave' again!

The woman who'd just shinned up the drainpipe, it dawned on Polly, was the same one who'd posed for the drawing on the cover of the missing magazine. She was wearing her hair differently – on the cover it had been loose, now it was in a surprisingly pristine French pleat – but it was definitely her, the masturbatrix.

At Inez's bedroom door, Polly felt as if she was tiptoeing over glass. She edged forward, a centimetre at a time, until she could see into the room but hopefully not be seen herself. To her surprise, and her guilty delight, the view was excellent.

Inez was lying on her bed, wearing the same dark blue silk wrap as this morning, and she appeared to be doodling a little sketch on an artist's drawing pad. The newcomer – who Polly now saw was wearing a pair of tomboyish dungarees, in a sludgy, military brown, but not much else – was standing by the window looking strangely ill at ease for someone whose entry had been so daring. She was smiling though, in fact she had a wicked look on her lovely, fine-featured face, but there was an air of diffuse discomfort about her posture.

'So, what's it to be tonight?' enquired Inez, laying her drawing pad and pencil on the bedside table and eyeing her visitor with what was clearly a look of hunger. 'Or rather, should I say "who"? Me or you?'

'Oh, you, definitely you,' said the blonde, looking for a moment as if she might faint with a matching desire. Then, to Polly's astonishment, she reached quickly down, cupped her brown-clad crotch, and gave herself a squeeze. As her fingers flexed, a breathy gasp escaped her lips . . .

Inez laughed and rose from the bed, advancing on the blonde as the other woman began to sway and softly moan. 'You're a dirty little girl, Severn O'Neill,' she said as she reached her, placing her own hand over her companion's still gripping fingers. 'You want to piss, don't you, you slut? Your bladder's full to bursting and it's making you so horny that you've got to rub yourself.'

Polly bit down hard on her own hand to stop herself from crying out. She could hardly believe what she'd just heard, or that it was the refined and ever ladylike Inez who'd said it. Oh, she knew the older woman was no angel, but she'd never known her use any kind of crude or off-colour language – the sort of words that sounded a hundred times coarser and more earthy in such a cut-glass, well-educated accent. Polly didn't know whom she now found more exciting: the unexpectedly forthright Inez or the embarrassingly beleaguered Severn? Certainly together they were a duo to stir the coolest blood. Oppressor and oppressed. Yin and Yang. Power and submission.

Polly knew how they felt. Well, how Severn felt . . . And she felt it right now, as her own bladder felt suddenly full.

'Describe how you feel!' ordered Inez again, and Polly herself felt almost compelled to speak.

'I want to pee . . . I need to hold myself . . . It hurts!' whimpered Severn, her voice sounding more girlish than Polly imagined it normally did. The young woman was pulling a face too, scrunching up her eyes, behaving like a baby. Even as Polly watched, she began to wriggle in a feigned attempt to break Inez's grip.

'I think I've wee-ed myself. My panties are getting wet,' the blonde girl went on sulkily. 'They feel all soggy.'

'Nonsense! That's just because you're horny!' said Inez, giving Severn's pussy another cruel squeeze.

The younger woman yelped and made a horrid, helpless gobbling sound, her brown eyes wide and bugging. 'I can't . . . Oh God, I can't . . .' she softly groaned.

'Oh yes, you can. Whatever it is,' replied Inez, turning away from her prey with an exultant grin on her face. 'And what's more you're going to do it for a little while yet.'

Polly saw Severn bite her full, beautifully pouting lower lip. Her expression was petulant but there was elation in her eyes.

She loves this, thought Polly, reaching down surreptitiously to cup her own crotch. Even the lightest touch seemed to bear down ponderously on her bladder. She tried another squeeze and felt a sensation like a hot yet icy dart.

Do I like it though? It was a tantalising question . . . Pressing again, and harder this time, Polly felt her clitoris quicken. She pursed her lips and fought once more the urge to shout.

'I want to wee,' muttered Severn again, sounding as if she'd reverted almost completely to childhood. 'Please let me wee, Mummy. It feels so horrid when I do it in my pants.' She was standing in the centre of the room now, one hand still clutching herself, and with the other twisting and fiddling at one of the fastenings of her dungarees.

'Well, in that case, you won't have to do it in your pants, will you?' Inez sounded thoroughly gleeful as she crossed to the sideboard. 'Although I have to say I'm sure that's all theoretical. I have a sneaking suspicion that you're not even wearing knickers, are you, Severn?'

Severn looked down at the carpet, her performance as a woeful, recalcitrant child a masterful piece of theatre. 'I . . . I can't remember,' she muttered, still squirming and tugging at her buttons. 'Might be . . .'

'Well, we'll check in a moment, but first there's something I want you to do for me,' said Inez, businesslike and, as she turned away from the sideboard, Polly could see what she was holding.

It was a tall glass, full of water, with ice cubes bobbing.

'No! Oh, noooo!' keened Severn, visibly grinding at her vulva. In the shadows, Polly helplessly aped the action and massaged her bladder.

'Oh yes, young lady!' said Inez firmly. 'You know how good this is for you, don't you? Don't you want to keep your system flushed? Keep that beautiful complexion?' She advanced towards the undulating Severn, her face set in lines that suggested a determined but well-meaning nanny. 'You really ought to drink at least a couple of glasses right now, to keep up your quota.'

To Polly's astonishment, she saw teardrops begin to well in Severn's eyes, and she continued to watch as they trickled slowly down the blonde girl's creamy cheeks. Severn was either a supremely competent actress or she'd thrown herself so far into her childlike role that she really did feel lachrymose.

'Must I?' she begged.

'Yes, you must,' replied Inez, dragging the girl's reluctant fingers away from her crotch and making her take the glass in both her hands. 'But if you behave yourself and drink it down, I'll do something nice.'

Reluctantly, and blinking away her tears, Severn put the glass to her lips. Her hips were still waving slightly as she slowly began to drink.

Oh God, that icy water! Polly's own bladder began to ache anew in sympathy. She could feel the onerous pressure re-doubling inside her just at the thought of all that liquid. And yet a maverick urge inside her made her wish she were Severn.

Especially when she saw Inez slide a hand inside the blonde girl's dungarees and begin to knead and pummel at one full breast. It looked like an animal, small and devilish, moving beneath the fabric. After a second, Severn spluttered and some water got spilt.

'Come on. Settle down and swallow it,' instructed Inez, her fingers stilling in their hidey-hole. 'You've got another full glass like this one to drink when you've done.'

Severn's eyes widened, looking both ecstatic and imploring. It was clear to Polly that the beautiful woman was almost soaring aloft on the delicious agony she must be feeling in the pit of her belly – but surely she couldn't endure a trial like this much longer. Polly could not begin to imagine how it would feel to tackle that second glass of water.

When the first glass was empty, with just the ice cubes rattling around in it as Severn trembled, Inez removed her hand from inside the younger woman's bodice. 'Very good, my sweet,' she murmured, then kissed Severn's lips. Polly saw Severn sag at the knees as her wet mouth was pillaged; and even when Inez withdrew and moved away, the blonde stood as if shell-shocked. Her posture was an ugly, splay-thighed crouch, yet she looked quite lovely.

'I should like you to be naked while you drink this,' said Inez, returning.

In her hiding place, Polly could no longer prevent herself from reaching down into her jeans to caress herself. The thought of seeing the magnificent Severn in all her bare glory, was just far too much for her.

With docility, but a great degree of obvious discomfort, Severn slipped out of her shoes, then her dungarees. She was indeed wearing not a stitch beneath the rough, utilitarian garment, and the body that was consequently exposed looked perfect to Polly.

The blonde girl's breasts were high and large, and almost stereotypically conical; but something about Severn's freshness and the delicacy of her nipples made her far from a cliché. She had a tiny waist, long slim legs, and a thick bush of glistening golden hair between her thighs, but the most provocative sight at that moment was her swollen little belly. The grotesque amount of fluid she'd been forced to swallow seemed to have pushed it out into a taut and prominent curve. It looked almost like an early stage of pregnancy, but the surest of instincts told Polly that was certainly not the case.

Inez clearly shared Polly's predilections. 'So pretty . . .' she murmured, running her fingers over Severn's bloated abdomen. When they reached the blonde girl's bush they appeared to press, and Severn groaned.

Polly groaned too, but inwardly. She could empathise with the sensations, even though her own need to pee wasn't really all that urgent. It was just a tweak to add spice to her sexual excitement, while Severn's state was clearly more parlous by far. Polly tried to imagine how long the blonde girl had been holding her waters, then wondered if it was a deliberate act. She pictured Severn drinking – tea, coffee, water, or whatever – and again and again resisting her natural urges. Again and again feeling the pressure, and the dark excitement, hike up and up.

The other woman was squatting now, her body shaking and swaying, her peerless skin clearly sheened with the copious sweat of pure strain. Or maybe on her thighs, the moisture was already more than perspiration? If it wasn't yet her piss it might well be sexual juices. She was tossing her head now, in a frantic state of torment.

'Now, my sweet,' murmured Inez, who seemed to Polly like a beautiful demon, remorseless and downright cruel, 'you must drink this,' she said, approaching Severn with the second glass of water. Fresh ice cubes seemed to chink in a rhythm of impending martyrdom.

'I can't!' wailed Severn.

'Yes, you can!' insisted Inez. 'And stand up straight. Behave like a grown-up . . . You must drink or I'll be extremely disappointed in you!'

Severn stiffened her spine, obeying Inez mutely, yet somehow assuming the mantle of a princess. Even in this most agonising of states, the young blonde woman was magnificent. Her belly was bulging with piss, yet she suddenly seemed inviolate. And Polly could see as much awe in Inez's face as she knew she would have exhibited herself.

Then, as Inez put the glass to Severn's lips and the young woman began to drink, her body shaking with a degree of stimulation that Polly could barely begin to contemplate, Polly knew that she herself – so inexperienced in even the most mild of these extreme pleasures – could no longer bear to watch the unfolding scene. With a last glance at the two women, locked in their strange and perverted communion, Polly crept from the landing as quietly as she could whilst still clutching her aching crotch.

Almost choking, Severn O'Neill felt some of the water escape her compulsively moving lips and trickle down the front of her body. Even the minute flow of it seemed to taunt her loins like a mighty Niagara.

Oh God, oh God, why the hell do I want to do this, she asked herself, feeling her consciousness drift into a changed state that seemed to exclude even Inez, her willing tormentress. She could feel her bladder swollen inside her, like a globe of lead resting in the cradle of her pelvis and bearing down ponderously on every sexual nerve-end in her genitalia. She imagined her clitoris to be standing out like a tiny digit from between her dripping labia, forced into obscene prominence by the infernal pressure behind it. Taking another drink of water, she seemed to feel that pressure increase exponentially, and the little organ push out even further, throbbing powerfully.

There was only one thing now that would bring the sensation to a pinnacle . . . if she could bear it, and not wet herself immediately, just from the thought of it. Thrusting the glass aside, she cried, 'Bring a bowl! It's time now! Do as I say!' aware as she did so that she had re-taken supreme control of the moment. Inez would hear that tone and do exactly what she was told.

Closing her eyes, she listened to the sounds of Inez leaving the room and stepping into the en-suite bathroom, in search of the required vessel. Even the tiny noises seemed to create a reverberation. Little impacts on the ball of water in her belly.

Time stretched and warped, and in moments that seemed to last long, distended hours, Inez returned with the large porcelain bowl which they always used on occasions like these. It looked not unlike a punchbowl, but had never held wine or spirits.

Pausing only to make sure the door to the landing was tightly closed now, Inez placed the bowl on the carpet. Severn manoeuvred herself, crab-like, over it. She hovered awkwardly in place, creating tensions in her muscles that only exacerbated the extreme arousal in her vulva. 'Finger me,' she commanded, completely in control of Inez, even if she no longer held sway over her own emotions. 'Stroke my clit . . . but only lightly . . . I want to see how long I can hold out against it.'

'Are you sure?' asked Inez softly, but nevertheless crouching down in readiness. 'Why not just come now, my darling? Surely you're ready? And you so deserve it.'

'No!' Severn commanded in a low voice, feeling slight tremors begin already, but fighting them. She wanted the most stringent of climaxes. She wanted the pleasure to be monstrous and all-consuming; so intense that she could almost imagine its strength could kill her.

Severn felt Inez's fingertip touch her. Soft as a feather yet agonising and tantalising. It was going to be harder to resist than she could have imagined. Than she could even believe. The caress was minuscule, but already far too much.

With a grunt of ecstasy, she let her pent-up waters gush.

'Oh God! Oh God! Oh God!' chanted Polly through gritted teeth and behind a muffling hand. Her other hand was between her legs and getting a thorough drenching.

After her flight from the landing, and back to the privacy of the bathroom, Polly had been unable to deny the imperative of her pussy. Wrenching down her jeans and knickers, she'd quickly straddled the toilet bowl and rubbed herself. And within a couple of seconds she been rewarded by an orgasm.

Now, though, as the sensations began to fade and dissipate, she felt a kind of disappointment take its place, a strange *tristesse*. She supposed that a part of it must be guilt at having watched Inez and Severn, and having taken a pleasure that now seemed faintly grubby and sleazy. Watersports were something Polly had never in a million years imagined herself ever taking part in, much less enjoying. But looking down at her glistening fingers, and smelling her own piss, she had to admit with some reluctance that the game had aroused her.

Washing her hands, and putting her clothes to rights, Polly tried to analyse the witch's brew that was her feelings.

Maybe she didn't feel blue because of the dirtiness at all? When she thought about it, the impression that gripped her was of shared fun more than anything . . . Little girl's mischief. A giggle. Pranks behind the bikesheds . . .

No, the melancholy came from having to get off on her own. Fucking with a partner was what she most missed, she realised, grabbing a hunk of toilet tissue and trying to convince herself that she wasn't going to grizzle. No matter how peculiar the practices that Inez and her friend had engaged in, at least they'd

61

performed them together. As a couple, in mutuality, and with obvious affection.

And I'm here, stuck on my own, feeling lonely and neglected. The only lesbian lover I ever had, I had to run away from, because of bloody Sanspareil!

She couldn't even make a pass at Inez now, either, as the older woman clearly had established women friends of her own. Even though she had seemed to be flirting with Polly the previous evening . . .

Shaking her head, and trying to clear it of the conundrum, Polly decided to return to her computers, even though it was very late. Back on the landing she could hear nothing now, and realised that the door to Inez's room had been closed to exclude her. Bits and bytes love me, she thought, shrugging her shoulders and finding herself smiling, in spite of everything. She felt almost cheerful as she plugged in her 'recreational' laptop and booted up again.

Almost immediately, she got a 'mail waiting' message.

'This is crazy! Nobody knows this addie,' she muttered, pressing to receive. Half in fear, half in excitement, she immediately remembered the mysterious 'Enclave'. How could she have forgotten? It, or they, or even, maybe, *she* were the only ones who knew her at this e-mail address.

After a few seconds of 'receiving mail' a message appeared – and Polly read the string of words in wonder and astonishment.

Welcome to our Enclave, Polly. You can be sure that you will be safe here. Safe from retribution as wielded by the forces of commerce, that is ... In other ways you might find yourself in peril. Amongst our company there are those well versed in the arts of correction, just as there are those whose *raison d'être* is the pursuit of pleasure. Perhaps they're the same people? Be sure that you'll find out, and that we'll be in touch with you again very soon.

There was no e-mail signature, just the single letter 'E'.

As she read the peculiar missive again, one word suddenly leapt from the screen and she studied it, aghast.

'Polly'?

How the hell could the Enclave, or 'E', or whoever the fuck they were know she was called 'Polly'? She hadn't signed the 'reply' message, and when setting up her free e-mail accounts she'd managed to avoid using her real name even once. There were ways a-plenty, of course, that a clever hacker could out-hack one of his or her peers, and thus winkle out a person's real identity, but Polly prided herself on a championship level of deviousness.

Who could it be? Was it Inez? She'd already intimated that she knew Polly had a guilty secret. And she was also, Polly suspected, hiding the extent of her own computer knowledge for some reason best known to herself.

Then Polly shuddered. She reached for the comfort of her Dictaphone and clicked it on.

'Right, it can't be Inez, because I've just watched her playing pissy games with her girlfriend . . . and neither of them looked as if they were in the mood to break off and start sending e-mails.' She paused, trying to work things out in her head.

'The message wasn't there when I left, so . . . it must have been sent while I was watching them. Which means somebody *else* sent it! Someone who's part of this "Enclave" thing . . .' Polly looked back at the screen and the words 'forces of commerce' suddenly popped out at her with sinister significance. 'And someone who seems to know that I've got something to hide . . .'

As the cursor flashed, she began to feel incredibly threatened and cold . . .

FIVE

Where to Next?

The next morning, Polly woke up feeling the same jolt of shock she'd experienced from 'E's message.

'What the hell am I going to do? What the hell am I going to do?' she whispered into the Dictaphone, then flung it aside, not getting any comfort in recording her thoughts whatsoever. The whole of the safe feeling she'd constructed for herself seemed to need rebuilding.

One of the first things she needed, obviously, was a new e-mail identity. She'd checked the route of the Enclave message and her own reply to it, but of course whoever they were, they'd used exactly the same sort of subterfuge that she had. Anonymous web-based e-mail providers and probably a series of multiple forwardings beyond that. Any attempt to find them would take a hack of truly enormous complexity, which could still fail. And even if it succeeded, it might not reveal anything all that helpful.

As she considered her options, it occurred to Polly that it was already too late to go through the rigmarole of setting up new accounts again. She'd been found, and if it could be done once, it could be done again. What was worse, there were even ways she could be traced physically, too. The high-tech surveillance depicted in movie thrillers was becoming all too real these days.

Living out in a mud hut in the wilds of Scotland or wherever, completely without technology, might well be the only real means of truly 'getting away' . . .

Suddenly even the thought of the smallest amount of hassle made Polly tired. Was it all worth it? Maybe she ought to go back to F&X, gradually reveal her progress with Sanspareil, and accept the smaller – much smaller! – rewards that she would receive as part of their team? It would be a lot easier than all this sneaking around like a fugitive and a felon, and that way she would at least have a chance to concentrate on her personal life. Discover her new self, and what she wanted. It might even mean she'd get another chance with Pat.

No! she found herself thinking, almost immediately. Not about the prospect of being with Pat again. That would be adorable, especially if she knew a bit more . . .

No, it was the thought of virtually giving away Sanspareil that made her baulk. Letting it be taken from her by some other developer – probably male – and then the kudos going to the company rather than her. Not to mention the possible financial rewards. Granted, the most sensible of her plans – to take the program to a rival firm – would still involve diluting the potential gains, but at least that way she had a bargaining stance from the outset. And there were certainly many computer firms out there, even quite monolithic ones, where the talents and worth of a woman might be valued more fairly.

'You're over-reacting again, Poll,' she told herself. 'It's this stupid place . . . It's enough to get to anybody.' She looked out of the window on another strangely monochrome day in Chandler's Haven, and thought again what a dark and sinister little burg it was. It never seemed to be light here, as if its natural state was night.

And yet she couldn't deny the reality of that e-mail – she couldn't ignore it. It was there in her data . . .

Thoughts whirled in Polly's head and she felt a peculiar sense of helplessness, which was something she had always hated in herself, and which she loathed even more now. When she'd run from London, and from F&X, she'd gone for it, seized the day, taken action – and now she was back again to dithering and worrying and just generally feeling powerless.

'Screw it, Poll! Think straight! Get your act together!'

It was no use going off at a tangent, even 'E' had said she was safe here. The only threat had been a veiled reference to what sounded like more kinky sex . . . and considering the fun that Inez and her friend had been having last night that wasn't a reason to turn tail and run, was it?

More a reason to stay, thought Polly, smiling and feeling more centred. Yes, she'd stick around, but be more scrupulous about her security, both computer and otherwise.

As seemed to be her pattern, Inez had not emerged from her room yet, and it was already afternoon. Obviously, she needs her beauty sleep after last night's performance, Polly thought, hardly daring to speculate what had gone on after she'd left the landing. But at least Inez's lie-in gave her a chance to check the burglar alarm.

Ash House had state of the art security. Inez had briefly shown Polly the control box, but a closer scrutiny now showed that the installation was quite sophisticated. There were motion detectors in the rooms, sensors on all the windows, a variety of settings available on the elaborate computer control panel.

No good if it isn't switched on, though, Polly grumbled to herself. There had been not a bell or whistle or flash at all last night, when a strange young woman had shinned up the drain-pipe and climbed in through the window!

'Is something wrong?' enquired Inez, from just behind her.

Polly spun around, trying not to look unnerved by her hostess's unannounced appearance or in any way surprised by the lateness of the hour.

The older woman was looking marvellous. Pervy sex must have that effect on you, Polly thought, taking in the sparkle in Inez's eyes, the gloss of her hair, and the sense of suppressed energy that seemed to pervade her exquisitely dressed body. Inez was wearing a pair of grey Capri pants in a heavy, textured shantung-like fabric, topped with a poplin short-sleeved blouse in a light, cerulean blue. It was a vaguely fifties look, and she appeared calm, relaxed and serene in it. There was no sign in her, even in the slightest, of the fevered, almost mania-driven seductress that she'd been the night before. She looked as cool as a dish of peppermint ice-cream, and just as delicious.

'I was just checking whether your alarm worked,' blurted out Polly, feeling a sudden, disconcerting urge to run her fingers down the sheeny cloth that covered Inez's perfect haunches.

'Oh really,' said Inez, unperturbed. 'It's in perfect working order. Why do you ask?'

Polly wondered what to say, what to refer to, then she decided on a portion of the partial truth.

'Well, it's just that I have some quite valuable equipment and software with me, and I don't want to take risks with it.' She felt herself blushing as Inez's perfect eyebrows went up. 'I should have mentioned it before, I know, but I've been so tired I just didn't think.'

Inez smiled. Her pale oval face was thoughtful, and unnervingly speculative. 'I don't think you have any need to worry down here, Polly,' she murmured, the smile still there, and taunting somehow. 'There's nothing to fear in Chandler's Haven, nothing at all . . . Well, at least not in the criminal sense –' The pause was infinitesimal, but Polly registered it like a fanfare of trumpets. 'There are some, shall we say, challenging people in town, but none of them would steal.'

Inez had laid no discernible emphasis on the last word, but Polly heard one anyway. Her thoughts raced again and, unbidden, her plans for flight resurfaced. Inez had to be implying that she *knew*, she simply had to!

'I – I didn't mean to imply that anyone local would do such a thing,' Polly stammered, 'but I'm concerned about outsiders. People from out of Chandler's Haven.'

Inez laughed, the note of it soft and sultry and reminiscent of her voice last night. 'I think you're being a bit melodramatic, Polly,' she said, taking Polly by the arm and beginning to lead her towards the kitchen. 'Anyone would think you were on the run from something. Now come along, let's get some tea. That'll calm your nerves.'

Polly followed mutely. She felt like a cornered animal somehow, all her thoughts of positive action and 'seize the day' in rags and tatters.

In the kitchen, Inez switched on the portable television with the volume turned down low, and settled Polly at the table, facing it. Polly looked at the shapes of people involved in some kind of afternoon talk show, but the TV pap made even less sense to her than it normally would have done. Some woman was shouting and hitting the man beside her, while the compère cheered them on.

'Here, get stuck into these,' said Inez kindly, placing a beaker of tea and a plate of sandwiches before Polly. 'I'm really not looking after you very well, am I?' With a shrug, she sat down facing Polly, with tea of her own.

'No, you're doing fine,' said Polly. Then she bit into a sandwich. It tasted like tuna mayonnaise and, as she chewed it, she discovered it was delicious. 'You're being wonderful, in fact. It's me that's imposing.'

'No way,' replied Inez firmly. 'I enjoy having you here, and I don't want you to worry about anything. I swear your software will be safe. That alarm is really efficient.'

'If you switch it on.'

Not for the first time since she'd come to Ash House, Polly wished she could call her words back. What she'd just made was a deliberately provocative statement.

Inez laughed again. A sensual, attractive, but nevertheless slightly rueful sound. 'Now what makes you say *that*, Polly?'

'Well, it certainly wasn't on last night, was it? At least parts of it weren't . . .' What was the point pulling back now? The damage was done . . .

Still smiling, Inez drew the teapot towards them, topped up their mugs, then added milk to each. The action seemed to take ages, but eventually she spoke.

'So you saw Severn climb in through my bedroom window, did you?'

Polly took a sip of tea, attempting to play her own waiting game. But the liquid was quite hot and it burnt her tongue and made her annoyed.

'I saw someone climb in through the window, so obviously the alarm *wasn't* on! It could just as easily have been a burglar, after your valuables. You ought to be more careful!'

'I thought it was *your* valuables you were concerned about?' Inez enquired mildly. She didn't seem to be deflecting the conversation, just making an observation.

'I am, but –'

'Do you want to know who Severn is?'

Inez's glance was very clear, very open – like a limpid blue pool. Without hesitation, Polly gratefully dived in.

'Yes. It's not often you see a beautiful blonde in dungarees shinning up a drainpipe.'

'Oh, that's typical Severn,' said Inez, her tone softer and more affectionate. 'Ever the tomboy. But underneath all that, there isn't a woman more feminine . . .'

I'll say! Polly was grateful that she managed to contain *that* thought . . . 'But why did she climb in through the window?'

'Probably because she knew I had a guest, and didn't want to disturb you by ringing the doorbell.'

Inez held Polly's look for a moment, then went on. 'Unless of course, we disturbed you later?'

'No! No, you didn't!' cried Polly, feeling turbulent blood rush up into her throat and face. She wished passionately that she'd worn a polo neck this afternoon, not a scoop neck top that seemed to deliberately frame her blush.

Inez graced her with another of her low, knowing chuckles. 'Of course I'm a dyke, Polly. I thought that was a given between us?'

Polly snatched up her mug again and drained the lot, not noticing this time whether it was hot or cold. It could have been paint stripper for all she was aware of it. Inez let her take her time, and simply waited, her expression amused.

'Well, yes, I did wonder,' Polly managed at last, the release of tension feeling almost euphoric. 'I even sort of hoped you were, actually,' she went on, noticing some crumbs that she must have dropped on the table cloth, even though she could barely remember having eaten her sandwich now. 'I've been . . . well . . . going through some changes myself lately, to be honest. And I rather thought it would be nice to talk them over with someone.'

'Good girl! Don't worry, you'll be all right,' said Inez quite matter of factly. 'Especially in Chandler's Haven . . .' She paused again, and Polly felt her heart rev, and a sensation of a lift falling out of control in her mid section. She was absolutely certain what her hostess was going to say next. 'You might say we're a bit of a lesbian enclave here.'

Well, I think I covered that one up pretty well, mused Polly, a while later, as she trudged up the road beside Inez, her hands in her pockets.

The 'magic word' had thrown her for a loop for a moment, even though something in her had been confidently expecting it, but she was pretty sure she hadn't revealed as much to Inez. She hadn't really had a chance, because the next thing her hostess had suggested was that the two of them go out together, visiting. To see Severn . . .

'You'll love Severn,' said Inez now, turning towards Polly and smiling encouragingly. 'She's fun, she's unpretentious, and she's scared of nothing.' Inez's dark eyes glittered suddenly. 'And she has no inhibitions, which is what makes her so great to play with!'

'Play?' Polly knew what Inez meant, but still couldn't seem to stop herself asking.

'Now come on, Polly, don't be so naïve. You know what I mean,' said Inez briskly, but not without warmth. '*Play*! Have sex. Do a scene with. You said you'd been going through some changes . . . Surely you've thought about it all? Read magazines? Tried to find out what it is we girls all do together?'

'Well, yes, I have,' said Polly stoutly. And it was true. She'd read books and magazines that Pat had given her; she wasn't a total idiot! She wasn't even a lesbian 'virgin', if it came to that.

'And I have been with a woman, you know! I'm not a complete beginner!'

'Well, I'm glad to hear it,' announced Inez, stopping in her tracks and forcing Polly to stop too by the simple expedient of grabbing her by the arm. For a slender, artistic woman, Inez was surprisingly strong. 'Let's see what you can do then, shall we?'

Then Polly was being kissed, and it wasn't a gentle, decorous, soft-focus kind of kiss either. Inez's hand gripped the back of Polly's head like a vice, while her tongue thrust into Polly's mouth, possessing it roughly. It was like no kiss she'd ever experienced before in her life; not from a man, nor even from Pat, who'd been as forceful as a man. What Inez subjected Polly to was nothing less than an assault. A sumptuous, mind-bending, oh-so-wanted assault, but an assault all the same.

And it was wonderful!

They stood by the edge of a narrow road, in the back of beyond, their mouths crushed together while Inez explored and probed with a tongue like a serpent. Polly went limp and she felt her cunt quicken to the force of her ravishment. A drench of nectar seemed to suddenly rush out of her and soak her knickers.

'Oh, you're so sweet, young Polly,' whispered Inez, her mouth travelling moistly over Polly's face and neck as her narrow hands made their way deftly between the fastenings of Polly's clothes. As Inez possessed her mouth again, this time more languorously, and more teasingly, Polly felt first her shirt and then her bra being pushed aside. Inez took a nipple between the very tips of her fingers and began to delicately twist and pull it in a way that seemed to connect directly with Polly's twitching, aching clitoris. It was as if both organs were being affected by the single touch.

Then, Inez suddenly laughed into Polly's opened mouth and Polly immediately understood why. She was standing there jerking her hips involuntarily, trying to rub herself off against Inez's thigh, almost without realising it.

'Yes, you're sweet, Polly,' said Inez, pulling away, her usual composure a little disarrayed, and her smooth face flushed. 'But you're also hot. Hot as hell! I can't wait to have you.'

Disorientated, Polly looked down the hill, back towards the twilight grey shapes of the dwellings, amongst which stood Ash House. She suddenly didn't want to go visiting Severn, no matter how beautiful and amusing the blonde girl was. All she wanted now was to be in a bedroom, getting undressed with Inez and exploring her svelte and elegant body. Which was something, Polly now realised, that she'd wanted all the years she'd known the woman simply as a friend.

Inez caught the look and gave Polly an apologetic grin. 'Oh no, young Polly, not tonight,' she said, then leant over and pressed a kiss as soft as a sigh against Polly's bruised lips. 'I have to be somewhere soon. I have an appointment. Why do you think I'm taking you to Severn's house? She'll take care of you . . . She'll see to your needs.'

For a moment Polly stood speechless, in shock, aware mainly that the elastic of her dislodged bra was pressing uncomfortably into the upper slope of her left breast. She reached into her clothing and righted it, then pulled her twisted shirt back into place too.

Then her brain re-engaged and she saw red.

'I'm not some needy, sex-starved little heifer who needs servicing, you know!' she stormed, then turned on her heel and began walking back down the hill, filled with a confusing muddle of mortification and piercing disappointment. She did want sex. She wanted it very much. But she wouldn't be patronised by anybody. Not even Inez, who she was now convinced she had a crush on. 'I've got plenty of work to do. I don't need "entertaining"!'

Inez caught her up, and took her by the arm again, although this time far more gently. Without much of a fight, Polly found herself redirected back the way they'd been going.

'Don't be like that, sweetheart,' said Inez, sounding genuinely remorseful. 'I'm sorry if that sounded bad. I didn't mean it that way. I just want you to be happy. To enjoy yourself.' She became a little more cajoling, giving Polly a swift kiss on the cheek. 'And you'll have a nice time with Severn, even if you don't have sex. She's a fascinating girl, and she's kind and funny. You really will like her.' Inez cocked her head on one side. 'And she's been so looking forward to meeting you. I told her all about you last night.'

'I'm amazed you had time!' countered Polly, then realised she'd given herself away as a peeping tom.

Inez chuckled, and Polly knew that the older woman had known she was being watched.

'Did you watch us, Polly?' Inez asked, slipping her arm through Polly's as if to ensure that she wouldn't bolt again.

Polly couldn't answer, but she felt Inez give her an encouraging squeeze.

'Don't worry,' said the older woman, almost blithely. 'Why do you think I left my bedroom door ajar? I wanted you to see what we did. I was hoping that it would encourage you to stop being such a wimp and come out to me!'

Polly digested this information. 'I'm not sure that I'm into the things you were doing, though,' she said finally, realising it was pointless to deny something that Inez undoubtedly already knew. 'It seemed a bit . . . um . . . kinky,' she added, knowing that wasn't quite the word she'd been looking for, but at a loss for a better one.

Inez laughed. 'Oh, not so "kinky" really, Polly,' she said, somewhat archly. 'And believe me, before long, you'll be redefining the parameters of what you once would've considered kinky. You'll find out that anything goes, here in this place, with my group of friends . . .'

'Maybe,' muttered Polly, wondering.

The two of them lapsed into an edgy, but not entirely uncompanionable silence for a while, and Polly tried to blank from her mind any trepidation she might have about the evening ahead, and concentrate on its possibilities. Severn was very lovely and clearly very imaginative – and Polly knew she couldn't deny her own extreme frustration. Why shouldn't she enjoy this unexpected gift that Inez seemed to be offering?

Severn's cottage, when they reached it, seemed to Polly to be far more welcoming and homely looking than most of the dwellings in Chandler's Haven itself. Although twilight was well fallen and there were no street lamps this far out of town, Border Cottage was lit by a porch lamp that glowed warm and yellow, accentuating its low doorway and the creamy, weathered stone-work. As they approached, the brown painted door swung open, and a smiling Severn stood in the entranceway, her arms out-stretched. She looked relaxed and innocently girlish in an over-washed and fraying vest, and drawstring pants, and her bright blonde hair was loose tonight, swishing glossily to her shoulders.

'Come on in, you two,' she said, her husky voice full of undisguised welcome. 'It's getting a bit chilly out. Do you fancy a glass of home-made plonk to warm you up?'

'I'm sorry, Sev, I can't stay,' said Inez, as their hostess led them to the fireside of a room that opened directly on to the outdoors. 'I thought I told you that?'

'Well, you did, but I always live in hope.' Severn laughed as she fetched a battered old tray, bearing a bottle and glasses, from an equally ancient-looking dresser.

'Yes, and I can imagine what it was you were hoping for,' countered Inez, turning to wink at Polly.

Severn quirked her eyebrows in response. 'Too right!' she said, then looked at Polly expectantly.

Inez did the honours.

'Polly, this is my good friend Severn O'Neill, small holder *extraordinaire*, champion winemaker, and goodness knows what else.' She touched Polly's back, and seemed to push her forward. 'Sev, this is Polly Sayers, who I seem to have known for a long, long time, but who I haven't really got to know at all until now. She's staying with me, and I thought it would be nice if she could become part of our little circle, or whatever it is we call it.'

'Hello,' said Polly, feeling suddenly bedazzled by the intense fervour in Severn's beautiful eyes. She held out her hand but the gesture seemed pathetically staid and inadequate.

Severn clearly didn't consider a handshake adequate either. 'And hello to you,' she said, then moved forward and kissed Polly full on the lips, not perhaps with the same insulting roughness that Inez had earlier, but certainly with a great sweetness and enthusiasm.

'There,' she said, as they parted, 'I like to get things out in the open right from the start, don't you? None of this shilly-shallying about and thinking "Is she or isn't she?" I'm a sassy dyke and I don't care who knows it!'

It was Inez's turn to laugh. 'Oh God, I wish I could stay now . . .' She hesitated and Polly saw a significant look pass between the two other women. 'But as you know, I have an appointment. And Madame doesn't like it when anyone keeps her waiting!' She moved towards Polly and, drawing her aside slightly, spoke more softly. 'Don't be afraid of Severn. She's sweet and kind. She'll look after you.' And with that, she too kissed Polly, then turned and left – flicking a teasing little wave to Severn from the doorway.

Polly swung slowly to face Severn. She felt nervous and, in a certain way, demeaned. She'd been dumped, passed on, left. It was ignominious.

'I feel like a parcel that's been abandoned,' she said, feeling a ridiculous urge to gnaw her lip like a petulant teenager – then giving in to it.

'Don't think that. Don't think that at all,' said Severn, her voice and her eyes frank rather than patronising. 'Inez knows full well what she's missing.' She began to move around the room, almost balletic as she switched on soft lamps and turned out the main light.

'Here, let's sit on the rug in front of the fire . . . Get to know each other a bit.' She gestured to what looked like a genuine cottage rag rug in front of a cheery open fire. Light from the

75

flames glinted all shades of plum and purple in the carafe of home-made wine.

'OK,' said Polly. Self-consciously, she removed her leather jacket and laid it over the back of a chair, taking a quick look around her as she did so.

The cottage sitting room was medium-sized, untidy and lived in, but not in any way squalid. The furniture was large and clunky and old, but perfectly right for its setting. The only jarring element, and the one that deeply disquieted Polly, now she noticed it, was a laptop computer that stood on an old desk in the corner, its backlit screen fluorescent in the half light. Polly saw a familiar screensaver, of a top-rated cartoon show, playing with the sound turned off.

'Come on,' said Severn softly, holding out a glass of wine to Polly from where she sat, elegant yet at ease, on the thick rag rug.

Polly sat, tucking her legs to one side, then took the glass. The wine within it tasted of all kinds of summer fruits, distilled then shot through with fine, biting fire. Its taste was succulent, but almost immediately she felt her nerve-ends pulsating.

'Wow!' was all she could manage as she set the glass aside, determined to take the drink very steadily.

'Good, isn't it?' Severn grinned and took a hefty swig from her own glass, clearly case-hardened to her own rocket-fuel potions. 'I thought it might break the ice.'

'Melt it, more like,' replied Polly, finding it impossible not to smile back. 'Oh God, this is such a strange set-up! I can't believe it's happening . . . What are we supposed to do? Start snogging straight away? Or shall we just get down to business?'

Severn let out a peal of laughter. 'Believe me, Polly, I'd like nothing better but, for your sake, let's not rush *too* fast.'

It made sense, but Polly suddenly felt rash. It could have been the wine, or just raw desire, or a defiant case of 'what the hell!' Looking at Severn's body, in its soft envelopment of clothing, she suddenly saw how thin the old white T-shirt she was wearing was. Dark, incredibly tumescent nipples seemed to call out to the tips of Polly's fingers, and make her lips prickle . . . Or could that have been the wine acting upon them?

'I'm – I'm not very experienced,' she said, watching Severn's reaction. 'I don't think I could do the sorts of things that you were doing with Inez last night . . .'

'We don't do it ourselves all that often,' said Severn imperturbably. It seemed that she too knew that she and Inez had been watched. 'It's just a role-play we'd promised ourselves . . .' She paused, and studied Polly closely. 'Believe me, I'm not really that kinky all the time. I couldn't keep up the tension. I like things nice and vanilla generally.' She seemed to think a moment, as if considering whether to say something. 'Now Ellen, she just adores "kink" . . . She lives for it. If you asked her to have vanilla sex with you she'd probably never speak to you again!'

'Who's Ellen?' asked Polly.

'Oh, just another of our friends,' replied Severn quickly. Polly had the impression that Severn was jealous all of a sudden, and it dawned on her that this 'Ellen' might well be the reason Inez had abandoned them. She decided not to press the matter. Why spoil the moment?

Severn clearly had the same idea. 'You look tense, Polly, how about a massage? I'm very good at it.'

It was Polly's turn to laugh. She had never heard anything more blatant. Or more inviting.

Severn chuckled too. 'OK, yeah, I know it's a cliché, but I really am a good masseuse, and I mix my own oils using home-grown herbs. Oh, go on, Polly, let me . . . I'm dying to get a look at you!'

This is mad, thought Polly. This woman's only the second ever that I'll have undressed for. I only set eyes on her for the first time last night, and I know nothing about her other than her sexual preferences. How can I do this? It's totally crazy. It can't be happening . . .

And yet it was.

As Severn rose gracefully from the rug, presumably to get her massage oil, Polly found herself unbuttoning her shirt and whipping out the tails from her jeans' waistband. Then it occurred to her that she ought to take her shoes off first and, as she tugged at her trainers, the laces seemed to deliberately knot and tangle. Wrenching at them made no difference, and she was still struggling when Severn returned to the rug, set down a folded pink blanket and a small glass jug of murky-looking oil, and sank down beside her.

'Here, let me,' she said, then without any effort at all, detangled the recalcitrant laces and slipped Polly's trainers off her feet. She then peeled off Polly's socks, rolled them up, and set them aside. 'Don't be embarrassed, Polly,' she whispered. 'I can see already that you have a wonderful body –' without hesitation, she reached inside Polly's shirt and gently cupped her breast, through her brassière '– and I'm sure it feels just as good as it looks!'

Polly still prevaricated. She thought suddenly of Pat, and felt obscurely as if she were being unfaithful to her. Which was nonsense, as Pat had never made any promises or protestations, and had been patently experienced. She's probably forgotten me completely by now, thought Polly, feeling a little pang of loss and pain, then shaking it off at the prospect of the gorgeous creature before her. Severn had begun to undress herself, clearly to encourage her by taking the lead.

As Polly had deduced, Severn wore no bra. She didn't need to. Polly had never seen, either in film, on TV, or in the flesh, in health club locker rooms, a woman with breasts more splendid. Large. Firm-fleshed. Exquisitely shaped. Polly notioned for a moment on the possibility of silicon implants, then dismissed it. She didn't imagine that dykes would approve of such a thing – judging by the pitifully small amount she knew about dykes, that was – and Severn's beautiful frontage looked far too natural to be shaped by surgery. Just one of nature's lucky ones, I guess, thought Polly, looking downwards.

Severn shuffled towards her on the rug and, once again, cradled one of Polly's breasts in her long slim hand. 'Don't take any notice of me, I'm just naturally big,' she murmured into Polly's

ear, her fingertips gently manipulating. 'Yours are perfect . . .
Simply beautiful . . . I'm longing to kiss them.'

And *I'm* longing for her to kiss them, was the thought that
suddenly dawned on Polly. Without quite knowing when it had
happened, her inhibitions had disintegrated, it seemed. With a
happy little laugh, she pushed her chest forward, to encourage
Severn's fondlings.

For a few moments, Polly enjoyed Severn's skilful handling of
her breast, and then the blonde girl released her, and drew back,
her smooth face slightly pinkened. 'Massage first,' she said, clearly
trying to sound imperious, but not quite achieving it, 'then sex. I
promised you the full treatment, and the full treatment you're
going to get!'

'I'm not sure I can wait,' said Polly, her mouth going a little
dry as she watched Severn remove the tiny G-string that had
been her only remaining garment. Polly had seen that beautiful
blonde bush before, but even so, the impact of its revelation was
undiminished. The burnished gleam of those soft, gilded curls
was a breathtaking vision.

'It'll be worth it,' Severn assured her, all the time running her
hands up and down her thighs and flanks as if expressing sheer
joy at being alive in such a body. Polly couldn't blame her. If her
own figure had been that good, she would have wanted to run
out into the streets and exhibit it publicly!

As it was, Polly began to feel nervous again. By comparison
with Severn, she was very ordinary, her body fairly well propor-
tioned, but, she felt, undistinguished. She wished now that she'd
been more stringent with herself in the gym and the swimming
pool.

'Your turn now,' said Severn, her voice low with anticipation,
even though she'd been so insistent that the sex should be
delayed.

Gritting her teeth, Polly pulled off her shirt, flung it aside, then
unclipped her bra before she could hesitate and renege. Keeping
up the momentum, she wiggled out of her jeans as fast as she
could and hooked her thumbs in her knickers' waistband and

whipped them off too. Naked, she stood in front of the fire, facing Severn and doing everything in her power to stop herself shielding her breasts and her pubis with her hands.

'Gorgeous,' breathed Severn, making Polly feel more confident simply by dint of the hot look in her eyes. Maybe the sex wouldn't have to wait, after all?

But Severn was resolute. Shaking her head slightly, she passed the old pink blanket to Polly. 'Spread it out, will you?' As Polly laid the blanket out, Severn caught her blonde hair into a ponytail with the help of a towelling covered band.

'Lie down now, sweetheart,' she urged, as Polly stood dithering beside the slightly ragged old blanket. When Polly looked questioning, Severn laughed and said, 'Face down first . . . Let's see how things develop, shall we?'

Polly did as she was told, responding to the slight take-charge note in Severn's voice. When she'd been with Pat, back in London, it had been the American woman who had always, without exception, directed the choreography of their love scenes. Polly sensed that what she felt, and what she would share with Severn, would be far more egalitarian, far more balanced and reciprocal, but she was still unsure of herself and what she ought to be doing next. Settling down on the blanket, she laid her face on her arms and just waited for Severn's next move, her muscles stiff and tense.

'Relax!' cried Severn almost immediately. 'I can see the knots in your shoulders from here. I'm not going to hurt you, believe me. You'll love this!'

I know I will, thought Polly, doing her utmost to allow herself to unwind. I will love it, and that's what I'm so goddamned afraid of!

SIX

Scented

'What's in that stuff?' demanded Polly as a scent so strong it seemed like smoke enveloped her. Severn hadn't even touched her yet, but the odours from the massage oil were almost as tangible as a caress.

'Well, it's a vegetable-oil base, with rosemary, lavender, camomile and clary-sage, all pounded up into it, then strained out again. So that you don't get covered in lots of icky little green bits,' said Severn, coating her hands in her potion, judging by the evocative, slippery sliding sounds she was making.

'Jesus Christ! I'm going to smell like a leg of lamb or a basted chicken by the time I'm finished!' replied Polly, the funnier side of things dispelling her apprehension. Severn's home-made unguent was very much like a culinary marinade.

'Don't worry, we can have a bath together afterwards,' whispered Severn, who'd moved like a wraith and was already kneeling over Polly, warm and close. 'That's a big part of the fun,' she added, leaning even closer and searing Polly's skin with the slightest brushing of a bare and tumescent nipple.

Polly felt as if she'd been zapped by a tazer. Until that moment, there had been a weirdly 'theoretical' quality to the interlude, even despite the mutual nudity and the initial touching.

But now she'd felt naked skin on naked skin, and everything was serious.

Even while she was still recovering from the incendiary contact of Severn's breast, Polly felt the blonde woman's strong hands settle on her shoulders and begin kneading. Slender but powerful thumbs moved in firm, deep circles, seeking out and dissolving tension and inhibitions. Severn's touch was purely businesslike and platonic as yet, but Polly could already feel its repercussions in her cunt.

She wanted more. She wanted everything. She wanted it soon. And if Severn wouldn't give it up and begin to move with a more sexual purpose, Polly herself would have to force the issue and seduce her. She shifted her hips, hoping it would be a message to accelerate.

'Keep still. Relax,' purred Severn, not pausing at all in her determined, professional pummelling, yet also managing to convey to Polly that the message was received. The tough, overlapping circles she made were as brisk as ever, yet somehow now they also had a fugitively sensual quality.

Polly endured the denial of her basest urges for a few moments longer, then spoke up again, rocking her pelvis as she did so. 'That's great . . . really great. My shoulders feel fine now . . . I think you should move on.'

The hands stilled, remaining in contact, two sets of five hot points, one poised on each of Polly's shoulder blades. 'Where to, exactly?' Severn queried, her low voice deeper, on the edge of raggedness but not quite succumbing to it.

'Lower,' murmured Polly, still rocking, indulging herself in the most discreet of all forms of masturbation. Her pussy was already burning, so tender that even the referred action seemed to create a riot in her flesh. 'The gluteus maximus,' she said roughly, lifting her bottom towards Severn's oily hands for emphasis.

'What a surprise,' purred Severn, taking her cue, and placing a hand squarely on each of Polly's buttocks. Her fingers curved outwards, her thumbs inwards, defining the cleft. She began to massage again, moving her thumbs in tiny circles. The motion was minimal but Polly experienced it like a thunderclap. This was it; this was sex with a woman, the first since Pat. Already longing to come, Polly mewed and clawed the blanket.

'Is that good?' whispered Severn, inclining over her, thumbs still delicately rolling and manipulating.

Polly wondered how many more women had experienced these marvellous sensations, this adept fondling. 'Yes, it's very, very good,' she replied, surprised and yet turned on by the sound of her own voice so gravel-deep and full of lust. She sounded like the accomplished seductress encouraging the novice – instead of the exact opposite, which was the true state of affairs.

And still the tiny circles persisted. Polly could feel her cunt gradually engorging as if the massage were a form of pumping action, forcing blood and increased sensitivity into her pudenda. She felt compelled to part her thighs, the lips of her sex had become so swollen. Of its own volition her pelvis began to tilt and rise. She felt like a she-dog offering up her scent to an interested bitch.

'Oh yes, my sweet, you're so ready,' murmured Severn, closer over Polly's back now, her magnificent breasts brushing and circling, just like her fingers. 'Do you want me to do you now? Or do you want some more massage?' The way she spoke made Polly sense no answer was needed.

'Now!' she said. 'I want it now!' Although what the precise mechanics were of what she was demanding, she did not know.

Without benefit of further instruction, Severn began a series of decisive actions. She ceased the massage, and grabbed Polly bodily by the hips, lifting her up until she was crouching on all fours. For a few seconds, she reached beneath, with both hands, and rubbed Polly's breasts in a rough, mashing action, then she released them, just as rudely, and caressed her flank. Dying for something more, indeed for anything at all, Polly groaned in protest.

'Oh yes, baby, yes,' said Severn, and Polly felt the cool brush of the backs of her fingers against her anus. 'Do you want it here?' Again the same flick. 'Or in your pussy? The choice is yours . . . But if I play with your butt first I can't touch your honeypot with the same naughty fingers . . .'

Coherent thought was a struggle, but what was left of Polly's higher reasoning was impressed by Severn's care and sensibility. It made her feel more tender towards the beautiful girl, and at the same time more lustful.

'In my pussy,' she grunted, angling her hips to facilitate her blunt instructions. Feeling deliciously sluttish she wiggled her body and offered her treasure.

'Just what you want, love,' said Severn, her fingertips already touching and probing at Polly's labia. 'You're beautifully wet, you know,' she went on, paddling in the moisture of which she spoke, slicking it up and down the length of Polly's channel, teasing her with a lightness and finesse of pressure that was as maddening as it was glorious. 'Do you want to taste yourself? Just a little lick . . . I know that I do . . .'

For a moment, the tantalising fingertips were gone and Polly heard a graphic sucking sound. 'Yum yum!' said Severn softly, but with obvious glee, and then Polly felt her nether parts once more being fingered. More comprehensively this time, as a copious sample was gathered.

'Here,' the blonde girl said, holding her narrow fingers just a centimetre or two from Polly's lips, then wafting them away again.

She's teasing me again, thought Polly, making me reach for it. Reach for myself. But hungry to know the taste of herself, she followed the bait like a greedy little beast.

Severn relented then, and allowed Polly to take the scented and anointed fingers between her lips.

Expecting a pungency born of her extreme desire, Polly was surprised by the innocuousness of her own intimate flavour. She tasted salt and an impression of something vaguely oceanic, but other than that, very little. She'd half expected herself to be strong, ripe and gamey, and yet somehow the very delicate quality of her taste was strangely addictive. When Severn repeated her sampling action and offered her glistening fingers once more to Polly's parted lips, it was impossible not to suck off the silky juices.

'Greedy girl,' chided Severn, pulling out her well-laved finger-tips. 'You're not giving me a chance to bring you off, are you? I can't make you come if you won't let me get inside you.'

Polly hung her head, breathing deeply. Her entire cunt was so sensitised now that if Severn so much as breathed on it, she knew she was likely to climax. And even though that was what she wanted to do, she was also enjoying the teasing, and the long drawn-out preamble.

'I need a moment,' she said, 'just a moment to calm myself. I don't want to come just yet. I want to make it last.' Flopping forward, she rolled on to her side, on the blanket, letting her legs loll wide apart so cool air could reach her clitoris.

Severn gave her an ambiguous look; it seemed to be half understanding, half amusement, and a great deal of something else that might just have been 'chicken!' Polly matched it though, keeping her own eyes steadfastly on the blonde. She had decided now that she wasn't going to be dominated.

'All right then. Time out for you it is,' Severn said non-chalantly. 'But I'm too turned on to wait. I'll have to make my own fun.' She made a graceful but telling gesture with her middle finger.

'Go ahead,' said Polly, trying to sound equally as laid back, but not feeling that way. It looked as if she was going to get a floorshow, which would make her more hot and bothered than ever.

Severn stood for a moment, like a statue carved in alabaster, and glanced around the room. What is she looking for, thought Polly. Does she need 'props'?

After a few seconds, Severn dragged one of the room's old overstuffed armchairs and placed it close up to the blanket where Polly was lying. The chair was a great, heavy thing, bulky and awkward, yet Severn showed little sign of effort in the manoeuvre and it dawned on Polly that the girl was extremely strong. All that digging and hoeing and working on the land, I suppose, she mused, admiring the sleek, toned power in the other girl's physique.

Satisfied with the positioning of her chair, Severn surprised Polly, not by sitting in it but by sliding neatly to the floor and settling there with her back resting against its front. Shuffling into position, Severn bent her knees, parted her thighs, then reached between them.

She's exhibiting herself to me, thought Polly in delight and wonder. She's showing me her pussy to taunt me because I won't let her touch mine for the moment. How can I watch this and retain even the tiniest bit of control?

'Do you masturbate much, Polly?' Severn suddenly asked, her voice studiedly casual as she began to comb apart the glistening blonde strands of her pubic bush. 'I do . . .' She cocked her head on one side, thoughtfully, then looked down, between her own legs, to better see her handiwork. 'And all the time really . . . I often have to break off when I'm working because I need an orgasm. I just seem to need them. I find it's difficult to concentrate when I feel horny . . . How about you, Polly?'

Polly licked her lips before she answered. Her cunt felt as if it was burning, and there was a reciprocal tingle in the very ends of her fingertips. She clenched her hands into fists to stop herself doing the deed right now. 'Yes, I masturbate,' she said. 'Quite a lot . . . Doesn't everyone?'

'Oh, I should say so,' murmured Severn, digging in even deeper. The curly golden hair was parted now, delicately combed away from the rosy niche it had protected. Severn had peeled back her labia, and was holding herself open, as if admiring the prominent button of her clitoris. 'Everyone I know is always at it. My friends . . .' She paused, looking up again and straight at Polly. 'The women in this town in particular. Nearly every time I call on someone, she's got her hand down in her knickers!'

Polly tried to imagine it. A whole community of women who felt free enough, and sufficiently sensualised, to masturbate at will, without a second thought. It was awesome.

'I suppose women all over are like that, but maybe not so up-front about it,' Polly posited, trying to sound as if she were making a serious observation, when all the time all she wanted to do was reach down and rub herself madly. But it had become a contest now, with herself, not to touch her clit until she was ready to let Severn do it. 'I'll bet there are women all over the place now, hard at it, bringing themselves off!'

Severn said nothing, but as Polly watched her, the other woman leant back more comfortably against her chair and closed her eyes. She appeared to be doing as Polly was, simply enjoying the coolness of the air against her clitoris.

How beautiful she is down there, thought Polly, shifting her thighs slightly to open herself more. I'd never much thought about what the cunt actually looks like, what a perfect creation of delicately sculpted flesh it really is.

The whole of Severn's vulva was glistening with fluid, and yet, when it seemed she was finally going to touch herself, the blonde girl made a big show of licking her fingertips in readiness. She sucked long and hard, lapping her tongue over each finger again and again, just as she'd made Polly take them into her mouth a few moments ago.

When Severn seemed satisfied that she'd lubricated her digits sufficiently, she opened her eyes, winked again at Polly, then bent to her work. Using one hand to continue to keep her sex-lips parted, she reached down and, with almost clinical precision, began to touch herself. First, she used a single finger to very lightly flick at herself, then she made a pad of two, and settled into a slow, leisurely action, back and forth, back and forth, back and forth . . .

Polly felt her own vulva swelling and flowing and responding as if it were she who was being fingered so expertly, she who was being slowly taunted and lifted . . . The desire to emulate Severn grew stronger and stronger and stronger.

'Why are you here, Polly?' said Severn suddenly, her voice perfectly pure and clear and modulated despite what she was doing between her legs.

Polly was shocked. The question was cool and calm, and in a moment of fear she understood the fullness of its meaning.

'I'm here because Inez thinks I should get laid, but hasn't time to bloody well attend to it herself!' she snapped. She felt both alarmed and yet, incredibly, even more stimulated. There was something threatening in Severn's question that tapped directly into her libido.

'I don't mean tonight,' said Severn, closing her eyes again as her hips began to weave and her bottom to circle against the floor, rucking up the rag rug. 'I mean why have you come here to Chandler's Haven? A woman like you . . . Inez said you had a great job back in London. Why have you left it?'

'I, er, I had a disagreement with the management. They were unfair. I couldn't stay.'

In a certain sense it was true. It *was* unfair that the program she'd written, that she'd taxed her brain to its considerable limit to perfect, could be taken away from her, just like that, and exploited by F&X Developments. OK, she'd worked on it in their time but the skill and the brilliance were hers alone!

Would Severn understand all this?

Of course, she'll understand, Polly chided herself. She might be frigging herself crazy at the moment, but she's a clever, astute woman the rest of the time. If I tell her what I've done, she'll weigh up the factors, and the morality. And she might think less of me . . .

It was no use thinking that Severn might not remember her question, Polly decided. The fact that the blonde woman had asked at all whilst mashing at her clitoris with her fingertips and grinding her bottom against the floor, showed that she had a very sharp and compartmentalised intelligence. Polly doubted that she herself could masturbate like that and still think straight, even if she'd tried.

'Life's unfair, Polly,' gasped Severn, bouncing and gyrating now. 'C– could you not have stayed and worked out a compromise?'

Could she have done? Yes, she could have. But she'd taken

the greedy path, become a thief almost, and now she had to hide out, down here, in this weird, dark little city by the sea.

'I don't know. I didn't stop to think. I just had to get away . . .'

Severn didn't speak for a few moments. She just gasped and grunted, and seemed to be having difficulty controlling all her muscles, much less the ones responsible for her powers of speech. Polly watched, enthralled in spite of everything, while the blonde girl took her hands away from her crotch for a moment, and, lifting her bottom, slid them beneath her. It took a second for Polly to realise what she was doing, but when it did, a fresh jolt of empathic excitement juddered through her.

What Severn was doing was parting her bottom cheeks and exposing her anus. Stretching it wide, so that when she sat down again, which she did, it would kiss the stone beneath her where the rag rug had been pushed aside. Polly imagined the cold unyielding texture of the stone against her own bare bottom, against her own tender little orifice, and she shuddered. It would be so stimulating, so dark and dangerous, so much an addition to the other pleasures that Severn was experiencing that Polly didn't know how the girl could hold out against her climax any longer.

But she did. Even as Polly gave in and pressed a hand to her own aching channel, Severn began to rock and jerk her body all over again, placing her fingers squarely between her thighs and visibly pressing.

'Oh glory halleluia, this is wonderful, Polly, this is wonderful!' she crooned, rolling herself against the stone, her trim buttocks distorted by the downward pressure she was creating to excite herself. 'This is the way I escape, Polly! This is my getaway. All I have to do is come!'

'Me too!' cried Polly, not sure what it was she was confirming, only sure that she could no longer wait to experience the sensations that Severn was enjoying. Beginning to pound herself, she lifted her pelvis, pushing and jerking reciprocally.

And as the crisis enveloped her and her cunt began to throb

and grab at some kind of divine inner space all of its own, she seemed to see the climaxing Severn overlaid with other images.

She saw Pat. She saw dancing rows of numbers and figures. She saw the abstract of freedom recede and danger personified walk towards her. She saw women, a mass of women, smiling and reaching for her.

Then she saw blankness. She could only feel. Her cunt was molten.

'Wow!' said Severn, a little while later, jolting Polly from the doze into which she'd drifted immediately after orgasm. At some time during this light slumber, she'd distinctly felt Severn come and lie beside her. Now as she woke fully, she realised she was in the blonde girl's arms. They were lying on the rag rug, their bodies both covered by the blanket.

'Yes, I agree. Wow back to you,' said Polly shakily, hardly daring to move, or even think, for fear of the consequences.

After a moment or two, Severn disengaged herself and sat up straight. Then she turned and looked down at Polly, her eyes wide and brilliant. 'I never did get to touch you,' she said, flexing her fingers suggestively. 'Would you like me to do you now? I'm sure I could get you to come again, no problem.' She waggled her blonde eyebrows like some pantomime lothario.

'I'm sure you could,' said Polly, sitting up beside her. The offer was tempting, but now the first fine sexual madness was over, she couldn't keep her thoughts from straying to other, more disquieting matters. Like the strangely pointed questions that Severn had been asking as she'd rubbed her pussy. 'But somehow I don't feel like it, just at the moment. I've had enough for now.'

Severn clearly tried to hide her disappointment, and just as clearly failed. This made Polly feel mean-spirited, like a prude or a killjoy. The beautiful girl's offer had been sweet and kind and genuine, an honest sensual gift that no red-blooded dyke in her right mind would have had to think twice about. Polly's self-opinion tumbled, and she reached out to touch Severn's arm.

'I'm sorry. I'm being a bit grumpy, aren't I?' she said, trying to sound placatory, but just feeling awkward. This was all so new, this game of love with women; she didn't know the rules.

'No, you're all right,' replied Severn with a smile as she placed her own hand momentarily over Polly's. 'It's me that's being greedy. But that's me to a fault. When I find something nice I want a lot of it . . .'

'But you're right. We could do it again,' said Polly, feeling vaguely let down, and very angry with herself for missing a chance she now realised she wanted to take. 'I think I want to.'

Severn removed her hand, then stood up. But she was still smiling. 'How about we finish that drink we started, and maybe have a bite to eat. Then let's see how we feel, eh?'

It made sense, but Polly was still disappointed and fed up with her own misjudgement. She smiled back though, and made as if to get up. 'Great idea. Can I help you with anything?'

'If you help, I won't even get as far as putting the kettle on,' Severn replied with a soft laugh. 'You just stay here and get your breath back. I won't be a minute.' She turned and made her way to the low door that appeared to be a scullery. When she flipped on the light switch Polly saw a sink and the corner of a big, old-fashioned fridge.

Severn pushed the door slightly shut behind her and suddenly Polly felt horribly alone in the room. The acute strangeness of her situation reasserted itself, and she wondered how she could come to be naked in the sitting room of a woman she'd never even met before tonight. How she could have watched that woman masturbate . . . and done it herself. She'd come so far from her days in London, and her abandoned life.

As she considered the changes, she noticed that the fire had burnt down a little, and she flung on another log, hoping she was doing the right thing. She had as little experience of tending a hearth as she had of being a lesbian. Then, wrapping Severn's blanket around her, she found herself thinking again of Pat.

Was this the life her first female lover had led? Instant rapport with a new, like-minded woman, leading to intimacy and sex within minutes of meeting her? Even though it was rather radical, it also seemed simple and remarkably honest. She thought of the mating dances she'd put herself through in the few relationships she'd had with men in her life, then shook her head, feeling profoundly glad those masques were over.

Feeling restless, she got up, still wondering where Pat was now, and how she felt, and who she was with. Polly couldn't imagine the American woman being alone and denying herself sex, just because some semi-casual 'thing' had foundered. Pat was more likely to feel angry, for about a minute, then find someone new.

I hope so, thought Polly, negotiating her way around the heavy old furniture in Severn's crowded sitting room. She acknowledged her own ambivalence. It would be nice to think that Pat was missing her, and missing the fact that there might have been something of real significance between them, but the better part of her really did hope Pat was happy again.

Like the proverbial moth to the flame, Polly naturally found herself drawn to Severn's computer, where it stood, on the table in the corner. Her hand moved automatically to the laptop's trackball, but then she halted herself, realising she really had no right to touch it. She of all people ought to understand the concept of computer privacy, considering the way her own various pieces of equipment were so assiduously secured, under lock and key, back at Inez's house. Even if someone had found them, every system had its own cryptic password.

For a moment or two, Polly watched the antics of the little yellow cartoon boy, wondering what irreverent witticisms he would be regaling his father with had the sound been on. It seemed odd to her that someone so obviously unspoilt, and close to the land as Severn was, should have what was clearly an up-to-the-minute and extremely powerful machine, but she supposed that, like herself, and a lot of other people, the blonde girl simply took pleasure in good equipment. Polly couldn't begin to imagine what type of programs Severn might be running, but if she had her own small business, she must do her own accounts and maybe produce promotional literature. Sure enough, there was an inkjet printer on the sideboard too, along with a scanner, and what appeared to be a particularly well-featured modem. Which was currently hooked up to the laptop, but with its status showing as 'on hook'.

She's on the Internet, thought Polly, feeling her own inner, mental computer begin to run again. She's on the Internet, and she knows I've just arrived in Chandler's Haven, and she's into sex games . . . Polly's heart thumped as she considered the notion that Severn might somehow be the person who had sent her the re-routed e-mail last night. The person who masterminded the so-called Enclave, and styled herself mysteriously as simply 'E'.

Don't be stupid, Poll, she chided herself, her fingers hovering once more over the 'trackball', the inset ball that was equivalent to a mouse on a desktop computer. Severn had been embroiled in a particularly all-consuming scenario with Inez at the time that the enigmatic e-mail had been sent, so that ruled out her as a suspect too.

Or did it? Polly wondered. Any computer could be scheduled to send messages or indeed perform any kind of task at a specific time. It was no big deal to set these things up. Maybe the e-mail had been sent by a scheduler that was programmed to dispatch it at a time when Severn had an 'alibi'? And when Inez had one too, for that matter? There was still no reason at all why either one of them might not be 'E'.

Without stopping to hesitate, Polly reached out and set her middle finger on the trackball. Then in the fraction of a second before the screen before her cleared of the saver, she thought again of what recent purpose she'd put that digit to. What wonders that finger could perform – both electronically and in the pursuit of female pleasure!

Then she forgot about such musings altogether, for on the screen was an image that was becoming disturbingly familiar. Set in the centre of a field of deepest, velvety purple was the single, white letter 'E', slowly revolving. Not stopping to waste time pondering the significance of what she was doing – she could hear the clatter of crockery in the kitchen – Polly guided the mouse pointer to the letter and double-clicked.

As she'd expected, the 'E' was the link to the next screen, which proved to be a browser-like space, with fairly standard toolbars and an array of rather cryptic-looking icons. She had time to take in only that one appeared to be rather like a stylised motorbike and another was reminiscent of the French symbol of 'La Liberté', because at that moment she heard an even louder rattling and sensed Severn's presence, in the room, not too far behind her. It was only long years of familiarity that allowed her to click the exit button and clear the screen again. Even so, the revolving 'E' was an accusation.

'Sorry!' she said, feeling her skin flush more than it had even while they'd been having sex. 'Force of habit. I work with computers. Did Inez tell you?'

Severn favoured her with a long, thoughtful look, and Polly felt deeply unnerved by the fact that it also contained an element of a smile about it too. It occurred to Polly that she'd been set up somehow; purposefully left alone with the laptop, so she'd snoop.

'Yes, she did,' replied Severn at length, nodding towards the rug, and moving to it, carrying her burden, another old tin tray, loaded with what looked like a fairly substantial cold supper this time.

Polly joined her, wondering how on earth she could explain her *faux pas*. It was the height of rudeness to start examining someone's computer and their data, even though hackers did it all the time, and in this case she'd almost been invited to . . .

The atmosphere was awkward for a moment, as strained as it would normally be when two strangers sat naked together on a rug. Severn snapped the spell.

'Don't worry, there's nothing secret on there.' She lifted a plate of sandwiches and offered them. Polly took one, and one of the mismatched smaller plates to put it on. 'Well, nothing that even you could have got into in such a short space of time. Inez said you were good, but I just wasn't away long enough.'

'Inez said I was "good"?' repeated Polly, taking a bite out of her sandwich, almost as a reflex, and vaguely registering some kind of tasty cooked meat filling. 'How on earth does Inez know I'm "good" with computers? She knows that's what I do for a living but I didn't think she knew enough to know whether I'm good or bad at it.'

'Oh, you'll probably find out that Inez knows a damn sight more than she lets on, you know,' Severn said, before pausing to chew her own sandwich. 'About a lot of things . . .'

Polly digested the statement while she continued to eat. The sandwich was excellent, she realised, the meat thick and hand-carved, the bread home-made if she wasn't mistaken. At length, she said, 'And what do you know about computers, Severn? That's quite an advanced machine you have, and you seemed to be on an intranet of some kind . . . a local network.'

Severn looked studiedly nonchalant for a moment, and it seemed to Polly that the blonde deliberately took a large bite of sandwich, so she couldn't answer straight away. As she chewed, a few crumbs tumbled down on to her marvellous breasts, and as a further distraction she brushed them off, making her firm flesh jiggle. Polly watched in fascination as a single crumb skittered its way down over Severn's tummy, then lodged itself in her golden pubic hair. There seemed to be nothing else in the room that Polly could look at.

'Yes, I suppose it is what you'd call a private net,' Severn said, seemingly unconcernedly, as she prised the breadcrumb from her bush and flicked it into the fire. 'A few of us in the town are on it. A sort of women's group.' She paused again, and looked up from her grooming activities and straight into Polly's eyes. Her own seemed full of secrets and excitement. 'You know . . .' she added, her voice warm and flirty.

A women's group? A group of lesbians? The mysterious 'Enclave'? Polly put her plate aside, suddenly no longer hungry.

'Inez mentioned that she had a circle of, um, friends,' she said non-committally. 'Would that be the same group?'

'None other,' said Severn, reaching for another sandwich and making Polly momentarily envy someone who so obviously didn't have to struggle to maintain such a magnificently svelte figure. 'Some of them make quite a big deal of it. Secret names and all that. It's called the Enclave, and we have a leader . . . Emperadora.' She giggled, and waggled her eyebrows as if, in her mind, fancy titles were silly and pretentious.

Polly had to agree. 'You must be kidding! Emperadora? What on earth kind of name is that?' As her companion began to giggle she let herself join in.

'Spanish for Empress, apparently,' said Severn, turning to the tray and pouring two cups of coffee. She poured a little milk in each and handed one to Polly.

Polly took the cup, and only after a moment did she realise she hadn't been asked whether she wanted milk or sugar. She opened her mouth to query this, but Severn was already speaking again.

'Mind you, the way she goes on, the word "Empress" is quite right for her. She just has a way of making you do exactly what she wants you to.'

'Who is she? This "Emperadora"? Will I get to meet her?' Polly took a quick sip of her coffee, which was as good as the sandwiches, then put the cup aside, too excited and slightly too alarmed to eat or drink any more.

'Maybe . . .' was all of Severn's reply. She was drinking her own coffee and looked over the rim of the cup at Polly, her eyes suddenly veiled and non-communicative.

She's hiding something, thought Polly. She won't say any more, I'll bet. She's already said too much.

'What do you mean "maybe"?' she persisted.

'Exactly what I said. Maybe you will meet her . . . Maybe you already have . . . I don't know.' Severn looked edgy now, and Polly knew that her surmising had been right.

'Don't you know?'

Severn shook her head, and as had happened with the crumbs, her splendid bosom shook invitingly.

'But surely you must know,' Polly went on, feeling like a terrier trying to prise its quarry out of a difficult hole whilst being distracted by a delicious roast dinner being waved about beside it.

Severn was idly fondling her own nipple now, her tongue sweeping her lower lip seductively as she did so. And Polly knew someone running interference when she saw it! 'How the devil can she make you do things if you don't know who she is? Surely you must meet to play these games of yours?'

Severn pushed her hands through her thick blonde hair, sweeping it back from her face, then sniffed her fingertips. 'That smell,' she murmured. 'I've washed my hands but I can still damned well smell it.'

'Severn?' Polly demanded, trying not to be swayed by her companion's sultry and ambiguous utterances. She had a feeling Severn wasn't talking about massage oil.

'It's like playing chess or some kind of strategy game in cyberspace,' Severn said at last, still studying her fingers. 'She directs moves by e-mail, sets up the encounters . . . and we never know whether she's been a part of them or not. It's very exciting.'

'But can't you work it out? By process of deduction?'

'None of us can be bothered to, Polly. Why spoil the fun?' Severn's smile was that of a patient aunt explaining something to a child who wouldn't or just couldn't get the message.

Polly thought about what Severn had said. It was fine, and it would have been great fun under other circumstances, but somehow she knew from the content of the e-mail that she'd received that 'Emperadora' had knowledge of far more than just her burgeoning sexual appetites.

Emperadora, whoever she was, seemed to know exactly what Polly had done in the real world, and what its implications were. The most dangerous of these was how vulnerable she was. How vulnerable she'd made herself, goddamnit! For someone into mind games, Polly was a perfect sitting duck, open to blackmail, coercion, and heaven alone knew what else.

It didn't bear thinking about but, somehow, Polly just couldn't stop . . .

SEVEN

Dial 'E' for ?

I let her distract me, thought Polly, as she lay in bed.

It was the following morning, she was back at Inez's house, and it was raining. With a forbidding downpour slashing against her window, there seemed little incentive to get up and go out, or even do very much of anything at all, so Polly was just chilling out and reviewing the time she'd spent with Severn.

I let her distract me just when I was beginning to find out something.

Polly had wanted to persist, and ask Severn more questions about Emperadora, and the games and messages, and the Enclave network.

Like who was in it? How far did it extend? What exactly were the games that they played? She'd felt certain, too, that Severn *did* know who Emperadora was, even though she'd continued to deny it. There had been so much progress to be made, but then Severn had begun to touch herself again.

'Why spoil the fun,' Severn had repeated, unselfconsciously letting her open hand drift over her breast, then cupping the globe of flesh, just as a lover would, and softly kneading. 'Life's too short for a whole load of questions, Polly. That's what I think

. . . I just take my pleasure where I can and ignore the whys and wherefores.'

Rapt, Polly had stared at her, entranced by the blatant diversionary tactic. Completely taken in by the sight of Severn's rosy nipple peeping out between her first and second fingers, as she massaged herself and began to wriggle her bottom to and fro.

'Let's finish what we started, Polly,' Severn had murmured, still caressing herself, and straying downwards to touch her lower belly now too. 'Life's too short,' she'd repeated. 'Let's just do it. You know you want to!'

And Polly had wanted to.

Half-crawling across the rug, she'd gone into Severn's arms as if it were a place she'd often been and found familiar. Then, panting with delight, she'd surrendered herself, and allowed Severn to kiss her senseless – whilst all the time rubbing exploring fingers across her bottom.

'Why don't we take a bath together,' said Severn presently, still gripping Polly's bottom cheek, her fingers delicately brushing Polly's anus. 'We can wash all this oil off ourselves and play around in all sorts of naughty ways in the water.'

Unable to stop squirming, Polly wasn't able to answer in words, but even so she sensed that Severn had got the message. The blonde girl released her, drew her to her feet, then led her by the hand out of the room and up a narrow winding staircase to an old-fashioned but well-appointed bathroom.

'I bet you need to pee, don't you?' Severn said casually, as she began to run the water and then dosed it liberally with bath crystals. 'Just help yourself. Don't mind me. I'm not embarrassed.' She gestured towards a huge, throne-like lavatory pedestal that stood in the corner of the room like a piece of modern, functionalist sculpture.

But I'm embarrassed, thought Polly, unable to forget the disturbing scene she'd witnessed between Severn and Inez, just last night. The simple action of urination was not without a special importance for the blonde girl. It was part of sex, and presumably watching it was too. Which made Polly deeply inhibited, even though she wanted to pee.

Severn laughed, as if she'd read Polly's thoughts. 'Don't worry, Poll,' she said. 'Just do it. I won't pounce on you. You'll be all right.'

Not really reassured, Polly took her place upon the lavatory. She was acutely aware of how the width of the mighty old pan parted her thighs, and how it made it all the easier for an observer to watch her flow. And regardless of what she'd said, Severn *was* watching.

'I don't know whether I can do this,' said Polly in a small voice. There seemed to be no point in trying to avoid the game her companion was playing. This was just another example of taking opportunist pleasure. Something that Polly devoutly wanted to do herself, if she was able.

'It's easy. Just rub yourself. Do you want me to help?' Severn moved away from the bathtub, an expression of excitement on her face.

'No! I'll be fine,' said Polly, a lot louder than she'd meant to. With a silent 'here goes!' she slid her hand between her thighs.

What surprised her the most, when she touched her pussy, was the extreme wetness she found down there. She was swimming in fluid, and she hadn't even started peeing yet.

Dear God, I'm an exhibitionist, she thought, and with the arrival of the notion came the truth of it. She was turned on by the thought of urinating in front of Severn, indeed, in front of any woman, and feeling hotter than ever, she felt her waters start to flow. A hot, pungent stream trickled noisily out of her, tinkling lightly on the porcelain of the basin, but in a spirit of devilment she did not remove her fingers. Instead, she continued to massage herself and wriggle on the toilet seat.

'Are you sure I can't help?' enquired Severn, much closer now.

'No . . . I'm fine . . .' murmured Polly dreamily. As she shifted her thighs again, she wondered whether to go all out and reach for climax.

After a few moments of rubbing and flicking and tapping at

her swollen clitoris, she decided to abandon it, though. One look at the fire in Severn's beautiful eyes and the creamy, firm-fleshed perfection of her body made Polly determined that the blonde girl was the handmaiden who'd serve her. The thought that such a magnificent creature could be brought to heel, and made to provide her, Polly Sayers, with physical pleasure was suddenly and uniquely intoxicating. She could have anyone, thought Polly; any woman, or even any man, on this goddamn earth, but she's mine for now. I'm going to make her work for me – she's going to give me orgasms until I'm sated.

And boy, did she ever! Polly reflected now, lying in her bed back at Inez's house, lightly touching a vulva that was still ever-so-slightly tender.

She recalled kneeling in the soapy water of the bath, clinging on the big brass taps for all she was worth, while Severn fucked her vigorously with three bunched fingers. It had been a sounder rogering than she'd ever had from even the best-built of her boyfriends and, in an odd way, even more intimate than being penetrated by a penis. Hands were intelligent, full of creativity and knowing, and it seemed to Polly with her new-found discernment, that a woman's hand was even more so. The hand of a woman was the instrument of ultimate power.

Of course, Severn hadn't only used her hands. She'd also used her lips and tongue, with enormous skill, on a number of occasions. And all Polly had had to do in return was –

Oh God, even now it made her blush! And it wasn't much of anything really. Especially not in the context of bathing and washing.

All she'd had to do was insert a well-soaped digit into Severn's snug anus.

'Oh, wow!' Polly whispered, feeling an intense urge to either giggle, or clutch her crotch, at the thought of what she'd done to Severn. And the reaction it had evoked . . .

She could still hear Severn's strangled groan of release and feel her, through the living medium of her body, rubbing furiously at her clit to extend and exacerbate the sensations.

'For Christ's sake, Sayers, leave it for now, will you?' Polly snapped, snatching her fingers out from between her legs.

It was no good. She just couldn't immerse herself totally in sex and forget about what she'd come here for. What she was supposed to be doing with her life, and her talents. Her 'baby'.

And she had a dangerous feeling Sanspareil was in jeopardy. That someone had traced her to this godforsaken place and might, at any minute, be ratting on her to her former employers. The police might be about to knock on Inez's front door, even as she, Polly the fugitive, lay here in bed, wondering whether to diddle herself. Again.

When the doorbell rang, Polly shot up in bed, her heart banging in her chest, almost as if she had had an orgasm.

No no no! It isn't them, she told herself, grabbing up her robe, and realising that after Severn had brought her home last night – in the most beat-up Beetle she'd ever seen – she'd tumbled into bed stark naked without even thinking of putting on her pyjamas.

The guest bedroom looked out over the gardens at the back, but when Polly peered cautiously out of the front landing window, she saw not the local constabulary at the door, but the innocuous and unthreatening figure of a young and rather wet postman. He was holding a wedge of letters and a small parcel in the lee of his oversized Post Office jacket, and looking nervous.

As there seemed to be no sign of Inez emerging from her bedroom – Polly was assuming the older woman had actually come home – Polly cinched her robe more tightly around her, and went down to get the post.

When she'd disarmed the alarm and opened the door, Polly found the young postman looking even more discomfited face to face than he had done when observed from above. But it was a discomfiture that was clearly laced with curiosity.

He knows Inez is a dyke and now he's wondering if I'm her lover, thought Polly, suddenly amused. It was quite titillating to be speculated about so racily.

Not yet, my lad, but I'm working on it, she told him silently as he proffered his delivery to her, rainwater dripping from his nose and the tips of his ears.

'Parcel to sign for,' he mumbled, those ears of his so bright red now Polly could almost imagine the moisture on them evaporating.

What is it about men and *us*? Polly thought as she signed the soggy clipboard. Why do they find the idea of two women together so arousing? It's illogical. We're declaring them redundant. No use to us.

Unwanted. Except as postmen, she added philosophically as the young man scuttled away, the vaguely hunched quality of his walk suggesting he had a hard-on as well as being soaked through and thoroughly miserable.

Polly studied the post she'd taken in. A few letters and bill-like brown envelopes for Inez. A small, brown-wrapped parcel about ten inches by three, anonymously labelled.

Plain brown wrapper, thought Polly with a grin. What's the matter, Inez, burnt out the motor on your latest vibrator?

She shook the package, but nothing rattled revealingly.

The last item made Polly forget all her frivolous speculations about her hostess's possible purchase of sex toys . . .

It was an official-looking letter, addressed to the Post Office Box that Polly had set up for herself, just before she'd left London. The envelope was pre-printed with the return address of the patent lawyer that Polly had engaged in closest secrecy and at great expense to herself.

With enormous trepidation, she slit open the envelope and began to read.

'And so, what do you think of her? You may answer freely; there's no need to censor yourself.'

The mistress laid the phone in its cradle and pressed the 'hands free' button, but it was some time before a voice issued from the speaker.

'She's very beautiful, ma'am. More so than I expected . . . but also different.'

The mistress smiled, concentrating for the moment on the voice itself rather than the words uttered. She loved the sound of that voice – usually so confident and so carefree – when it was tempered into schooled obedient tones in order to answer her. The very management of the syllables was a subtle form of restraint, a reminder of the power the mistress wielded over the speaker, and others like her. It was a part of the games they played; the balances they constantly adjusted and recalibrated for greater and lesser purposes. She found herself excited just by the drawing of a breath.

'In what way?' she prompted, hearing the breathing at the other end of the line – amplified by state of the art equipment – now grow a little ragged. 'Please expand upon your answer. I'm fascinated.'

There was another long pause, but the mistress didn't reprimand the slave at this point. She'd found that kindness and courtesy could be as strong a weapon in her arsenal as any amount of verbal or physical abuse. The gentle tone was, if anything, more menacing. It threw the subservient off balance, and made it difficult for her to know quite what to expect. The mistress knew that others of her ilk didn't generally subscribe to such a policy, but then, not prone to modesty, she knew she was greater than they were.

'I didn't expect her to be so amenable, mistress,' said the slave at last, her respiration even more disturbed.

The mistress smiled again and idly pressed a key on the computer keyboard beside her. She considered sending an e-mail to the subject of the conversation, even as they spoke of her, but then changed her mind and, seeking something more facile, closed the window again. A few further keystrokes brought up a simple card-like game.

'What do you mean by amenable? Is she friendly?' The mistress clicked the mouse button quickly, pleased that so many cards already had their values exposed.

'Yes . . . No –' The slave hesitated and the mistress could almost imagine her biting her beautiful lower lip nervously. She imagined other actions too, and would have bet good money on the fact that they were taking place in reality. She had known the woman on the end of the line for quite some time.

'My dear,' she prompted, the gentle words silky but firm.

'She – she didn't seem at all shocked by another woman coming on to her. She seemed quite at ease with it. As if she wanted it. As if she were used to it.'

'Maybe she is?' observed the mistress, turning over card after card now, on a winning streak. 'Maybe she has had experience with women? Maybe she's been touched before you got your greedy little paws on her?'

There was another long hesitation, and the superb audio system picked up the sound of rustling and of a body moving slightly.

'Perhaps so, mistress,' came the voice again, tense and shaky.

'You have had your paws on her, haven't you?' enquired the mistress, winning her game in what was a very brief space of time, even for her. Growing bored, she closed the program and stared for a moment at the letter slowly revolving on the screen. 'You have carried out your instructions, haven't you, my dear? You know I'll be disappointed if you haven't.'

'Yes! Yes, ma'am, of course I have!'

The mistress let the slight impertinence go. There was a quality of ambivalence in the voice of the slave now. Was the woman lying? It was possible. The slave might not even have approached the target sexually. She might not have had a chance. But it didn't really matter what the truth was as long as the slave had thoughts that were lurid.

'In that case, what is her body like?' the mistress asked, her fingers going, almost without any thought on her part, to the buttons on the front of her shirt. 'Would *I* like her?'

'Oh, yes, ma'am!' the slave gasped. 'You *would* like her! She's got plenty of flesh on her, but she's not fat. She's got lovely breasts and legs. Smooth skin. She's very sensitive.'

The mistress formed her inner picture easily. She would have liked to have tested that sensitivity right now. Unbuttoning a couple of buttons, she slid her hand inside her shirt and found one of her nipples. It was hard, like the pit of a fruit, and touching it sent exquisite silvery shards of feeling through her body. But schooled in her disciplines, her lips and voice remained unbiased by them.

'And how did she seem generally?' she enquired. 'In herself . . . in her demeanour?'

The mistress could almost taste the slave's frustration across the airwaves. The woman was hungry now, excited. She wanted blatant words, graphic details, outrageous requests that would require even more outrageous answers. She was ready to talk foul and dirty; nominally at the behest of her beloved mistress, but really for her own gratification.

But the essence of me being your mistress is that I control you, thought the mistress, continuing to strum her own nipple and ride the sweet sensations that it gave her. This was the game that she loved to play with her slaves. Denying them what they wanted until exactly the moment she wanted them to have it. She could imagine her companion at the end of the line rubbing and diddling herself compulsively, but needing the conversation, the delicious obscenities, to induce a crescendo.

Not until I'm ready, my sweet, she told the slave silently, knowing that the woman on the other end of the line was fully aware of that fact.

'She seemed a little nervous . . . preoccupied. As if she had something on her mind.'

'Did she indeed? How interesting.'

And it was.

Knowing that certain strategies were at work gave the mistress the keenest satisfaction. Ignoring the slave hanging on her every word, she opened her shirt and bared her breasts to the thin, clear light that was streaming in through her window. It was a wet day, but the freshness in the air seemed to add to her pleasure somehow. She wondered what the 'subject' was doing right now? Whether her preoccupations were all-consuming or whether she still had a little time for the fleshly pleasures?

Beginning to fondle both nipples now, the mistress glanced at the digital clock in the corner of her computer screen. It was almost noon. The subject should be up by this hour, and the post would most definitely have been delivered at the house at which she was staying.

Was she panicking? Was she even now preparing to run again? The mistress thought not. She had an idea that the attractions of Chandler's Haven would hold the girl a while. Keep her *in situ* for the next round of developments. The idea of that, and the anticipation of it, only added to the mistress's growing arousal and, remembering her slave still waiting patiently, she cupped and stroked her breasts with a touch of roughness.

'Are you nude?' she said abruptly, enjoying the quaint, old-fashioned terminology. It sounded ruder somehow, than the word 'naked'. More insulting. As if she were reducing the waiting woman to a painted cipher, and denying her as a person.

'N– no, mistress,' came the stuttering reply. The words were juddery, but the mistress recognised happiness now that the conversation had returned to sexuality.

'Then what are you wearing?' asked the mistress softly, calming her own voice as she relinquished her breasts and began unfastening the zip and button of her trousers. 'Describe it to me. Every detail.' Without making a sound, she dragged down her own clothes until they were a bundle round her ankles.

'I – er . . . I'm wearing jeans, socks, panties, a T-shirt and a bra,' said the slave, sounding as if she were shamefaced to be so well protected.

'That's too much, my dear,' said the mistress calmly – as she pressed a finger to the tip of her aching clitoris. 'Take off everything below the waist, but leave the rest. And when your crotch is naked I want you to spread your legs wide open. As wide as you can get them . . .' She paused, ostensibly to think, but in reality to regain control of herself. Her cunt was puffed and slick now; she was very close to orgasm.

'Where are you sitting, slave? In what kind of chair?'

'I was sitting in an armchair but now I'm standing up, taking my things off.'

'What things? Specifically?'

'My knickers, ma'am.'

'Are they wet?'

'Yes, ma'am.'

'Very?'

'Yes, ma'am.'

'Then lick them. Taste your own wetness.'

The slave made a small, telling sound. The tiniest of deeply fraught whimpers.

This is exactly what she wants, thought the mistress, her own cunt trembling.

'Please do it, my dear,' she murmured, her voice revealing nothing.

There was another short silence.

'And how do you taste?'

'Salty . . . just a little bit. Not much of anything really.'

'Thank you for not lying, my dear,' commented the mistress, smiling. 'I know of others who would have exaggerated. Just for effect.'

Imagining the discreet flavour of the woman at the other end of the line, the mistress took time out to decide what the next move would be. She stroked herself lightly and very carefully, picturing a variety of demeaning tests she could put her willing slave through, conjuring up clear images of a half-bared body, bent and jerking.

'I want you to get astride the arm of your chair, my dear,' she said at length, 'but don't sit down yet.'

The sound of shuffling issued from the speaker.

'Are you ready?'

'Yes, ma'am.'

'Now, I want you to lubricate both your middle fingers. Use saliva, or cunt juice, I don't care which . . . Then I want you to reach around behind yourself, and push a finger into your anus. Then from the front, put the other in your snatch.' She heard a gasp of outrage but, impressively, no denial. 'Then sit down, on both your hands, with both holes plugged.'

There was another silence, longer this time, and punctuated with small, squeaky sounds of awkward movement. After a few moments, there came a groan, soft and heartfelt.

'Are you in position, my sweet?' the mistress enquired, when it appeared that her slave was finally settled.

'Yes, ma'am.'

'And how does it feel?'

'Uncomfortable.' The voice was contained, almost choked.

'Only that?'

'And . . . exciting. I feel stuffed. I want to come.'

'All in good time,' murmured the mistress creamily, parting her own legs and positioning herself more comfortably. 'But, for now, you must stay quite motionless, and simply listen . . .' She licked her own fingers, then replaced them squarely between her legs. 'While I describe the things I'm doing to myself!'

Closing her eyes, she began to slick herself in earnest.

Up in her bedroom, at Inez's, Polly read the letter again and again.

What did they mean 'irregularities with her application'? She'd thought it was all sorted out and going smoothly, and now they needed to see yet more detailed specifications of the software! And just who was this new person who was dealing with her file? This Ms C. Ignoto?

Polly felt choked with panic. Was this merely a simple hiccup at the patent lawyers, or was it the first iceberg tip of something more disastrous? What if F&X had been making enquiries and got in contact with the lawyers, asking them to stall? But surely they wouldn't do that, would they? Wouldn't they take a swifter, more direct form of action?

But you know this business, Poll, she told herself as she set up her laptop and her portable bubble-jet printer and began preparing a more detailed specification, as requested. People are always playing sneaky tricks on each other – it's more or less a given thing! The standard practice . . .

And yet she had a feeling that her own paranoia was

exacerbating the situation. These notions that she was being watched, and controlled somehow, by some omnipotent sex goddess who lived in Chandler's Haven. Someone who could even be Inez, or maybe Severn, but also some female as yet unmet and unknown. Some female overlord who knew her every dirty secret. It just didn't make sense but she couldn't dismiss the possible connections.

Throughout the late morning and early afternoon, Polly worked assiduously on the specification document. Every detail had to be perfect and fully described, or the resulting patent, when she got it, could turn out worthless. She was grateful she'd had the foresight to bring with her the appropriate stationery that she needed.

By the time she'd finished, she'd also come to the conclusion that to send the document back to the lawyers by post was probably not a good idea. She considered registered mail, but then decided it would be worth going the extra mile, just to be on the safe side. She'd send the damned thing in by motorbike courier and be done with it.

'What are you looking for? Can I help?' enquired Inez breezily from over Polly's shoulder a little while later, when Polly was flicking through the Yellow Pages, in the hall.

'I wanted to order a motorcycle courier,' muttered Polly, taken aback. Inez looked perfectly normal and cheerful, as if nothing unusual ever happened in Chandler's Haven, and she wouldn't even dream of passing Polly on to one of her lesbian girlfriends for an entire evening of frantic sex-play. Polly had a feeling that if she even mentioned such a thing, Inez would probably say she was imagining things.

'What for?' said Inez, with a casualness that sounded manufactured to Polly. The older woman was dressed in one of her beautifully cut designer trousers and top outfits again, this one a soft pink that looked amazing with her sleek, dark hair.

'I've some papers to send to my lawyer,' Polly said, hoping Inez wouldn't press for specifics. 'Just work stuff, but I wouldn't want them to go astray.'

'Well, you should use the service I sometimes use,' said Inez, taking the directory from Polly and putting it aside. Then, from the pin-board above the phone, she took down a card, 'Here, try these. They're very efficient. I always send for them whenever I have artwork to deliver.'

'Well, I suppose that would be all right,' said Polly doubtfully. In view of her earlier notions about the possibility of some kind of conspiracy, of which Inez may well be a part, it seemed like madness to let her hostess take control this way. Even so, Polly held her hand out for the card.

'Let me,' said Inez, and before Polly could protest she was already dialling what was presumably the courier service number. 'Yes! Hello! Could you send someone round to Ash House, Chandler's Haven? It's Inez Parker here and I've got a package to send to –' she covered the receiver '– London, I presume?' she said to Polly. And when Polly nodded, she went on and made the arrangements.

Too late now, thought Polly, as Inez chuckled and exchanged pleasantries with whoever was on the other end of the line. Which made Polly then wonder if the person answering the phone at the courier service was yet another of Inez's lesbian friends. It's as if they're spreading a net around me, or weaving a web, Polly mused, her excitement stirring even as she almost smiled at the apposite terminology.

'There will be a courier here in fifteen minutes. Is that it?' asked Inez, putting down the phone and knodding towards the well-sealed and carefully addressed envelope in Polly's hands, a slightly smug expression on her face. Clearly organising other people's lives gave her enormous satisfaction.

Especially their sex lives, thought Polly wryly, realising that Inez hadn't asked a single question yet about last night.

'Yes,' she said, turning the envelope over again and wondering if it would be safe in the hands of some unknown courier, and not a nationally recognised company.

'Oh, don't worry,' said Inez, as if reading her thoughts, 'it will be perfectly safe. I've sent all sorts of valuables via this service.

Come on, let's have some tea while we wait for the courier to arrive.'

'So, what do you think of Severn?' said Inez, apropos of nothing, when they were settled in the kitchen with their tea.

Although she'd been half-expecting the question, Polly was nevertheless taken aback. What could she say? That she thought Severn was a sweet person? A fine masseuse? One of the hottest fucks imaginable, given her own inexperience in the realm of woman to woman sexuality?

'I like her,' she said at last, stirring tea that contained no sugar to dissolve. 'She's good company. Kind. Honest. What more could one ask for?' She looked at Inez, challenging her to comment and to take the matter further.

Inez laughed, then took a biscuit from the plate of chocolate and cream fancies she'd put out to accompany the tea. Trying to be a proper hostess for a change, thought Polly idly, following suit.

'What indeed?' said the older woman, snapping her biscuit in two and popping a piece in her mouth. She chewed with such an obvious pleasure it made Polly feel uncomfortable. Why did everything now seem to have a blatantly sexual context?

'She's very beautiful too,' added Polly, knowing she wouldn't be let off with just bland social niceties here. 'Very sensual . . . She was very sweet to me.'

'I hope you had sex with her,' said Inez, quite calmly, before attacking the rest of her biscuit with the same gusto as before. 'I promised her that . . . She'd be disappointed if she didn't get some action!'

'Inez!'

Inez laughed again, her teeth looking very white, almost predatory in the watery sunshine that was now coming in through the kitchen window.

'Don't "Inez!" me, Polly,' she said, still chuckling. 'You know you're interested. You know you want to find your way around in this. To meet women. Have sex with them.' She reached out and put her hand over Polly's, on the table. 'Don't go all prudish on me now. It won't wash. You *know* you're a dyke!'

'OK! I am one!' Polly shook off Inez's fingers, feeling cross, but somehow relieved at the same time. 'And Severn was fabulous! I must have come a dozen times! There, are you satisfied now?'

'For the moment,' said Inez speculatively, as she made as if to pour them more tea. The doorbell, however, saved Polly the embarrassment of more questions.

'There, that's your courier,' announced Inez, leaping to her feet and on her way through to answer the door before Polly could hardly draw breath and follow.

By the time Polly had reached the front door, Inez was actually out in the street and talking quietly to the courier, who had returned to his bike and was now sitting astride it, entering details on to a clipboard.

If I didn't know better, I'd say she fancied him too, thought Polly, deeply puzzled. Was Inez bi-sexual, then? Did she enjoy men as well as women? It didn't seem likely, given what Polly had gathered of Inez's preferences so far, but then again, here in Chandler's Haven, nothing could quite be ruled out of the equation. Hesitating to break up such an intimate-seeming conversation, Polly held back and observed her hostess's dark companion.

The courier was clearly tall. His length of leg alone indicated a six footer at least, and his body appeared lithe and athletic, even when encased in a suit of heavy, no-nonsense working leathers. There was no way to see the man's facial features, as he still wore his helmet with the visor only slightly raised to permit his voice to be heard, but something in his proud, almost militaristic bearing suggested he was good-looking and very much aware of the fact. Despite her recent discoveries, Polly felt a fleeting twinge of interest.

Oh God, she thought, am I bi too? Aren't things complicated enough already without not being sure of what I am and what I want? As Polly watched, Inez laughed and slapped the courier lightly on his leather-clad thigh, and he shook his head as if amused by something she'd said. They looked completely relaxed together, which confused Polly even more.

After a few more moments of this exchange, Inez turned towards Polly, where she stood in the doorway, and called out, 'Hey, Polly! I thought you were in a hurry for your letter to get there? Come on! Time is money! Chop chop!'

As Polly moved forward, she realised that both biker and bike were even more imposing close up. The machine was big and sleek, something Japanese, she suspected, done out in a livery of mostly black with the faintest frosting of bronze. Its rider wore all black, like a carapace, plain, hard leathers. He held out the clipboard to Polly, and gestured for the envelope.

Strong silent type, huh, she thought, effecting the swap and beginning to fill in the relevant particulars on the fortunately very clearly set-out form. I used to like all that stuff before I found out there was a better way, she told him silently. Nevertheless, she still felt a troubling frisson of response.

When it came to the payment section, Polly hesitated, thinking momentarily of the traceability of credit cards. It didn't seem worth worrying about, considering that this transaction would lead to all sorts of other ways to track her down, but the pen still stalled.

'Oh, just put it on my account,' interjected Inez to the courier. Then she turned to Polly. 'It's OK, you can settle with me later. Don't worry.'

With that the business in hand appeared completed. The courier took back his board and placed it, along with the letter, inside one of his panniers. Then, with a small salute, he flipped his visor fully down and flicked the bike's ignition. Stepping back from the truly thunderous roar of the powerful machine, Polly was left with the fleeting impression of a strong mouth surrounded by a surprisingly pale complexion.

A moment later, after a sequence of small, economically effected movements – the kick away of the bike's stands, a twist of the throttle, and a strong push from a sternly booted foot – the bike was pulling away and already streaking up the road in the direction of the motorway.

As Polly turned, she saw an expression of longing in Inez's eyes that was nothing short of hunger.

'You know him, don't you?' demanded Polly without thinking. 'Goddamnit, Inez, you *more* than know him. I thought you didn't like men? What's going on?'

'Oh, yes, Polly, I *know* that courier,' said Inez, laughing once more. A rich, throaty laugh that confirmed all Polly's suspicions. 'And in the biblical sense, too, I suppose you'd say . . .' She pressed her hand to her throat, and her fingers flexed sensually.

'But you're a lesbian . . . I didn't realise . . . Are you bi-sexual?'

Inez continued to laugh, shaking her head as the biker had done before her.

And then it dawned on Polly. It was obvious really. She thought of those firm lips she'd seen, and their reddish tint. The extreme and immaculate pallor of the skin around them. The smoothness.

'It was a woman!' she cried, everything slotting neatly into place. The spasm of interest she'd felt redoubled, twisting inside her. 'That courier is a woman, isn't she? She's one of your friends!'

'Of course Ellen is one of my friends. Why else do you think I vouched for her reliability? I'd far rather entrust something important of mine to her than some stupid, greasy yobbo of a man who I don't know from Adam,' said Inez, the moue of distaste on her confirming that she certainly was *not* bi-sexual. 'You do see that, don't you, Polly?'

'Yes, I'm sure it makes sense,' replied Polly as they re-entered the house and headed for the kitchen and the resumption of their tea party.

She wasn't sure, though, whether Inez's declaration made sense for her at all . . .

Inez's group of cronies seemed to be gaining access to her in all sorts of ways, and not only ones that were sexual. The members of the Enclave, whoever and however many they were, had made implications, and issued subtle hints and threats, that they knew the reasons for her flight, and that there were questions to be asked about her project. Worse still, they now had a further link to her, in the real world, via her patent lawyer.

Are they working with F&X somehow? Are they watching me? Watching my moves? Waiting to pounce?

And what of this new one, the biker goddess, thought Polly, remembering the long stretch of those leather-covered legs as the woman had effortlessly straddled her powerful machine.

Where did she fit in? Was she a key player? When would she turn up again, as it surely seemed she must?

And it hadn't escaped Polly's notice that both 'Emperadora' and 'Ellen' began with an 'E' . . .

EIGHT

Lean Machine

'Have you ever ridden pillion with her?'

It was some time later, when they were eating their evening meal, that Polly voiced a question that had been on her mind since they'd watched Ellen roar away on her motorcycle. There was something about the machine's power, and the need to hold the rider, that suddenly obsessed her. And filled her with a need to overcome long-standing fears.

Inez laid down her knife and fork and reached for her wineglass. 'Once or twice,' she said, taking a sip from her glass. 'She's very particular about that bike. She doesn't let just anyone ride with her. You have to be very, very good in order to get an invitation.'

Good?

What the devil did that mean, Polly speculated. Good in bed, presumably, but she sensed there was more to it than simply a bit of kissing and fondling and sucking. She thought again of the hard aura that had seemed to hang around the mysterious female courier. It had a lot to do with the leather, she supposed, which in and of itself carried a multitude of nuances. People who wore leather were into a special kind of game. And even in her inexperience, Polly knew a little bit about them. She remembered things that Pat had said, when they'd been lying in bed, kissing and cuddling and fantasising; things she'd read in books that Pat had recommended she read. Pat herself had worn leather, but Polly had parted from her too soon, she realised now, to know the true significance of it . . .

'How good?' she asked after a moment. She felt like pressing Inez for answers in the hope that what she discovered would push away her sudden feeling of loss and melancholy.

Inez took another drink of wine, and Polly noticed that the older woman beginning to blush a little.

Bingo! Polly sensed that exactly the distraction she needed was on its way.

'Very good,' said Inez, with obvious caution.

'In what way, Inez?' persisted Polly, feeling stronger, as if she'd somehow shifted her companion into the very mode that she adopted in Ellen's presence. That she herself was acquiring the biker's mode – and that of Pat.

'Ellen likes to play games.'

'But doesn't everyone in Chandler's Haven play games?' Polly ran her fingertip to and fro around the base of her glass. 'What makes Ellen's games so significant? What's so special about her?' Is she 'Emperadora', she wanted to ask, but withheld the question. It would soon be easy enough to work it out.

'What do you know about sex, Polly?' asked Inez, leaning back in her chair, her eyes assessing and her moment of slight weakness clearly over. 'I mean all the different colours of it . . . Not just the things most women – and men – do in bed?'

'I know that people do some pretty unlikely things for pleasure,' offered Polly. She paused, then dashed on impulsively, 'Like you and Severn, the other night for instance. To taunt someone when they're dying to pee doesn't at first sight seem like a way to give them pleasure, does it? And yet it obviously does, or you wouldn't have been doing it.'

'*Touché*. Obviously you do know enough,' said Inez obliquely.

The moment stretched out, like a wire, as if Inez were determined to hype up the tension. Finally, Polly had had enough.

'So, is it sadomasochism then?' she said, biting the bullet, and hoping she was right. She knew she was, really, but it was still a stretch to say it, and make it real. 'Does she like to hit people? Ellen, I mean.'

Inez gave her a long, long look, and Polly's confidence quailed. She had a feeling that her assessment of Ellen's predilections was probably far too simplistic.

'That's a very small part of it,' said Inez, confirming Polly's suspicions. 'So many people think that sadomasochism is simply about beating each other. But there's more, so much more. It's so much richer an experience than that.'

'I don't understand,' said Polly, although it was partially a lie. She knew there was more, and she found the concept almost unbearably fascinating, but she wanted to hear the details from Inez's cool, perfect lips.

'It's about power and trust, Polly,' Inez said, assuming an expression of almost rapt contemplation. For a moment, Polly thought of religion. Of zeal and obsession. It was all here, she realised, and it thrilled her.

'Giving power and taking it,' went on Inez, 'Trusting, and respecting the trust put in one . . . It's quite hard to describe until you've experienced it first hand.'

'It hurts though too, I suppose?'

'Oh yes, my dear,' said Inez roundly. 'Of course it hurts. But you'll soon find that's a plus, not a minus.'

Soon? Polly thought, when she was back in her room, back at her computer, tweaking at what seemed like a never-ending series of small program bugs that would have to be eradicated before she could claim that her software lived up to its 'matchless' name.

After her brief discourse on the delights of a relationship based on corporal punishment, Inez had rather abruptly switched the subject back to Ellen's motorcycle. Polly had felt a little frustrated by this at first – as something in her was beginning to fire up at the thought of penetrating a new sexual mystery – but she had to admit that Inez made the act of riding pillion sound fairly thrilling too. In the end the older woman had said that Ellen would most certainly give Polly a ride if she asked her for one but with the implication that a certain price might be asked.

Don't be insane, Polly, she told herself, heaving a deep sigh, closing the program, and turning from the screen. She was making far too many screw-ups for it to be worth working tonight. And yet it seemed so crazy to get her mind all tangled up in thoughts of something she might not like anyway, especially when she needed her head perfectly clear, and her wits about her.

At any moment, her world and her career might come tumbling down in ruins about her, and here she was, wondering what it might be like to have a leather-clad woman spank her bottom. Or whatever Ellen's chosen practice turned out to be.

What seemed like the hundredth time that day, Polly thought of Pat again. There had always been that edge in their relationship, she reflected. That spark of danger, and challenge that kept the adrenalin flowing. Polly had the sure feeling that if she and the American had stayed together much longer, she might have ended up being beaten by Pat. There had been unequivocal hints in the magazines and books Pat had shown her, and in the subtle currents of the way they'd always been together. Polly felt an arrow of regret pierce her heart at what she'd lost.

But just when she was considering trying the Web again as a diversion – deadly slow as it was when using a mobile – a sound outside made her spirits lift and her pulse race madly.

Just drawing up outside was a roaring, growling motorbike.

Polly ran to the landing window and looked out. She knew who it was, but some child-like twinge of fear compelled her to check, just to make sure. She felt almost sick with excitement when she looked out and saw that a now familiar figure was on the point of dismounting from the gleaming Japanese motorcycle.

Standing, Ellen Allenby, as Polly had since discovered she was called, looked impossibly tall. The shadows and highlights on her dark leather suit seemed to elongate her figure and make her look menacing and mythical, and her shiny black helmet wouldn't have looked out of place on a space marine. It wasn't all that many steps to Inez's front door, especially for someone with legs as long as Ellen's, but even in those few moments, Polly got an impression of the mighty Amazon's stride. Her gait was elegant, yet extremely efficient and almost manlike. Polly felt something stir in the pit of her belly, like a serpent of yearning. She could hardly wait to see the woman up close – and without that helmet.

Inez beat her to the door, however, and was just ushering the newcomer inside as Polly half-ran down the stairs. She was just in time to see the ceremony of the unveiling.

In a smooth and clearly long-accustomed action, Ellen lifted the black helmet clear of her head, then shook herself to loosen her squashed-down hair. Polly felt her breath catch as the other woman noticed her.

Ellen Allenby had a face as powerful and distinctive as her body. Her cheekbones were high, her jaw was strong, but despite that she was womanly. She had skin the colour of cream, dark brown eyes, and her hair appeared to be brownish-black too. But it was presently damp with sweat, making her strong dark curls gleam and shimmer as she moved, like a twentieth-century Medusa.

It was only when Polly reached the bottom of the stairs and made her way towards the newcomer that she realised again how almost unnaturally tall the woman was. Polly was medium height herself, and Inez was about an inch or so taller, but Ellen Allenby towered over the pair of them like a goddess, looking down on Polly as if she were surveying a lower form of life.

Or I could just be imagining things again, thought Polly, when the woman gave her a warm, slightly crooked smile.

'So this is the "Polly" I've been hearing so much about, eh? The computer genius getting away from it all, out of town?' Passing her helmet to Inez, as a knight would to his squire, Ellen held out her hand to Polly, clearly as much in challenge as in welcome. 'Ellen Allenby, pleased to meet you,' she said, grasping Polly's hand firmly, about a second before it reached the optimum position, which put Polly at a disadvantage, and a little off balance.

'My pleasure,' she said, feeling shaken as much emotionally as physically.

Ellen didn't reply immediately, but there was an answer in the long, calculating glance she bestowed on Polly. *It could be. We'll have to see . . . You're already on probation.*

'Come on in to the lounge, you two,' said Inez, putting aside the helmet and reaching for the jacket that Ellen was already shucking off. 'Let's have a drink, shall we? Get comfortable and have a chat.'

'Just a small one,' Ellen said quietly, her low, resonant voice sounding vaguely amused. 'I'm driving . . .' She nodded towards her helmet, her dark brows arching significantly.

'A spritzer then,' suggested Inez, something in the lightness and breathiness of her tone suggesting to Polly that she too was nervous of the majestic Ellen.

'Marvellous,' replied the leather-clad giantess, walking ahead of them into the sitting room.

As Inez fussed around getting the drinks, Polly had an additional chance to observe the new arrival. Ellen had immediately thrown herself down into an armchair, and she just sat there for a few moments, eyes closed as she lay back and passed her fingers through her damp black hair in a gesture of unwinding. She appeared perfectly relaxed, but not slouched; quite at ease, yet ready for anything. The strongest impression Polly received was that of a female soldier, but a non-conformist, not part of the rank and file.

Even Ellen's clothing bucked the system in a certain way.

In the meagre knowledge of lesbian forms and hierarchies that Polly had learnt from Pat, and from the books that Pat had lent her, she had gleaned the notion that the female powerbrokers always wore black. Classic black leather, as a kind of totem, an instant symbol. But on observing Ellen Allenby more closely, Polly saw that the tall woman's clothing – a leather vest or jerkin-type garment, worn with leather jeans and chunky boots – wasn't actually black, though it had first appeared to be so. The colour was, on closer inspection, a deep, dark brown, a sort of black overlaid with a bronze frosting which, Polly realised, with a strange pang of pleasure, was exactly the colour of the motorcycle outside. It seemed that in a society of rule-breakers, Ellen Allenby was still unusual.

But just as Polly was making these inner observations, and congratulating herself on her insights, the tall woman opened her eyes and stared back at Polly, her expression amused.

'What's the matter, Polly?' she said, stretching out her long legs in a graceful feline flex. 'Never seen a woman this big before?'

Polly blushed. Then felt herself seem to blush more, because she was blushing. Her skin felt puce, and she could hardly frame a syllable.

'God, I'm sorry, I was staring,' Polly said in a rush, aware that she was in danger of sounding like a gushing adolescent. She had never seen any figure quite as imposing as the woman who sat before her, male or female. 'But . . . well, yes, you are quite tall for a woman.'

'True,' was all Ellen said in reply, then, 'Thanks, love,' when Inez handed her a drink.

Inez gave a glass of the same to Polly, but it might have been a vial of turpentine for all the impact its flavour made on her. She was still pink-eared and gobsmacked in the presence of Ellen Allenby.

'So, what are you working on at the moment, Polly?' asked Ellen at length, after subjecting Polly to another of her extended, yet strangely benign scrutinies. 'I should imagine the sort of work you do is difficult to take a break from, isn't it? That it's in your blood somehow?' She took a sip from her glass, then passed the back of her fingers across her lips in what was almost a parody of the same gesture as a man would make it.

She's playing with me, thought Polly, trying desperately to organise an answer. She's taunting me, not quite being what I expect her to be, and yet hinting at it. I wonder what Inez has told her about me?

'Oh, just a software program, nothing interesting,' she replied, knowing it was perilous to even say she *was* working. This woman could very well be Emperadora – in fact, probably *was* Emperadora – and that person seemed to know far more about Polly than just her sexual aspirations.

'What kind of software?' the Amazon persisted, her voice acquiring just a little sharpness, right at the edge of perception. Polly felt her guts melt – in fear and anticipation. 'I'm not a totally ignoramus where computers are concerned, Polly. I use one every day, I surf the Net, I know the jargon.'

'Well, it's something a little new,' began Polly, then went on to recount as much as she dare about Sanspareil, and its fairly revolutionary structure. She withheld the program's name, of course, but was aware, even as she spoke, that she was dancing on a precipice and could well be setting the seal on the doom of her enterprise, and indeed of her future. But Ellen Allenby, with her long lean body and her powerful eyes, seemed to put her into a truth-baring trance like a human version of Scopolamine.

'Sounds fascinating,' the tall woman said when Polly ran out of steam. 'A thing like that must take a lot of time and concentration . . . Hours and hours of work. How on earth did you manage to develop it? And have a "day" job, and a life? That's quite an achievement, Polly. You must've had to make some sacrifices?' The last sentence was delivered as a very light question, and Polly felt her metaphorical feet losing their grip on that notional ledge.

'Oh, it didn't take that long,' she said, fudging the issue, knowing she was transparent to this woman.

'Then you really are a genius,' observed Ellen with a laugh. Raising her glass to her lips, she looked at Polly over its rim. 'Or a nasty little liar.'

If Polly had been hot before, she was on fire now. And not just with sexual excitement. Inferior as she was in size and strength, she suddenly wanted to leap up and smack Ellen Allenby in the mouth. Then she had another vision, and seemed to see a chihuahua yapping around the fetlocks of a Great Dane, and she felt an almost hysterical need to laugh instead.

'Oh, it's "genius", I think,' she murmured, miraculously getting hold of her composure.

Ellen tipped her glass in Polly's direction, and Polly suddenly realised she'd held her own in this first of probably many engagements.

'How do you fancy a ride out on my motorcycle, Polly?'

Polly had never ridden on a motorbike and, up until that moment, she hadn't ever wanted to. But suddenly the idea of riding pillion behind Ellen seemed infinitely safer than refusing and risking the possibility of incurring the woman's enmity in some way. Plus it would give her a marvellous excuse to put her arms around Ellen's waist and experience the very strength and substance of her, something Polly realised she'd been wanting to do since the moment she'd first set eyes on her. Which, confusingly enough, had been while she'd still superficially believed that Ellen was a man . . .

'Well, what do you say?' the tall women prompted, making Polly realise she'd been woolgathering again.

'I – I've never been on a bike. I wouldn't know what to do.'

'You don't do anything,' said Ellen with an unexpectedly kind smile, 'except hang on while the bike and I do the work. It's simplicity itself, believe me, Polly. You'll enjoy it. You strike me as a woman who can appreciate a taste of danger.'

Now what the fuck does that mean? Polly thought, although on a sub-level of her consciousness she knew.

It wasn't just a blast on a motorcycle that Ellen Allenby was suggesting, but another experience, a far more hazardous one, *after* the ride.

'OK,' said Polly, not granting herself time to get the fear. 'But what about a helmet? Do you have a spare?'

'Inez has one kicking around somewhere,' replied Ellen smoothly, turning to Inez, who Polly now realised hadn't spoken once since they'd come into the room.

She's been watching us though, thought Polly, turning to Inez and observing an expression of intense interest on their hostess's smooth face. It's like an experiment to her. She's set me up again. Maybe Ellen isn't Emperadora after all? Maybe it's Inez?

She was barely given time to digest this possibility, because at that moment, Ellen rose sinuously to her full, magnificent height, and said, 'OK, let's go then!' She turned to Inez, who had got up too, and inclined gracefully down to give the shorter woman a brief but telling kiss. On the lips. 'You don't mind, do you, love?' She touched the place where she'd kissed with the tips of three fingers. 'We'll have another time, eh? Promise.'

'No problem,' said Inez, and Polly saw a silent message pass between the two women that only confirmed her belief in a set-up. Even though right now she suddenly wasn't sure who by . . .

'I'll get the helmet,' Inez murmured, then left the room. Ellen followed, gesturing to Polly to fall in behind her.

In the hall, they both shrugged into their jackets, and Polly was obscurely pleased that she too had leather to wear.

'Nice coat,' commented Ellen, zipping up.

'I treated myself,' said Polly, not sure why.

'Quite right. One should always indulge oneself,' Ellen said, snapping up the various fastenings on her boxy yet subtly flattering bike jacket.

Out in the street, with Inez's helmet on her head, which was enough to induce claustrophobia itself, Polly experienced a sensation of complex fear unlike anything she'd ever really experienced before. When it came to it, she was frankly terrified at the thought of being on Ellen's motorcycle, and the feeling was not unlike the one she'd gone through moments before a minor operation she'd once had, that had entailed a general anaesthetic. It was a complete unknown. She simply could not imagine what it would be like to streak along the road, her safety and her very balance in the hands of a woman she hardly knew, and yet already held in awe.

And yet there was exhilaration about the prospect too. It was dangerous, but the pump of her heart made her feel high. High, and somehow desperately excited too. There was a sexual aspect to it, definitely, but also an intellectual peril ahead that only added to the sheen of eroticism.

As she buckled the helmet straps, under the supervision of Ellen, Polly finally and fully recognised the blend of feelings.

She'd felt like this just before she'd burnt her boats, handed in her notice and quit F&X to make her getaway.

'Wow,' she murmured, and even though the helmet had muffled her voice, she saw Ellen eye her curiously.

'Ready?' the other woman enquired, and when Polly nodded, Ellen swung astride the bike, and gestured her to follow.

Polly did so, and was shocked, but almost indecently so, when she realised how firm the seat felt when pressed against her vulva. It was wide, too, and moulded the seam of her jeans snugly up against her clitoris.

'OK?' enquired Ellen, twisting to face her.

Polly nodded again. God, how Ellen must love this feeling, she thought, settling down more solidly. It was hard to imagine what it would be like when the engine actually fired, but Polly knew that at any moment she would find out.

'Just relax, Polly,' said Ellen, putting her face as close to Polly's as their position allowed. 'Hold on, put your feet on the pegs, and don't try to balance – just let me do it. Put your trust in me completely and you'll be perfectly safe, I promise you.' And with that she snapped down her visor, straightened around, and fired the engine.

In a moment of piercing clarity, Polly realised that the latter part of these instructions might apply later in the proceedings too, but then it was too late to try to analyse or question. While Ellen's feet were still squarely planted on the road beneath them, Polly put hers on the pegs and gripped the other woman round the waist, and held on tight. She thought she heard Ellen laugh then, but the rampaging engine noise made it difficult to be sure. A second later, in a fast, but perfectly synchronised series of actions and adjustments, Ellen set the bike in motion and they shot away, along the road, in a breath-stopping burst of acceleration.

Oh shit! This is fabulous, Polly thought, another couple of seconds later, when the first shock was over and it dawned on her how good she felt. After one moment of panic, she felt no urge whatsoever to try to balance for herself; she simply became one – clichéd as it sounded – with the bike, and Ellen.

In spite of the roar of the powerful machine and the inner roar, the reverberation of the engine that surged through her entire body, the impression Polly got of their progress was that of a 'flow'. The bike seemed simply to pour itself along the road at high speed; to glide under only the lightest of control by Ellen. There was no element of brute force, just the subtlest of coercion.

And that's how she'll be with me, Polly thought, thrilled by both the speed, and the flashing by of the country hedgerows on either side of them, and by the firm hard feel of the peerless body she was clinging to. Ellen was a rock astride her machine, a column of perfect stability, yet alive to every facet and idiosyncrasy of both the road and the machine. This perfect mastery and confidence transmitted itself effortlessly into Polly, and thus, engaged in one of the most hazardous activities in which she'd ever participated, she felt as safe and sure as she'd ever done in her life.

It was a disappointment when the machine began to slow, and Ellen coasted the bike to a halt in a secluded road, back in Chandler's Haven.

'My place,' she said, nodding to a narrow, dark stone house set back a little way from the road when they had both dismounted. She didn't say 'do you want to come in?' but simply fished into her jacket pocket, then tossed Polly a single door key. 'Let yourself in while I put away the bike.'

As Ellen wheeled the sleek machine away to her garage, Polly pulled off her helmet and did as she was told. With much trepidation. She'd had her ride, and now she had to pay for it; and all she had was only the most rudimentary knowledge of what was expected of her. It suddenly occurred to her that she was terribly afraid of pain.

Once beyond the black-painted front door, Polly found herself in a long, narrow hall not unlike the one at Inez's house, and when she reached for a light switch she found it lit only a single lamp, half way along one wall. Stepping a little further inside, she saw paintings and drawings, in simple classic frames, hung upon the wood-panelled wall, and smelt the subtle odour of jasmine-scented furniture polish.

The art was by a number of hands – including Inez's, Polly noted – but the theme of each piece was always the same. An unsurprising one, given what she'd recently learned about Ellen.

The images were of women being punished. Women bound. Women under duress of a kind Polly's subconscious eagerly recognised. It was an abstract form of home to her, she realised dimly. Not one that she'd ever want to live in all the time, but one she had always been destined to visit. And footsteps behind her told her that abstraction and reality were on the point of merging.

When she turned, Ellen was almost upon her, deep in her personal space, brushing her with leather-clad arms as she too removed her helmet. The tall woman's dark, almost unnaturally glossy curls unfurled, kissing her broad shoulders, and she looked down on Polly, her brown eyes huge and mesmerising.

'You know what I want from you, don't you, Polly?' she said, taking both the helmets and placing them on a hall table. 'You know why you're here,' she went on, lifting her hand to Polly's face with a tenderness that was as unnerving as it was unexpected, then stroking her cheek with all the delicacy of a doting mother.

'I think so,' whispered Polly, feeling her own breath whisper back at her because Ellen's face was now so close. A second later their skins touched, Ellen's cheek smoothing against hers in a caress.

'I want to hurt you, Polly,' she said, pausing to brush her lips over Polly's hairline, both of her hands now forming a cradle for Polly's face. 'I want to hear you cry and sob and plead with me . . . I want to hear that because it makes me wet, do you understand me?'

'I don't know . . . Sort of. I'm not sure,' stammered Polly, afraid not of the uttered threat, but because her head was being held in two of the strongest hands she'd ever encountered, and she had a feeling that Ellen Allenby could snap her neck like a stick of chalk, if she really wanted to.

'I think you are, sweetheart,' said Ellen, her voice infinitely gentle as one hand left Polly's face and slid down, almost like a conjurer's, beneath the collar of her jacket. Polly felt deft fingers slip inside her shirt, then just as cleverly inside her bra. Within the space of a second, Ellen was holding her naked breast.

At first the touch was light, merely an encirclement of the flesh, then the taller woman began to knead and fondle and grip. It wasn't pain yet, but Polly knew that the margin was close.

'Soon,' said Ellen softly, clasping Polly to her and kissing the top of her head even as she squeezed and played with her breast. 'Very soon, Polly . . . There won't be long to wait.'

But just as Polly's crotch was beginning to heat up and to seep, Ellen released her. 'Come along, little one,' she said almost sweetly. 'Come on, baby, I can't wait to make you cry.'

Ellen led Polly upstairs and straight to what was obviously the master bedroom; a surprisingly feminine room decorated in shades of spice and cream. Looking around, Polly saw nothing untoward. No shackles, no stocks, no obvious whipping benches or instruments of torture, just a big, wide bed with heavy wooden head and foot boards, a couple of old leather-covered armchairs, and the usual chest of drawers and wardrobe. And yet the pleasant room had a palpable air of threat about it, an atmosphere of danger that was all the stronger for its bland accoutrements.

Moving with economy and purpose, Ellen crossed immediately to a large well-polished chest of drawers and took out a small pile of garments that she then held out to Polly.

'I'd like you to put these on, my sweet,' she said, then seeing Polly's puzzled expression, she added, 'It's just something I like. A part of the game . . . Just think of them as props.' As Polly studied the clothing, Ellen crossed to a wardrobe and reached inside, then came back with a pair of boots.

'These too,' the tall woman said, putting them on the top of

Polly's pile. 'You can change through there in the bathroom.' She gestured to a half-open door at the other side of the room. 'Take all the time you need. There's no great need to rush. I'm sure you'll be worth the wait.'

Bemused and unable to speak, Polly darted into the bathroom with her bundle and then shut the door.

The clothes were the last thing Polly had expected. She'd imagined – if she'd consciously imagined anything – that Ellen would require her to be naked. The fact that she wanted Polly dressed, and in so unlikely a style, was more frightening, in a way, than the prospect of the actual physical beating. It was somehow menacing and mysterious. Unknowable.

Polly examined the dress first. It was grey, plain, old-fashioned and shapeless, yet curiously made from a far from unpleasant fabric. The style was that of a prison garment, yet the cloth – a fine wool – had a soft, expensive feel to it. It was institutional, yet from a fantasy institution. As were the underwear, the stockings and the boots.

The bloomers in particular were extraordinary, straight out of a Victorian melodrama: voluminous and knee length, with a button fastening at the waist. More conventional in appearance was the suspender belt which was white cotton, and perfectly plain, but beautifully finished. The stockings were a total surprise too – knitted wool, but very fine, to complement the dress. Polly had expected something sheer but she realised now that nylons were too clichéd.

Putting the costume on, rather than just examining it, was a borderline for Polly. She had a feeling that if she were simply to refold everything and step back out into the bedroom, and say 'I've changed my mind', that it would be accepted, with no hard feelings, and she'd be allowed to leave.

But she couldn't do that. Her cunt had already come to life and demanded that she make provision for its requirements. That she had to go through fire first seemed to matter not one jot to it.

The dress felt strange, yet comforting; the stockings, suspenders and bloomers just peculiar. In an age of form-fitting Lycra and undies as light as thistledown, to be both trussed up, and yet enveloped in what seemed like yards of loose fabric, felt distinctly unnerving. The weirdest thing of all was how erotic the costume seemed to her.

No bra, Polly thought, touching her breast through the soft grey fabric and finding her nipple hard. The 'prison' dress fastened down the front, all the way down to its loose, dropped waistline, and she was painfully aware how completely accessible that made her. Ellen could just unfasten all the buttons, then reach in and handle her breasts.

It was the same with the voluminous knickers. They were ridiculously baggy too, and had a long slit at the side, and loose legs. Deft hands could easily get in and grope her sex.

And she had no doubt that, notwithstanding anything else she did, Ellen Allenby would want to spend time playing with her cunt.

Lacing up the soft leather boots, which were a touch on the big side, but not too bad if fastened tightly, Polly could suddenly not think of anything *but* being touched down there. She seemed to see an image of Ellen's long, pale hands manipulating her – both of them at once, some fingers caressing while others probed. She wondered what it would be like to feel both orifices filled.

'Oh God!' Polly whispered, jumping up, and realising that with her boots done up, she'd automatically begun to touch herself. She'd been massaging her vulva through her bloomers and her prim grey frock.

'Concentrate, you stupid mare!' she told herself. 'Focus on what's definitely going to happen and not just the things you want to.'

This woman's going to beat you, she thought, just because she wants to – and it gets her off.

Standing before the bathroom mirror, Polly smoothed down the dour grey skirt and straightened the bodice and the sleeves. What do you look like, she asked of her image, feeling the increasing sense of being in prison attire or an institutional uniform. Jailbird, she thought, smiling nervously and feeling ever so slightly hysterical.

As she gave the dress a last primp, Polly began to wonder what Ellen would be wearing when they faced each other again in a few moments' time. Would the tall woman be in uniform too – prison wardress, headmistress, policewoman? – and if she were, would she, Polly, be able to take the resulting effect seriously?

Oh God, what if I spoil it all? What if I laugh and destroy the mood? Polly thought, clenching her fists and feeling as small and anxious as the little poorhouse girl whose costume she wore. She turned away from the mirror, then swivelled back again, adjusting the dress again.

I must go out! I have to go out, she told herself, feeling the enormity of what she had committed herself to thundering down upon her. The truth was, she was an utter cry-baby where pain was concerned. She snivelled if she as much as stubbed her toe. How on earth would she cope with whatever Ellen saw fit to inflict upon her? Which would be some sort of smacking or hiding to say the very least.

What if she's got whips? Riding crops? School canes? Any one of those will half kill me! What the hell am I going to do? Why the hell did I come here?

You came here because she's beautiful, observed a cool, calm, almost serene voice inside her. Because you want to find out if she is Emperadora. Because there's a slim hope that she might let you see her naked body. Because she just might, if you let her do what she wants, let you touch her and caress her.

Yet Polly continued to hesitate, her hand on the door handle. She could still change her mind, put her own clothes back on, and tell Ellen it was all a mistake. Yes, she could still behave like a coward and miss the chance to experience something that life might never offer her ever again.

When Polly entered the bedroom, she was both surprised and relieved to see the tall, dark woman still wearing the suit of brown-black leather that so became her. Ellen had changed no part of her costume at all, except that the front of her sleek, body-shaping jerkin top was unfastened now. Between twin panels of hide, her unbrassièred breasts gleamed pale and free.

Polly stifled a gasp, aware that she was both salivating and exuding fluids from her more intimate anatomy. Ellen Allenby's breasts didn't have quite the stunning, near-conical perfection of shape that Severn's did, but they were glorious, both womanly and tender, a triumph in their own right. Her nipples were smallish, but beautifully upstanding, two delicate rose-brown studs. As Polly gawked at them, Ellen lifted a slender hand and gave one breast a squeeze.

'Come in, Polly,' said the tall woman, her voice soft yet authoritative. 'Don't lurk by the doorway. I can't see you properly there.'

In Polly's absence, Ellen had lowered the lights, and the room was moodily shadowed. Oblique radiance from one or two lamps seemed to dance on the polished leather that clothed the tall woman's body, and made the creamy flesh of her breasts and midriff glow. Polly approached her in genuine awe, her own body shaking. She didn't quite know what she was supposed to do when she actually reached Ellen, but she had an irrational instinct to just drop down to her knees and grovel.

'You shut the door on me, little one,' said Ellen, her voice resonant with amusement and the subtlest hint of menace. Reaching down from her towering height – Polly estimated that she was topped by at least six inches now, allowing for her own flat footwear, and the chunky heel on Ellen's boots – the dark-haired woman gently cupped Polly's chin with her left hand and made her look up. 'You must never do that again,' she went on, all the time absently fondling her own breast with her right hand. Polly felt almost more afraid of the fact that Ellen could so calmly caress herself at such a moment than she did of the potential ordeal that lay ahead of her.

'I'm sorry,' she whispered, unable to prevent herself leaning in towards the slight contact. Ellen's hands were unexpectedly soft and beautifully kept, the fingers like air against Polly's heated skin.

'I know you are, love,' replied Ellen, still touching Polly, yet still massaging her own breast also. Polly could not take her eyes off that leisurely, understated circling. 'I know you would never intentionally do something bad. Something wicked . . . It's so often circumstance that leads us astray, isn't it? Don't you think so?'

Lulled into a condition of dreaminess by Ellen's touch and her nearness, Polly was suddenly pulled up sharp again. There had been a crisp edge of emphasis in that last question somewhere, a slight bias that had nothing whatsoever to do with doors and issues of privacy.

Oh God, how much does she know? Polly thought, panic thrashing in her bosom like an unbroken horse. Is she Emperadora? Does she know about Sanspareil? About F&X? About everything? She felt herself begin to tremble violently now, the agitated motion most likely being transmitted through Ellen's fingertips too.

Polly hung her head, fear of discovering the truth preventing her from seeking answers in Ellen's dark eyes. Instead she stared fixedly at long, creamy pale fingers, topped by the most business-like of severely trimmed-back nails, manipulating a nipple as ripe as a berry and as dark as a jewel.

'I'll bet you've done all sorts of bad things, haven't you, Polly?' the voice like silken velvet purred on. 'Committed crimes? Cheated and lied? Performed any number of small acts of thievery?'

Struck dumb, Polly could only nod her head and enjoy the way that made Ellen's hand caress her cheek.

'So you are a thief?' Ellen enquired, a slight note of triumph in her tone now. She didn't allow Polly to answer, though. Instead, she curved her fingers around Polly's face, and Polly felt her lips parted and pressed open by Ellen's strong thumb. Penetrating, the slender digit felt much bigger than it actually was somehow; it seemed like a cock or a dildo, insidiously forcing her mouth open. Polly made a choked sound as she felt herself start drooling.

135

'Are you sorry for the things you've done, Polly?' asked Ellen in reasonable, perfectly normal tones as she molested Polly's mouth with her thumb and continued to play with her own stiff nipple.

Polly made a sound that was supposed to be 'yes' but which came out like the grunt of some degenerate, subhuman being. It was impossible to talk when her tongue was immobilised and her mouth full of spittle.

'Good! That's good, my sweet,' replied Ellen, clearly understanding her perfectly, 'and it deserves commemorating. A breakthrough like that should be marked, so it will always be remembered, don't you think so?'

Polly grunted again, her powers of speech still under Ellen's complete control.

'I knew you'd understand,' Ellen said softly, removing her thumb from Polly's mouth and gently stroking her lower lip. 'Let's get started, shall we? The night is young, Polly, but we've a long, long way to go.'

NINE

The Long Good Night

According to Polly's limited preconceptions Ellen should have been cool and stern and hard now. She should have assumed the persona of a dominatrix, haughty and unyielding.

What the hell do I know, though, thought Polly, feeling sweat break out in her armpits and at her hairline. I've only read books, and picked up the gist of things from Pat; I've no real experience to draw on. Stealing a glance at Ellen, she looked for signs of a metamorphosis.

But Ellen's demeanour hadn't changed at all. To Polly's nervous eyes she looked serene, unremittingly benign, and almost mild in aspect. Which, paradoxically, scared Polly more than anger would have done. At least when people were angry, their drives and emotions were crystal clear to you.

'Kneel for me, will you, Polly,' said Ellen gently, spinning away on her booted heel and walking to the bed. Once there, she sat down, leaning back a little with her arms braced at either side of her, supporting herself. It seemed almost a position of display, somehow, because it made her unfastened top slide away on each side of her torso and gape open. Her flawless breasts were a splendid challenge to the warm night air.

Not sure if there was a certain way to do this, and certain that whatever way she chose would be the wrong one, Polly sank awkwardly to her knees, her body wavering with unnatural tension. Once down, she didn't quite know what to do with her hands so she clasped them tightly behind her back.

'Good! You did that well,' said Ellen, flexing luxuriously, as if she were about to indulge in some favourite passion of hers. Which indeed she was, Polly supposed, twisting her hidden fingers.

'I like that pose, Polly,' the tall woman went on. 'I actually have to tell most of my submissives to clasp their hands behind their backs, but you've done it without any prompting. We seem to understand one another already, don't we, little one?'

Do I answer? Polly thought. Am I even allowed to speak?

'It's OK to answer,' said Ellen, softly laughing.

'I – I hope so . . . I –'

What did she call Ellen now? Was there some special title required?

'You may call me "mistress",' said Ellen, standing up again and sweeping the spirals of her gleaming dark hair back from her face. 'It's a cliché, sadly, but I like it, and it's appropriate.'

'Yes, mistress,' chimed Polly. The word didn't feel like a cliché to her at all somehow. It was as if it were entirely new, and freshly minted into her lexicon.

'Do you know what I'm going to do to you, Polly?' enquired Ellen as she approached, seeming four times as lofty now Polly was downgraded.

'No, mistress. Not precisely.'

'Well, I'm going to punish you for all the crimes you've committed, Polly . . . and perhaps add a little extra for all the crimes you might commit in the future.' Ellen was directly in front of Polly now, which meant that Polly's eyes and nose were dangerously close to Ellen's leather-clad crotch. The urge to rock forward and rub against the leather was almost unbearable. Polly wanted to kiss the delicious V there in desperate homage. Insane as it was, she realised all of a sudden she was half in love.

'Do you think you might commit more crimes, Polly?' the

goddess enquired, her hand digging without warning into Polly's hair and pulling her forward. The very proximity that Polly had lusted after was instantly effected and, though she could smell only leather, inside her mind she smelt Ellen's fragrant cunt.

'Yes, mistress,' Polly murmured, pressing her open mouth to the gleaming leather and the ridge of the heavy zip. If Ellen had permitted it, she would have used her teeth to open the fastening.

'Well, I'd better smack you hard then, hadn't I?' the tall woman said, ruffling Polly's hair and pressing her hot face closer in.

To her own surprise and embarrassment, Polly discovered that, quite without realising it, she'd begun to cry. Even though she hadn't even been punished yet, not even in the slightest way, she was blubbing like a baby against the front of Ellen's trousers. And it wasn't from fear, it suddenly came to her, but from purest affection.

How can I care for this woman? Polly thought, snivelling against Ellen's crotch, and wanting to kiss it with even greater passion. I hardly know her, and if I were to say I was in love with anybody, shouldn't it be Pat? Pat, the one who'd initiated her and set her on the true and righteous path?

It shouldn't have been possible but she seemed to have become filled with an instantaneous devotion to the tall woman who held her, and she nodded in agreement with Ellen's casual suggestion of rigorous punishment.

'There there,' murmured Ellen, her fingers nevertheless quite forceful against Polly's scalp. She was getting off on a worshipping face pressed to her groin, that was clear, and the honesty of that only made Polly want her more. 'I can't say it won't hurt, my sweet, but I promise you'll feel better for it afterwards.'

With what felt like one last regretful push, Ellen then released Polly and took a couple of steps away from her. 'Get up now, and lift your skirt. Show me your knickers,' she said, her level voice lightened by a playful edge. 'Exhibit yourself to me, little girl . . . Come on, let's see you show some grace.'

Grace was the last thing Polly felt capable of, but she tried.

Getting up was marginally easier than getting down had been, and she tried to lift the grey woollen skirt as slowly and elegantly as she could. As she held it bunched at her waist, she was aware that in any other set of circumstances, such an order would have been ludicrous, and she would have been laughing hysterically at both herself and Ellen, but right now it seemed both serious and appropriate. She stole a glance at herself in a tall mirror that stood some way away, across the room, and saw a very young-looking woman, almost a waif, with her skirt hiked up.

'Very nice. Very pretty,' said Ellen, approaching again. When she was close, very close, deep within Polly's personal space, she reached down and laid a fingertip against the snowy white cotton, at the exact point where Polly's vulval slit began. 'Open,' she instructed, then proceeded to push the pristine fabric inwards between the folds of Polly's labia. Almost instantly, Polly felt the cloth get sodden, as Ellen pressed on in search of her hidden, swollen clitoris.

Opening her thighs necessitated that Polly set her legs apart, and to allow Ellen access meant assuming an ungainly posture. But there was no question of refusing, or not obeying the order perfectly. As Polly squatted slightly, the finger pushed in further.

'More,' ordered Ellen again, her digit burrowing and finding its target with unerring accuracy.

'Oh God!' gasped Polly, as Ellen's fingertip flicked and circled around her clit. Of their own volition, her hips began to wave, destabilising her posture and making her stumble and lose the very contact she craved.

'Careful, little one,' Ellen said, her voice harder as she grabbed Polly by the arm, held her steady, and plunged in again. Once more, Polly found her clitoris beleaguered. 'Stay very still. Completely still. No jiggling about, no waggling your hips . . . and, most of all, no coming!'

How can I not come? Polly thought, fighting every urge in her body as the tall woman skilfully frigged her. She could feel her juices pouring out on to the white cotton between her labia, soaking it profoundly and making the friction all the more exciting and multi-textured. Even as she fought it, her vagina clenched, and she bit her lips trying to control the inner reaction.

'Polly!' warned Ellen softly, and Polly realised the other woman had felt the spasm.

'Touch your tit,' Ellen went on. 'You've got a hand free, little one, use it!'

Polly laid her fingers around the curve of her own breast and cupped herself tentatively.

'Inside. Open your dress. Hold the nipple between the tips of your fingers.'

Fumbling with the grey dress's buttons, it took Polly a few moments to get the front of it open, and when she'd achieved the objective, she hardly dared put her hand inside. Ellen was still strumming her mercilessly, and the combination of nipple play and being fingered was too explosive. If she touched her own breast, Polly was convinced she'd have a climax.

'Don't you dare,' purred Ellen, her lowered face close, and Polly knew exactly to what her tormentor was referring.

She had to ride through this ordeal, and not orgasm, or she'd be banished.

With the deepest of trepidation, Polly took hold of her own nipple – and tried to work her way through the most elaborate computer algorithm she'd ever calculated in an attempt to suppress her raging arousal. The complex strings of code kept breaking up and re-forming as Ellen's finger danced and flickered.

'Oh, you're good, little one,' murmured Ellen, her lips almost moving against Polly's brow, her fingertip ceaselessly gyrating. 'What are you doing in there?' She kissed Polly's temple. 'How are you distracting yourself? What are you thinking about?'

'Code,' Polly forced out, through gritted teeth. She was beginning to lose ground.

'Code?'

'Computer code . . . for my latest program.'

'Ah, that,' breathed Ellen, and almost immediately Polly regained control of herself as her mind skipped into 'fear of retribution' mode.

Ellen too seemed to be aware of the shift and, with no further comment, she pulled her hand from Polly's crotch and wiped her fingers on the white cotton of her bloomers. After effecting a graceful turn, she backed away and sat down on the bed once more.

'Drop your knickers. Show me your cunt,' she ordered bluntly, beginning to fondle her own breast once again.

Re-gathering the full grey skirt into a new bundle, Polly turned her attention to the waistband of the full knickers she wore. They buttoned at the side, with a long deep slit there, but they were also lightly elasticated too. She wondered whether to unfasten them or just push them down. What kind of effect, or display, would most please Ellen? Fiddling with the fastening, she risked another quick look at the taller woman.

'Guess,' ordered Ellen. 'You work out whether to unfasten them or not.'

God, she's a fucking mind-reader! Polly thought, in a sudden burst of defiance. She knows everything and I know not a bloody thing at all! How on earth can she expect me to second-guess her?

Ellen laughed again, the sound clear and light with amusement. 'Oh, go on! Take a stab at it! You're going to be punished anyway, it doesn't make much difference.'

Yes, I am. Of course I am, Polly thought, still plucking ineffectually at her waistband. Then, making a split-second decision, she slid her thumbs inside it and eased the great, clumsy white garment down her thighs as far as just above her knees. If she was going to be exhibited, she might as well make it in the most demeaning way. Feeling decidedly proud of herself, she hitched her skirt even higher, displaying her suspender belt and crotch with a flirt of mild bravado.

'Oh, yes!' hissed Ellen, her smile widening to meet Polly's bold look. 'You are such a minx, my sweet. So naughty . . . but you do catch on quickly.'

Still holding her skirt up with one hand, Polly laid the fingers of the other against the edge of her stocking tops, subtly framing herself for her mistress's further pleasure. If this was a game, she was learning the rules, enjoying the challenges . . .

But just then, a tiny, extraneous noise set her heart bouncing.

Oh shit! They weren't alone. There was someone else in the house! Ellen had had an ace from the pack tucked away all the time . . .

Slowly, the just-pushed-to bedroom door began to open and Polly braced herself for the pits of humiliation. Being seen by some stranger, some woman – or worse, man! – with whom she *wasn't* totally besotted.

The doors swung slowly, the effect almost cinematic and unnatural to Polly's anxious eyes, as her anticipation ramped up and up and up . . .

With a studied nonchalance that would have done its mistress proud, a large ginger cat prowled into the room and, ignoring Polly completely, sidled up to Ellen and pressed its flank to her booted calf.

Polly laughed, dropped her skirt, and almost fainted with the intensity of her relief.

'Don't laugh at Freak,' reproved Ellen immediately, albeit mildly, as she picked up the cat and cuddled him close to her naked bosom. 'He's a very noble beast and he's very mindful of his dignity.' Still caressing the tomcat she gave Polly a square-on look.

It's a test. Another test, Polly thought. The game doesn't just end because the cat wanders in. I can't call a stop to this just because I've been distracted. I have to hold fast, stiffen my resolve, and act as if nothing's happened. Snatching up her skirt again, she resumed her humiliating pose.

'There now, Freak,' whispered Ellen, kissing her cat and then setting it on its paws again. 'You have to go now. Mummy is busy. She'll play with you later.'

The cat gave her a look that seemed almost complicit, as if it had seen such scenes a hundred times before and found them mildly amusing, then sashayed away, its tail up, its gait insolent.

At the door, it hesitated and looked around once then was gone. Polly let out her breath, knowing she'd passed another test.

'Do you like cats, Polly?'

Polly thought about it, then gave an honest answer. 'I don't know. I think so. I don't know much about them.'

'I'll introduce you to Freak later then, shall I, when this is over?'

Polly nodded, brooding much more on 'this' than the eventual introductions. And she sensed a turning point too, a switch of mood both in the room and more specifically in Ellen. The fun and games were over, and now the business ahead was serious.

The tall woman didn't wait for Polly's answer and Polly suspected that one wasn't expected. Moving with her light, predatory tread, Ellen came across the room and stood close again, her hands instantly taking rude possession of Polly. Her breasts were felt up, then her crotch, and finally her bottom; and it was at this last site that Ellen seemed inclined to linger. She cupped and manipulated the twin lobes of Polly's buttocks, as if assessing the resilience of the muscle there and its suitability for punishment. Once or twice she pinched and Polly only just managed not to squeak out loud. It was very clear now that silence was a prerequisite.

But not for Ellen, it seemed.

'I was right,' the tall woman said, her voice arch now, self-congratulatory, a little cool. 'You do have a deeply delicious bottom . . . I could tell, even through your clothes, that you're a choice one.' Using both hands now, she squeezed and lifted and circled. 'Oh, it's a lovely one . . . Such a lovely, lovely bottom.'

There was something about the way Ellen said the word 'bottom' that excited Polly. Bottom. Bottom. Bottom. The tall woman invested the word with such a round and fruity enjoyment, rolling the syllables around her tongue with extreme relish, as if it were a mouthful of luscious wine. Falling from her lips the word sounded both mysterious and infinitely rude.

And the actions that accompanied it were vested with much the same qualities. As Ellen handled her, Polly could almost imagine that the prime focus of her eroticism rested squarely in the cheeks of her backside. It wasn't that her cunt and her breasts had lost their involvement, in fact she seemed more sensitised than ever in those areas too, especially her clit which seemed to swell and throb with every move of Ellen's fingers. It was more that Ellen's attentions elevated the bottom to an equal level, and increased the susceptibility of all Polly's erogenous zones.

'Has anyone ever punished you here before?' enquired Ellen, gripping both cheeks hard now, and first lifting – raising Polly precariously on to her toes in the process – then pulling them apart.

Polly groaned as she felt her anus stretch and pout. 'No. No, mistress. Nothing other than a quick slap or two when I was a child, and then with clothes on.'

'So you've never been struck on the bare bottom then?'

'No, mistress.'

'Oh God, how I'm going to enjoy this!'

The tension increased, and Polly whimpered and grabbed her own crotch.

In a movement like lightning, Ellen released her and dashed her hand away. 'Do not ever touch yourself without my permission, do you understand?' she said in a low voice that was both flat and strangely ringing. 'Your body is mine tonight, slave. Completely mine. I have dominion over it, and you only touch it when *I* give you leave to.'

'Yes, mistress,' whispered Polly, feeling slightly faint and overpowered by the heavy pull of desire her cunt exerted on her fingers. If she'd wanted to masturbate before, the urge had been but a passing whim compared with the compulsion that gripped her now. She felt as if her sex might explode at any moment.

'Now, let's not waste any more time, shall we?' Ellen was brisk and businesslike, her fingers like vices on Polly's upper arm as she led her to the bed. Polly shuffled as she went, hobbled as she was by the pulled-down knickers. 'Arrange yourself over the foot of the bed. Use a pillow over the foot-board if you need to,' Ellen went on, giving Polly a light shove – not enough to make her fall, just sway a little and feel ungainly.

The wooden foot-board of the bed looked hard and unyielding to Polly, and mindful that she would have more than enough discomfort soon without that, she tottered around the head of the bed first, and snatched up a pillow. The crisp yet soft pillowcase felt all of a sudden very familiar and comforting, and she experienced a momentary urge to hug the thing and perhaps snivel into it, feeling sorry for herself. A second later, the fleeting urge left her when she considered the possible consequences. She knew she wanted what was about to happen to her, wanted it with a yearning she was totally at a loss to understand, but she was still realistic enough to know that she wasn't yet ready for the worst that Ellen could deliver. A milder session would be more than enough to get them started.

With some care, Polly draped the pillowcase over the hard upper edge of the board, then turned cautiously towards Ellen to see what was required next.

'Now arrange yourself, slave,' she said, moving closer, the faint sardonic smile back on her face, her eyes alight.

Slave? I suppose that's part of the cliché too, Polly thought, not actually disliking the nomenclature. It felt right for the moment, and for the scene.

Arranging herself was more difficult than she'd expected, she realised in a moment. The bed was old-fashioned and quite high. To get herself over the foot-board at what she hoped was the right angle, she had to stand right on her booted toes. Which meant she was almost teetering, and felt destabilised, without control. Which was probably exactly how Ellen wanted her to feel, she reflected stoically as she went over and pointed her toes to get the best position.

'Oh very good, slave. Very fine,' said Ellen, coming close and placing her hand on Polly's bottom. Polly flinched, half expecting the contact to be a blow, but Ellen's hand only flexed and began to knead her flesh again, like an addict getting a fix of a so-adored substance. It was clear to Polly that the woman had a passion for bottoms, and couldn't get enough of the sight and feel of them. Polly began to relax, but tensed back up again when a finger strayed across her anus.

'And isn't this a sweet little character?' Ellen said teasingly, poking at the little aperture in determined little stabs. 'I have friends who are going to love this, slave. I can't wait for them to see you, and start to play . . .'

Friends? What friends? Polly thought, fighting to control herself, fighting not to gurgle with lust as Ellen fiddled with her bottom.

Then, just as soon and as shockingly as the contact had begun, it was over. Ellen moved briskly around the room, leaving Polly prone and abandoned, and waiting. She heard the small sounds of preparations. Small ominous sounds that made her cunt and breasts tingle. A few moments later, Ellen was back, and had her hands on Polly again.

'Now we need to make the final adjustments,' she said as she worked, rearranging both Polly's body and her clothing. First, she reached underneath Polly's torso and pulled open the front of the dress, then she gathered in the fullness of the skirt so that Polly's bare crotch was resting against the pillow that supported her. The feel of the fabric against her skin was tantalising, like a whispered caress, a sly reminder – if that were needed – of her intensely eroticised state.

The last preparation of all was made when Ellen took both Polly's arms and stretched them out, above her head, across the counterpane. 'You might want to grip on to the cloth,' she told Polly as she backed away slightly, then with no further warning the much-feared ritual had begun.

Polly shrieked aloud when a sensation like being struck by a block of wood exploded squarely in the middle of her left buttock. A second later it detonated in her right one too, then repeated, twice in succession, first right then left. Appalled, and half-stunned by the pain, Polly listened to her own shouts as the blows continued and her bottom flamed.

What is she hitting me with? A small portion of Polly's brain remained lucid enough to ask the question as the blows rained down and down, then sharp enough to answer it a moment later as realisation dawned.

It was Ellen's strong hand that was belabouring her bottom and turning it into two tender mounds of heat. The human hand, an instrument of such graciousness and benison, was inflicting more savagery than any implement possibly could. Polly realised that she was crying helplessly, and yelping and jerking at every stroke.

Ellen herself remained silent throughout the process, but, despite all her own noise, Polly could still hear her tormentor's breathing. It was slightly heavy, and a little uneven, and the thinking Polly, deep inside, knew this wasn't simply a product of exertion. Ellen was turned on, and turned on powerfully, by her efforts.

And by my pain, Polly thought, bucking high from the foot-board as a particularly fiendishly aimed slap caught her hard on the under-hang of her bottom. My pain is making her wet. My pain is making her ache and become engorged, Polly observed, almost detachedly, as another blow found the same under-hang but of the other cheek this time and she squealed out loud like a piglet being strangled.

Not that she's the only one who's wet and swollen, Polly mused in wonder as she jerked back down on to the foot-board again and a spasm in her own crotch seemed to call out to Ellen's. Astonishingly, Polly could feel her arousal welling and cresting like a powerful storm deep in her belly. Her vagina was liquid, her clit a bloated, throbbing bead.

As Ellen smacked her anus, she howled, 'Oh God!' and climaxed heavily.

For about a minute, Polly floated in a sea of sensation, not really analysing its individual facets, but just letting the power of the ebb and flow wash around and through her. If anyone had asked her, she wouldn't have been able to tell them whether she was still in pain or not. The waves of stimulus were just too huge to get a handle on.

The only thing she did know was that Ellen was no longer

hitting her. She was no longer even touching her. Yet she was close, Polly began to realise as a few shreds of her faculties began to coalesce and she reoriented herself in space and time, over the end of the bed. She could hear the breathing again, the broken rhythm, the slight gasping quality; and she could smell the leather of Ellen's clothing, her sharp 'green' cologne, and her pungent, aromatic sex.

'Mistress?' Polly whispered, then realised that her throat and lips were so dry that the sound had not come out. And she still had no strength to move from where she lay in order to investigate her lover.

Lover?

Oh yes, thought Polly, focusing in on the still glowing after-pleasure that suffused her sated cunt. No matter how it had been induced, she'd been brought to climax, she'd been made love to . . .

Suddenly she heard the gasping again, then small rustles and scrapings, then a tiny joyous cry. Summoning the last dregs of her energy, and, as she moved and felt her body hurt, a hidden well of fortitude, Polly set her feet on the floor, pushed with her arms, and stood up straight.

Only to find that her mistress, the mighty Ellen, her tormentor, was on the floor.

The tall woman was sitting there, her back against the foot-board, her long legs splayed, her head tipped back a little and her beautiful lips parted. Her eyes were closed and her hand was moving inside the leather of her trousers. As Polly watched, one leg flexed convulsively, the heel dragging on the carpet.

'Oh, mistress, let me!' cried Polly, falling to a crouch immediately, her pounded buttocks shrieking. Hardly aware of what she was doing, and working purely on instinct, she dragged at Ellen's leather trousers until they were down around her ankles, noticing as she did that the woman wore no stitch of underwear.

Then, awkwardly, in a mad tangle of tensing limbs, twisted clothing, and with a beaten body that seemed to sing with residual agony, Polly nevertheless managed to force her face between Ellen's legs and claim her treasure.

'Oh God, little one!' shrieked the magnificent Amazon – as Polly sucked.

Polly woke up first – which didn't surprise her given it was the first time she'd ever woken up in bed with another woman. She'd never even spent a whole night with Pat, and yet she'd docilely agreed to share the bed of this woman she'd only just met and who had punished her grievously.

Sunlight, unusual as it seemed in dour Chandler's Haven, was pouring in through the windows of Ellen's bedroom, slightly hazed by the thin gauze curtains that were drawn to give a modicum of privacy. Polly remembered the thick velvet curtains being drawn last night while she and Ellen had been playing – or whatever one called it in these circumstances – so the tall woman must have pulled them back to let in the thin light of the high watching moon.

Lying inert for a few moments, Polly was almost afraid to look at the woman who lay beside her. She was still in total awe of Ellen, even though their embraces, once in this bed, had been far more egalitarian than Polly would ever have believed possible with someone to whom she'd so completely subsumed her will. Keeping her body still, and her eyes averted, she explored her companion with her remaining senses, and her memory.

Taste came to mind first. Polly suspected that, in the normal course of events, Ellen had a quite mild and naturally sweet flavour between her legs; but being encased in leather for several hours, excited, had made her ripe and pungent by the time she'd lain back and allowed Polly to give her head. Polly had felt her mouth water in response, the dryness borne of tension and suffering completely hydrated by the saliva that sexual hunger had generated. She'd lapped and slurped at Ellen like a beast at the trough, barely feeling embarrassed at all by all the noise from her attentions.

Her actions too had been free and uninhibited. She'd dug into

Ellen's crotch with her fingers, to open her, then grabbed her buttocks and probed her anus as she'd licked her. It had all seemed perfectly appropriate, and almost poetic, while she'd been doing it, but she blushed now thinking how gross she might have seemed. Cautiously, she touched her face, imagining that she could still feel the sheen of her saliva and Ellen's flowing juices.

The skin of her cheek was dry and warm, however, and all she could smell was a very faint aura of baby soap on her fingers. The same scent that now emanated from the woman beside her, warmed through by the cosy presence of two bodies in one bed.

Still staring at the abstract patterns of light drifting through the wispy curtains, Polly listened to the soothing sounds of Ellen's breathing. The individual breaths were smooth, regular and deep, each one in immaculate aural symmetry with the last; the respiration of an athlete, a supremely fit woman. A woman asleep, in perfect harmony with her life.

Unable to resist any longer, Polly turned slightly and admired her bedmate.

In sleep, Ellen was totally abandoned, totally relaxed, the kicked-away sheet hiding nothing of her magnificent beauty. She had one arm curled back over the pillow around her head, exposing the tiniest wisp of dark hair right in the hollow of her otherwise shaven armpit; the other was resting lightly at her groin, fingers splayed and with one dipping uninhibitedly into her crevice. She wasn't masturbating, but when she woke, she might well begin to. Polly knew how much Ellen loved her own touch. Last night, before sleep, they'd lain side by side, each of them rubbing themselves to one last sweet orgasm.

Even as Polly watched, the pioneering fingertip jerked, then began to probe and burrow, and feeling guilty Polly turned away, feigning sleep. When Ellen began to gasp, Polly groaned inside and bit her lip.

Oh, little one, I know you're awake, Ellen Allenby thought contentedly as she rubbed herself.

Memories of last night's session rose in her mind and added to the pleasure of the moment. The young woman beside her had been a true find, a perfect proselyte. Scared, yet responsive; awed, yet eager; born for the game. Not for the first time, Ellen blessed the long-standing lover who had so cunningly brought them together. Oh, she had been right when she'd said that Polly was a treasure.

Tapping at her clitoris, Ellen moved her long legs against the mattress and flexed her buttocks. She considered putting on a show for her new young friend, granting her the beneficence of a wild display of lewdness. But then self-interest took its toll, and Ellen admitted that what she truly wanted was to make use of the fabulous creature at her side. There would be plenty of other opportunities to be kind, but not so many to savour a Polly who was still virtually uninitiated into the mysteries. The girl would never ever be as fresh as this again.

Abandoning her vulva with some regret, Ellen made a determined show of waking up, stretching, murmuring, beginning to rub her own face and hair lazily. Would Polly 'wake up' too? Or would the girl show the extreme intuition she'd shown last night, and remain 'asleep' for her new mistress's convenience?

It would be quite a leap for Polly to put herself in such a vulnerable position, but, Ellen reflected, this was someone who wasn't afraid of taking leaps of all kinds. Acting rashly, and taking risks, was very much Polly, it seemed. If she'd preferred the safe life, she wouldn't have been in Chandler's Haven. Ellen thought again of that friend they shared, and smiled with pleasure.

Sitting up, Ellen turned to stare at Polly, just as she knew Polly had stared at her earlier.

The young woman was remarkably beautiful, but in the ingenuous style of someone who had only the barest inklings of her own potential. Ellen could imagine that Polly thought herself to be 'OK', 'not bad', 'fairly pretty'. It was only an outside observer who could appreciate her lusciousness. She had the look of a fallen angel about her, a corrupted pixie. Her short red hair was thick, and feathered around her face like a flattering little cap. Her eyes were large, her nose was straight, and her mouth was small. But only small in the way that the sweetest fruits were always the most miniature. And beyond those lips lay a tongue that was fey and mobile. Ellen clasped her own crotch again as she recalled its sovereign skills.

And I might have some of that again soon, she thought indulgently, lifting the sheet.

The body was as good as the face. Rounded but well shaped, with good muscle-tone, exceptional breasts, and a juicy cunt. The thighs were long and pale and simply cried out to be lashed.

As Ellen watched, the tiniest tremor seemed to pass right through Polly. Her thespian skills were good, but not that good. She was obviously awake.

Little madam, thought Ellen, smiling again as she peeled away the sheet entirely. She had a vision of herself as some stereotypical silent movie villain, mugging outrageously and twirling his long moustaches as he loomed over the cringing, shrinking heroine. Although Polly Sayers, she suspected, would never be a victim. A submissive, yes, but a willing one. The sort who secretly, when it came down to it, really controlled the scene.

Moving as quietly as she could, not wanting to fracture the pretence, Ellen reached into the drawer of her bedside cabinet and drew out a set of cleverly crafted restraints. They'd been made by a man who lived in Chandler's Haven, a man of many talents as well as special proclivities, and their design was quite specific to this bed. They allowed for securing women to it who were a good deal shorter than Ellen herself; and because the bed was long, the straps themselves were lengthy too.

Hush, little one, mimed Ellen as she loomed over Polly. Just play your game a little longer and you'll play right into my hands. Then moving as silently as that rolling-eyed movie villain, she secured the restraints in place, clipping the ends of them to certain small steel rings in the bed's head and foot-boards. Returning to Polly, she thought, I'm ready when you are, baby.

Almost as if she'd heard the silent imprecation, Polly 'stirred', artfully stretching her arms out above her head, across the pillows. Needing no other signal, Ellen darted immediately into action.

As quickly as she could, she buckled each of Polly's wrists into the cuffs at the head of the bed and, as the girl began to struggle for real, she did the same at the foot of the bed, although it took a good deal of strength and dexterity to snare the second jerking leg.

'Wha— what are you doing?' demanded Polly, and Ellen had to admire the degree of authenticity of her acted surprise.

'Surely you don't think you paid the whole of your penance last night, do you?' Ellen said, watching the widening of Polly's eyes and the dark dilation of her pupils. The girl was fully aroused already, and she couldn't have been awake all that long. 'If you consider your transgressions, you'll realise you still have a helluva lot to pay for. Your crimes are real, little one, I think we both know that full well.'

A look of real fear, a different fear, passed across Polly's face for a moment, but Ellen smothered that by touching the girl's white thigh. It was only the lightest touch she allowed herself, but she swept it upwards infinitesimally. Tantalising Polly's sex with only the smallest note of suggestion.

Pulling away, Ellen reached again into her bedside drawer and brought out another of her favourite items. As she uncoiled the fastenings, she imagined what might have happened if Polly had become curious in the night and investigated. If she had allowed that delicious streak of unscrupulousness in her, that Ellen found so endearingly arousing, to get the better of her. A lesser woman than Polly might have gathered her clothes and run for the hills on encountering that hoard of toys, but Ellen knew that, even if she'd found them, Polly would still have stayed.

'What's that?' demanded Polly, although Ellen suspected that the girl knew full well what it was. 'What the hell are you going to do with it? I want to know. You have no right to do this!'

Bravo! Ellen thought, her own cunt moistening spontaneously. Polly was entering into the spirit of this to a degree that both astonished and delighted Ellen. The girl was acting again, but so skilfully it just didn't jar.

'This —' Ellen exhibited the device before Polly's eyes '— is a ball gag. And I'm going to put it in your mouth because I don't want to listen to your questions and protests for one minute longer.' Sliding her hand behind Polly's head, she lifted her, then pushed the round rubber ball against the barrier of the girl's closed lips. Polly fought the pressure for a moment, or at least appeared to, then opened her mouth. Once the way was clear, Ellen very carefully slid the ball in and secured it. With equal attention, she arranged the fastenings so that they wouldn't dig into Polly's head when she laid it back down on to the pillow.

'Now I can do whatever I want to you and you can't do a thing about it.' Just voicing the words gave Ellen a long-familiar jolt of excitement. The oozing of her cunt became a slippery, almost river-like flow.

Before her on the bed, the hips of her acolyte began to weave . . .

TEN

Bound

Oh God, what have I done now? Polly thought as she tried desperately to contain her urge to struggle.

The trouble was she hadn't *done* anything. She'd allowed things to be done to her. She'd lain inert, simulating sleep, wondering what Ellen was up to. She'd let this happen, when she could have avoided it – and now she wasn't sure that she actually wanted it. And it was too late now that the huge round gag was in her mouth.

And that was the aspect of the situation that was so monstrous, yet so exciting. Her mouth was completely stopped up. She couldn't speak, or even move her lips. The orifice was closed off entirely. While between her legs, the orifice there was laid wide open. Her cunt was exposed and totally vulnerable, a dribbling maw.

She could quite distinctly feel her own juices oozing out of her. In fact, she was flowing faster than she'd ever flowed before – just when there was not a thing she could do to either disguise or conceal it. The lubrication welled from her glands in her vulva, making her anal groove and the just-exposed underhang of her bottom glisten, not to mention wetting the white sheet underneath her.

The worst thing of all – yet also the best – was Ellen's scrutiny. The tall woman was kneeling on the bed and looking down at her. Those fiery brown eyes were entirely focused on Polly's wet cunt.

'Dirty little girl, you're drooling on my bed,' Ellen said silkily, moving in a little closer and putting her fingers between Polly's spread legs.

Polly felt a combing action and, when she looked down at herself, she saw that Ellen was meticulously dividing her pubic hair, so she would be even more exposed. When the cooler air hit her inner membranes she bucked and heaved.

'There, that's better!' replied Ellen in answer to Polly's muffled, unintelligible protests. 'But it's not quite enough somehow . . .' She cocked her head on one side, her spiral curls swaying and brushing her strong shoulders. 'I want your clit completely exposed. I don't want to have to keep uncovering it.'

Polly shuddered, unable to control her spasms of dread and lust in any way. She so agonisingly wanted to close her legs, yet lying there, open, like some kind of pagan Sapphic sacrifice, was more exciting than anything that had ever happened to her before. Involuntarily, she began to imagine how Ellen's wishes might be achieved. She closed her eyes and hideous images formed behind her eyelids.

When she opened them again, it seemed as if her worst imaginings might have come true. Ellen was leaning over her again, yet another confection of straps dangling from her fingers. Polly saw fine chains, thin strips of leather, a pair of clamps. She tried to cry 'No!' but the intrusive gag made it into a gurgle.

'Hush now,' said Ellen, placing a hand squarely on Polly's thigh and holding her down where she was jerking and rising in her bonds. The touch was steady and calming, yet even as it began to do its work, Polly sensed its quality change. Ellen's fingers grew more languorous and lingering; they seemed to creep infinitesimally towards Polly's naked sex.

'Now keep quiet, little one,' said Ellen, 'and settle down. I'm going to arrange you just exactly how I want you.'

Polly's eyes bulged in their sockets, and her plugged mouth worked around the gag, seeping saliva, as she watched and felt her own privates being manipulated. The device, contraption, call it what you would, consisted of a pair of delicate but firm clamps, their gripping surfaces padded with soft leather, which were attached to an adjustable retainer fashioned from chain and a narrow hide strip. Ellen slid the retainer under Polly's hips and brought the clamps around to the front. Polly shook her head when she realised how the device would function, then worked her hips as Ellen fastened the clips in place.

The tall woman worked deftly in spite of Polly's struggles, and it was oh so obvious that she'd used this method countless times. Polly wanted to scream, but not with pain, when she was finally trussed . . .

Moaning behind her gag she looked down at the obscene image of her own displayed body, and absorbed the firm but exciting pressure that the clips on her outer labia exerted. She was being held right open like some surrealist piece of art. Her clitoris was gleaming, prominent, enormous, the very centre of the room.

'Oh yes . . .' whispered Ellen, crawling half over Polly and putting her face very close to the engorged and glistening bead. Polly felt a huge urge to move, to push her clit upwards and jam it against Ellen's half-parted lips, but suddenly she knew that such an action was taboo; she had to stay perfectly still.

For long moments, moments that felt like aeons, Ellen's face hovered above her cunt. She could feel even breathing wafting against her clit like a will-o'-the-wisp caress. Deep in her vagina she felt the first strong clench begin to gather.

'Oh no, little one, not yet,' said Ellen, laughing softly as she straightened up. Half-frenzied, Polly wondered whether her mind had been read, or whether Ellen had actually seen her vulval membranes moving. It didn't seem to matter which it was, she could only want and want . . .

'I get what I want first. Then we'll see about servicing you, my sweet,' Ellen said, almost conversationally, as she climbed off the bed, then reached beneath it, out of Polly's sight-line.

Oh please . . . Oh help . . . What now? Polly thought, then her question was answered as Ellen showed her another implement.

This item was far from being yet another arcane and perverted artefact, such as Polly had anticipated. It was just a bedroom slipper, a plain flat mule, made of wine-coloured leather, but even so, Polly feared it utterly, and began to struggle in her bonds, both grand and intimate.

'No no no, not your clit, my darling,' said Ellen, leaning over Polly's face, her eyes dark, aflame with lust, yet strangely kind and tender. 'That would be far too barbaric. Not many women like, or can even tolerate, such an extreme degree of torment.' She hesitated a moment and, reaching down in a gesture that Polly half thought was imaginary, she delicately drew her fingertip across Polly's clitoris. 'No, it's your thighs I'm going to punish for you this morning, my love. I'm going to make them nice and red and sore.'

And yet, as Ellen slipped into position and tapped the sole of the slipper against her own palm, as if testing it, Polly knew that she would experience the punishment ahead as much in her genitals as she would in her thigh muscles. Everything about her was focused down there now, in the pink, wet, exposed slit of her pussy. In the swollen, completely exposed pearl that seemed to stand out between her legs. There was a maverick voice crying silently in her head for the blows to be struck there.

Then, suddenly, 'slap!' and it had begun. Almost without Polly noticing the movement, Ellen had raised an arm and brought the slipper down fast and hard. Polly stood up on her heels, within the leeway of her bonds, her right thigh on ragged fire. She would have shrieked if it hadn't been for the gag, and her muffled squawk was ludicrous. In the open niche between her legs, her vagina clasped and released and her clit jerked like a pulse.

More blows fell and Polly seemed to float in a maelstrom of sensation. The bite of the slipper made last night's hand-spanking seem like a gentle massage by comparison, and it seemed all the harder and more emotionally affecting for being laid upon her thighs. A slap on the bottom was a caress somehow, a coming home of the hand upon the flesh; a blow to the thigh seemed to strike the psyche too: it was seen as well as suffered.

Yet the more she burnt and writhed, the wetter her sex became.

She began to make silent internal deals with Ellen.

If I let you give me ten more slaps, will you touch me? How about twenty slaps, or twenty more, a round red fifty?

If I promise to come here and let you beat me senseless every night and day for the next year, will you just touch your tongue to my clitoris for half a second?

If I pledge my body to be yours for ever, will you just please bring me off?

After another strange, extenuated period of time, one during which Ellen murmured a soft, constant litany of praise that afterwards Polly couldn't remember a single word of, the steady barrage of smacks to her inner thighs ceased.

Drifting, Polly could hardly tell whether she was in pain or ecstasy any more. All borders and distinctions of sensations seemed to have been moved, redrawn or blurred. She knew her thighs were blazing but she couldn't really decide whether the feeling was good or bad.

All of a sudden, from a great distance of strangeness, Polly realised she was no longer being hit. Lifting eyelids that felt leaden, she looked up blearily and into Ellen's face.

'Ah, my pet, you're so strong,' the powerful but lovely woman said, from far closer than Polly had expected. She was crouching over her, right at her side and, as she bent to lick the perspiration from Polly's slick and streaming face, Polly felt firm breasts brush against her heated skin. 'It's been far too long since I had a woman who could stay with me.' She ran her fingers around Polly's mouth, circling the gag, teasing her with the softest of touches. 'This looks beautiful, you know,' she went on, her tone almost musing as she fingered the gag's restraining straps. 'You might not be able to imagine that, but it does . . . It's a different beauty.' She brushed Polly's sweaty hair back from her face, then kissed her brow.

Polly moaned and struggled a little, riding the pain in her thighs as she did so. Ellen's gentle caresses were far more of a torture than the beating had been. To be tied up like this, and exquisitely nurtured, was a subtle agony. She wanted to embrace Ellen, fold herself around her, draw one of those strong, skilful hands towards her crotch, where her exhibited clitoris was bursting.

'Patience, little one. Not long now,' said Ellen, drawing away. 'It's just that I'm so reluctant to give you up. You're so juicy. So very, very luscious . . .' With that, she ran a single closely manicured fingertip along the inner edge of one of Polly's peeled back labia – and Polly arched in her bonds as if she'd been goosed with a cattle prod.

Oh God, so close! So close! Thrusting her hips madly, Polly tried to knock Ellen's finger sideways so it landed on her clitoris, but the dominant was far too clever and too fast to oblige her.

'This is such a jewel, Polly,' said Ellen, her voice husky as she put her face near to Polly's pinioned cunt-lips and the sexual bead nestling between them, 'and big, too . . . Such a big one . . . So tempting . . .' She breathed heavily, her breath puffing out, and Polly gurgled behind the gag, pushed yet closer to the edge by the zephyr drifting across her beleaguered membranes. For one fabulous moment, she thought Ellen was going to kiss her there, but then the tall woman sat up straight and tapped her hard on her sore and tingling thigh. Polly grunted and protested, the existing flame stirred.

'Hold fast a little while longer, sweetheart,' Ellen said, rising from the bed and reaching for a towel that was draped over the end of it. As Polly watched Ellen wiped her own long, muscled body free of excess sweat, the sweat she'd worked up beating Polly's inner thighs red raw. When she was done she returned to her Pandora's box of a drawer. 'Now how shall we finish?' she murmured, reaching in and rummaging around.

Polly felt faint with desire and with the effort of wondering what new manifestation of fiendishness might come out of that drawer. She was almost surprised when it wasn't more straps and buckles – but what did appear made her belly surge with dread. A dark, hot dread that only added to her arousal, instead of defusing it.

Ellen ran her fingertips lovingly, almost possessively, over first one object, then a second, caressing both as if they were sentient and aware of the pleasure. From what Polly could see of them, both items were dildoes of one kind or another, and both more thoughtfully crafted and better constructed than any of the fairly basic vibrators that she'd ever sampled. It was clear from their shapes that each had a different and very distinct purpose.

They're meant for two different holes, thought Polly, groaning inside as her eyes took in the specific contours of each of the two toys.

But whose holes?

The question was redundant really. Polly felt anew the powerful urge to squirm, fight, resist, deny what was so obviously going to happen to her. It was unthinkable, well nigh impossible that her body could take such strain . . .

The first dildo was of black latex construction and cock-shaped. It wasn't especially long, but its circumference was fearsome, almost as thick as a young woman's wrist. Polly could imagine its stretch filling her, pressing and pushing at the walls of her vagina while the wider circumference at its slightly flared base played real havoc at her entrance.

Dear God, she thought suddenly, almost laughing in shock, despite her predicament. Should she be thinking this? What was wrong with her? She felt a confusion that made her far more tearful than the pain did. Just when it seemed that she'd finally decided what she was, she'd felt a sudden and deeply surprising yearning to have a cock inside her . . .

As if she'd sensed Polly's doubts, Ellen smiled, then put the huge, man-like dildo to her lips and licked it slowly. 'Don't worry, Polly,' she murmured, still running her tongue around the realistic head of the *faux* tool. 'No harm in this, my sweet. There's no man on the end of it. We've reclaimed it . . .' Rolling her eyes theatrically, she sucked the black rubber knob with an obvious joy and vigour.

A different kind of confusion replaced the first. Ellen was a dominant, wasn't she? A mistress? A butch dyke? Whatever? Surely it wasn't right for her to be sucking and slavering over the cock-like toy in this way? Polly frowned, using the crinkle of her forehead to ask the questions that her mouth wasn't able to.

'Forget preconceptions, my love,' said Ellen softly, still fondling the dildo as she spoke. 'There are no rules for us. We're bigger than categories and roles. We do what we want here. Surely you know that, little one?'

We? Does that mean the *both* of us? Polly thought, feeling the germ of a different emotion inside her. A pride and elation at being likened to the gorgeous, almost mythical creature in front of her, a naked icon of omnipotent female power. To be a part of whatever Ellen was suddenly made all concerns outside this bedroom seem quite meaningless.

Calmed by the strange sense of inclusion, Polly was better able to face her speculations on the function of the other dildo. It was also made to penetrate, clearly, but its shape was shorter and squatter, and had a very tellingly formed flange at its base.

Oh shit! Polly thought, and a second later she couldn't contain a laugh that sounded gross and animal-like when forced out around the gag. The irony of that single word almost made her forget that the curiously shaped plug would most probably end up inside her body. Almost, but not quite. The thought of its introduction made her buttocks clench involuntarily.

Jesus Christ, the thing's huge! I can't take it!

Fingering that shorter, more indecent plaything now, Ellen raised her fine dark eyebrows as she looked at Polly. Then, as she visibly seemed to put an end to her prevaricating, the tall women performed a minute yet potently telling shimmy.

Oh my, thought Polly, her desire and devotion to her strange new friend suddenly enhanced by a nerve-tingly streak of awe. Forget preconceptions, Ellen had said, there are no rules . . .

It's not for me; it's for her! How can she do that? Surely *I* should . . . *I'm* the sufferer . . .

But Ellen just laughed again, as if she'd heard all Polly's questions and protests. 'You've a lot to learn yet, sweetheart,' she said almost merrily as she started rummaging in the drawer again.

And learn Polly did. Feeling strangely detached from her physical torments and appetites, she watched closely as Ellen began to lubricate the phallic dildo. The tall woman applied a copious slathering of a clear, silvery gel to the sex toy, coating it again and again as if she were getting off on the action itself. She even paused to taste the gel, licking her fingertips with her long red tongue, then smacking her lips as if she'd just tasted a juicy woman. It was all a performance, Polly realised, and done for her benefit.

When the toy was prepared to Ellen's obviously stringent requirements, she came towards Polly again, her dark eyes fiery with purpose. 'Now this is going to be a bit of a struggle to get inside you, young Polly, and it'll probably feel extremely uncomfortable at first,' she said as she twirled the dildo into alignment, close to Polly's vulva, 'but I think you'll find it's worth it, in the long run, so just bear with me.'

As if I could do anything else, observed Polly, her voice tart in her own mind, contained by the gag. She felt first the shock of contact, then a steady pushing pressure as Ellen introduced the penis-shaped contraption into her. The thing was far bigger than she'd realised and her vagina felt traumatised and violated. Fresh waves of sweat broke out on her body as she fought the pleasure of it.

She had a filled cunt; filled by a manlike thing. She shouldn't want that; she should abhor it utterly, but her swollen clitoris told her an entirely different story. The sensations that wracked her sex scaled up to a new, yet higher level. Of their own volition her hips once again began to rise and weave, making the portion of the dildo that remained outside her do a silly, loathsome dance. The ugly black protuberance seemed to silently insult her.

Just as the flange of the other toy would soon insult another orifice.

But Ellen would not consider it demeaning, of course. She wants this! Polly thought, experiencing – to her utter astonishment – a pang of jealousy. Clenching her inner muscles around the *faux* cock, she tried to imagine a second latex intrusion inside her bottom, stretching her to just the same degree but with darker, nastier overtones. Her clitoris throbbed at just the thought, crying out for contact.

'Now it's my turn,' murmured Ellen, turning away for a moment and bending forward, just like a ballet dancer, to expose her backside to Polly. As Polly watched, she smeared yet more lubricant in between the cheeks of her bottom, and liberally into her anus, making spontaneous sounds of pleasure as she moistened herself.

More show, thought Polly, wanting to look away, because her need to climax was becoming unbearable, but unable to. Only the gag kept her from groaning long and loud when Ellen squatted and took a long white finger into her bottom.

The tall dominatrix let fly an uncouth grunt, then immediately straightened up again, turned and advanced on the bed. With a grace that Polly knew she herself could never possess in a thousand years, Ellen flung a leg astride Polly's restrained body, facing away from her, then knelt forward and reached for the greased black plug.

Polly's eyes bugged as she watched Ellen immolate herself, pushing the stubby little dildo slowly and lasciviously into her body. The tall woman had an exquisitely delicate anal portal, and the sheer width of the plug seemed too great, at one stage, to gain entry, but with a good deal of grunting and panting and huffing the task proceeded.

It took a few seconds, with intense strain tautening the long planes of Ellen's elegant thighs, but then she pushed harder and the bung slipped home inside her. The dominatrix cursed out loud in a long, elaborate profanity, and Polly felt a surge of pain from her abraded upper thigh, where Ellen brushed against it. A few moments later, though, Polly forgot her own sufferings, even though they increased as Ellen swung around, changed her position and sat down facing her, her shoulders shuddering tellingly as she settled.

What a strange tableau we must make, thought Polly, her mind flying high and clear above her staked-out body. Ellen was sitting open-thighed across from her, inclining slightly backwards, weight still on one hand, her bare legs bridged across Polly's secured ones. She and her mistress were a chimera, many-limbed and bizarrely mated.

The tall woman's cunt was almost as vulnerably displayed as Polly's was. Her bulging clit and convoluted lips were pink and coated with gel and juiciness, and while Polly watched her she flicked herself briefly, then began to undulate.

Saliva bubbled from around Polly's gag as she both saw and felt the rhythm of a curious body dance. Ellen rocked and circled her buttocks like some perverted, anal-erotic Salome, stimulating her own rectum as she leant forward to jiggle the dildo in Polly's vagina. The dreadful medley of sight and feeling was almost a martyrdom. She was being deeply and crudely penetrated while a cunt of the most exquisite deliciousness was being exhibited before her, and Ellen's own cries and groans and curses only increased the anguish.

As she ravished her own bottom, Ellen regaled Polly with a stream of luxuriously foul oaths, contorting her mouth and face until she looked more alien than human. Her head tossed slowly from side to side in time to her pelvic undulations, and her curly black hair looked like some dark weed slick with sweat.

Polly too felt as if *in extremis* she was turning to fluid. Perspiration was pouring from her in visible streams, tears were dripping from the corners of her eyes, and saliva was dribbling continuously round the edges of her gag. Sexual juices were overflowing from her opened-out vulva, blending with the silky lubricant to create a wash of copious fluids. She was almost certain that her hyper-stimulated bladder was leaking piss too.

She felt abandoned, shipwrecked, marooned on the terrible

high point of her own frustrated need to come; she felt ready to burst or lose her mind or die if she didn't climax soon.

'Oh baby, baby, baby . . .' she heard her tormentor babble happily, then, to her horror, she realised that Ellen seemed to have forgotten her and had now started to masturbate. The bucking, jerking, gyrating woman had a hand between her legs and was rubbing and pinching her clitoris in time to the cadence of her own licentious gymnastics. Her milk-pale face was red now, and her firm, magisterial mouth had slackened.

In a last defiant burst of outrage, Polly spluttered behind her gag, feeling pure anger rather than submission at being so callously treated.

The sound seemed to shake Ellen, who focused immediately and almost appeared to physically rise from her fog of selfish lust.

'Oh, little one,' she whispered, her voice little more than a croak, as she gave Polly a smile of perfect, lucid kindness. 'Oh, little one . . .' she softly repeated as she withdrew her hand from between her splayed-out thighs.

In a swift sure movement, she put her finger on Polly's clit . . .

'What on earth happened to you?' enquired Inez, as Polly walked into the sitting room at Ash House, trying not to look as if she'd been involved in some kind of terrible accident.

Her beaten thighs made it difficult to move comfortably, but it was much more than the simple bodily pain that was affecting her thoughts and consciousness. That moment on the bed, during her unnatural congress with Ellen, was still echoing and reverberating inside her. If she had been asked, now, to describe how she felt in its aftermath, she would have struggled for the words.

The orgasm had come not as the kind of rending explosion of pleasure she'd been expecting; rather it had been like music, soft and sweet and magical, a river of silver notes rippling through her cunt. She had still been floating there, smiling round her gag, when Ellen too had finally joined her, coming splendidly and shrieking loud.

Afterwards, when Ellen had released her, they'd moved around each other cautiously, yet in a state of wonder like a pair of newly hatched erotic creatures stretching their wings. And Polly was still convinced she'd had a special impact on Ellen.

'Polly?' prompted Inez, still staring at her.

Polly stared back, feeling a sense of exasperation. When would Inez stop pretending like this? Playing these little charades of innocence. 'You know full well what happened to me! You handed me over to your friend, the butch dominatrix! We've been playing Monopoly and pressing wild flowers . . . What else would we have been doing?'

'Temper, temper,' murmured Inez, rising from her seat, her body looking chic and shapely in grey linen slacks and a silky white vest top. 'Just because you allowed Ellen to get a little bit carried away with you, you mustn't be tetchy. You could have said no, or left at any time. I think you know that, don't you?'

Of course she knew it. She just didn't need smirking Inez to remind her. 'Yes, I was fully aware of that, thank you. I made my own choices.'

'Sit down,' said Inez. Her cool face seemed to become gentler somehow, much more sympathetic. 'I think you need a drink. I'll get you one. Just relax.'

'But it's only –' Polly hesitated. Not once in the time since she'd woken up this morning had she even bothered to look at a clock. She'd taken a leisurely shower, allowed Ellen to dress her in a long, loose skirt – because her thighs were too sore for her own jeans – then feed her breakfast and bring her home in an unexpectedly luxurious Mercedes saloon, and never in all that time had she thought once about the passing hours. When she looked at the clock now, and saw it was midday, she wasn't surprised.

'Just the one,' said Inez firmly, already at the drinks tray and pouring. 'Think of it as an aperitif. It won't be long until lunch. I'm just doing a snack, I hope that's all right. We've been invited out to eat this evening, and I took the liberty of accepting for both of us. You don't mind, do you?'

Whatever, Polly thought, too turned over by all that had

happened to her to even care about it. 'Fine,' she said, sinking into an easy chair and wincing. Her thighs weren't really all that sore, it was just the strangeness of the sensation that jolted her senses.

As she made herself as comfortable as she could and watched Inez fussing with fresh ice cubes, Polly did suddenly find herself dragged back into the real world. There were things she had to check up on. E-mails it might be advantageous to send. For one thing she had to make sure that the documentation she'd sent had actually made it to her patent lawyer. No matter how she'd trusted Ellen sexually, in the cut-throat world of electronic commerce, Polly really trusted no one. She'd compartmentalised her paranoia for a few hours last night and this morning, but her worries were still at large and bearing down on her.

'Drink this,' said Inez, handing Polly a measure of whisky, then sitting down in a chair opposite her. 'When I said "what on earth happened to you", I didn't mean physically. I know about that. Ellen e-mailed me this morning, while you were showering.' She paused, took a sip of her own drink, and nodded to Polly to drink some of hers. 'No, what I meant was . . . what on earth *happened* to you? You look as if you've been lit up from within by a one-thousand-watt light bulb. You look as if you've been transfigured. You look like you've seen God!'

Polly took a sizeable drink of whisky, finding its smooth yet smoky kick extremely pleasant. She never usually drank the stuff, but something about what Inez was saying could well be right – she felt as if *something* had at least augmented her senses.

And yet she felt a need to hold back some of what she felt from Inez. She was grateful to the older woman, and she still didn't know how she could adequately repay her, at the moment, for her hospitality. But Inez herself hadn't been exactly frank, had she? Polly still felt that her friend was holding a great deal back herself. That there were subtle agendas behind that sophisticated yet laid-back façade, and even though Polly felt that Ellen was the obvious candidate to be the mysterious Emperadora – who may or may not know all about her misdemeanours – Inez could not be ruled out of the running either.

'It was quite something,' she said cautiously, applying herself to her drink and wondering if it would ease the stinging in her legs.

Inez seemed to accept that. 'You're a very lucky girl,' she said thoughtfully, swirling the amber fluid in her own glass. Polly looked across at her sharply, detecting a strangely wistful undertone.

'But you're lucky too, aren't you?' she said, studying Inez more closely. 'You've, um, done things with Ellen, haven't you? At least that's what you said.'

'Oh, I have,' replied Inez. 'I've played the games . . . And sort of enjoyed them in the arse-about way that you do enjoy such things . . .' She looked up, her eyes so clear and candid that they quite surprised Polly. 'But I don't think I've ever really got to the heart of it somehow. Not the way you have. That's obvious . . . I've never seen God!'

Polly had to laugh at the older woman's frankness, and Inez joined in too, but, a second later, a movement on Polly's part proved to be unwise.

'Oof!' she said, flinging down the last of her whisky as the soreness in her upper thighs flared in the aftermath of a minimal contact.

Inez put down her glass, rose from her seat, and came to kneel in front of Polly. 'Let me look,' she said, plucking at the hem of the borrowed black skirt.

Polly hesitated. Right at this moment, even if she hadn't been sore, she really didn't feel like getting sexually involved with Inez. She felt over-faced for the moment – as if she'd dined too well on orgasms.

'It's all right,' said Inez, her voice wry as she shrugged her shoulders. 'I'd like to . . . but I'll leave you alone. You need a rest from all that, at least for the next hour or so.'

The two women laughed again, and Polly allowed Inez to lift the edge of the flowing jersey skirt that Ellen had lent her.

'Oh, that looks rather hot,' murmured Inez, staring intently at Polly's rosy pink thighs. There was a look of slight amusement on the older woman's face, Polly could have sworn it. Her expression was arch, even a little bit patronising, but strangely it was also quite attractive. Against her expectations, Polly felt a whispering stir of interest. After all, Inez was staring at her French knickers, which were also borrowed from Ellen and consequently loose. Glancing down at herself, Polly saw pubic wisps escaping from beneath the ridden-up satin.

Inez had clearly seen the same thing. Polly saw her long, artist's fingers flutter as if wanting to investigate, and the older woman sighed, very slightly, almost under her breath.

I could say 'yes, go ahead' right now, thought Polly, and she'd touch me exactly how I wanted her to. I have the power now; she's the one who's kneeling to me.

For a few seconds Polly debated her options. Given the word, she imagined that Inez might slip her fingertips inside the loose legs of Ellen's very plain, flesh-coloured satin knickers, then burrow in, through Polly's bush, and find her clitoris. The tiny organ was still sensitised from Ellen's attentions earlier, not exactly sore, simply hyper-stimulated and a little tender. It would take but a second or two for Polly to come to climax.

Enough already, she told herself, shifting in her seat then flicking the long black skirt down lightly across her legs. She didn't want sex now; she wanted to get back to her computers!

If Inez was disappointed, she covered the emotion consummately. 'Would you like me to get you some soothing cream for that? I have a very good balm in my bathroom; Severn made it. You know how good she is with herbs and oils and things. And if that doesn't work I'll get Violet to take a look at you.'

'Who's Violet?' asked Polly, getting up rather peremptorily and forcing Inez to back away and straighten up too. I suppose she's yet another member of the Enclave, Polly silently added, feeling quite sure that this was the case and that she would soon meet Violet herself.

'Oh, she's a dear friend of mine,' said Inez, her composure intact as ever as she collected the glasses, ready to rinse them. 'And coincidentally, she's the one we're having dinner with. She used to be a state registered nurse and if we're ill, she always looks after us.'

Oh, I'll bet she'll look after me, thought Polly a short while later, studying the little pot of white ointment she held in her hand.

Inez had given Polly the balm, then left her to it. She was in the kitchen now preparing the light lunch she'd promised. Polly had undressed, and was about to anoint her legs. As she hesitated, she couldn't help but speculate about Violet.

The homely type, Inez had said. Fond of cooking, household crafts, and making things. A bit of a busybody, but in the nicest possible sense.

Well, I'll take that under advisement until I've met her, thought Polly firmly, dipping her finger into the pot of white goo. If she's anything like the rest of you she'll soon be trying to get into my knickers.

But whatever Violet's sexual peccadilloes were there was no reason to worry about them for the moment and, as she applied the skin balm, Polly's thoughts flipped over to Severn.

There was no denying the young woman's skills as an amateur apothecary. As soon as the silky ointment met Polly's soreness, the sting abated. The stuff was a miracle, and Polly slicked it on gratefully and copiously. It was absorbed quickly too, leaving only the barest film of residue.

Thanks, Severn, I owe you one, Polly thought, then found herself grinning. It didn't take much imagination to work out what sort of 'one' would satisfy . . .

Her discomforts dealt with, Polly slipped on her light cotton dressing gown, and decided it was time to check out her e-mail, and see if there were any new developments with the Enclave. It hadn't escaped her notice that Inez had mentioned that she'd received an e-mail from Ellen; and if the tall woman Emperadora, there might well be post for Polly herself from the mysterious matriarch. Something cryptic, no doubt. Implying that she knew all about the astonishing interlude at Ellen's house, yet in no way committing herself to actually having been there.

There might even be some clue as to whether Polly was being paranoid, or whether the enclave of women down here in Chandler's Haven really did know about what Polly was working on and the rather dubious nature of its ownership.

Thankful that, despite all that was happening, she'd still had the presence of mind to charge batteries for her various bits of kit, Polly hooked up the laptop she used for ordinary work to her mobile phone and dialled into the anonymous e-mail account she'd used the other night and got such a goddamn shock from. She didn't really expect to receive anything other than something from Emperadora, or perhaps an update from one of the mailing lists; but as the 'checking for messages' legend flashed, her heart began to churn. What would Ellen, or whoever it was, have to say this time?

Eventually the slow baud rate yielded up her messages and, as she studied what had been downloaded, Polly felt the lurching of her guts as a trapdoor seemed to fall away beneath her.

There was no message of sexual innuendo in the name of the Enclave, and no message regarding the latest happenings in the computer world. But what sat on the screen was both the worst thing she could have received, *and* well-nigh impossible – because she wasn't sure that she'd ever actually told anyone that secret name, except her patent lawyer.

In the sender box was the word 'E-Tech', presumably a company title, yet unfamiliar to Polly; but in the 'subject' box there was a word that was heart-stoppingly familiar – the one that had brought her all these miles and miles from London.

The subject of the e-mail that she'd just received was listed as 'Sanspareil'.

ELEVEN
Dinner for Five . . . or Six?

Sanspareil?

Who the hell else knew she'd called her project 'Sanspareil'? She'd never told anyone at F&X about it, not even Pat, although many times, when they'd been together, she'd longed to share the secret and ask the other woman's opinion on what she should do with it. But in the end caution had prevailed, and she'd accepted the fact that as a company trouble-shooter, Pat was the last person she should confide in.

But how else could the name have become known to anyone? She had used it briefly, when she'd first been fooling about with the germ of the idea at F&X, but as soon as she'd realised that she was on to something very significant, she'd encrypted all her files so thoroughly that not even the cleverest of the company's other hot-shots could have broken their way into them. And when she'd left she'd done the most rigorous cleaning-up job after herself; one that no file reconstruction program she knew of could make anything of.

Yes, she'd covered her tracks will all the skill at her disposal – which was considerable, and as good as anyone in the business, she believed.

Yet there it was, in black and white, her code name 'Sanspareil'. And what was worse, the e-mail was addressed to her by name.

Dear Ms Sayers. With regard to your project 'Sanspareil', we believe that here at E-Tech we are in an ideal position to help you develop and market your project. With us, you would enjoy a secure, creative environment where you would have no cause to fear certain industry threats that might be made against you. We are sensitive to certain critical considerations in the areas of 'creative ownership' and 'moral rights' and we feel that with us you will be protected against any repercussions of what was possibly a rash action on your part. Equally, by forming an association with E-Tech you will be placed in the happy position of being able to reap the full benefits of your remarkable skills and hard work, much more so than should you market the product alone or take it to any other major commercial player. You will shortly receive our full proposal, and an invitation to meet with us in order to discuss it.

The signature line said only 'E-Tech' with no personal name.

Polly had never heard of them. She couldn't recall even a single reference to the name, and she prided herself on being well informed, and well connected. She read the message again, and found it even more sinister than ever. It seemed strangely mannered and punctilious for a communication medium like e-mail, where informality was everything, and the only thing she could liken it to were the mysterious messages from Emperadora and the Enclave. The significance of the initial 'E' wasn't entirely lost upon her either.

But how can they be linked? Polly pondered, clicking rashly on the 'reply to message'. The hints and intimations made by the Enclave group seemed to suggest they knew something of her doing a runner with Sanspareil – but for the life of her she could not work out how they had found out about it. It seemed so unlikely; a group of women living a quiet if rather bizarre life in a backwater such as Chandler's Haven, who were really in cahoots with what sounded like a seriously major, if highly secretive, computer company. It didn't make sense, and it seemed impossible to make the connection.

The grating 'klonk' sound of an error message shocked her out of her musings, and what she saw on the screen didn't seem to make much sense either.

Unable to reply. No location or location withheld.

'This is fucking stupid! You had to come from somewhere!' she regaled the offending message when she'd clicked the cancel and was left with the pontifications of E-Tech.

Feeling panicky and sweaty, Polly quickly checked the message source, and unsurprisingly found that it had originated with a Web-based e-mail service that provided anonymous mailing. Which stood to reason, as that was exactly the method of obfuscation she was using herself, except that the provider they were using was one she'd never heard of, and seemed to have a software firewall against incoming e-mail. Then she ran a few different diagnostic programs – some standard, some crafty wrinkles of her own devising – to see if she could get any further than that, but the same denial of a location came up with each and every result. Whoever E-Tech were they'd chosen their e-mail service with diabolical care; it might be hackable, but it would take far more hours than time and her phone batteries would allow. In desperation, she logged on to the Web and tried to do a search for E-Tech, but even after using several engines, and waiting ages, nothing turned up. She wished she dared deploy the search module of Sanspareil itself, but if she'd been 'found' this way, to use it in the wild was utter madness.

Polly couldn't believe it. That was *twice* now. First the Enclave and their mysterious messages, and now this lot! It just seemed impossible that these people could beat her this way, at something she was supposed to be so hot at. They'd got to her, but she couldn't get to them. At least not in the cyber sense. Although maybe there were other avenues she could try?

What about the direct approach? A confrontation with either Inez or with Ellen, who was the standout choice for being Emperadora, the Enclave leader. Why not just march up to either of them, and tell them she knew what they were up to? And that she wasn't prepared to be blackmailed.

The trouble was that any bold protestations and stances were all very well in theory but, in practice, they were a mug's game. Technically, she'd stolen Sanspareil, even though she was the one who'd created it, and the consequences under the law could be a nightmare.

Polly glared at the name. 'E-Tech'. This was all very cloak and dagger, very sneaky and film noir somehow. But what if the E-Tech offer were genuine despite its unorthodoxy? She could do a lot worse than work for a big firm again, especially if they'd give her a better profit share.

That was the other avenue. She could play along. Just wait and see what E-Tech offered. And just wait and see what moves the Enclave made too . . .

'All right then, you lot,' murmured Polly into her Dictaphone, using the familiar method of recording her thoughts to calm and centre herself. She'd made her decision and, though it seemed a mad one, she was glad she'd made it. 'E-Tech, the Enclave, whoever you are, the ball's in your court now. Do your worst. I'm ready for you . . .' She paused a moment and thought ahead to the evening, the prospect of which made her body tingle. 'I couldn't care less. I'm going to a dinner party. I'm going to enjoy myself!'

'So who else is going to be there tonight?' Polly asked idly as Inez drove them to Violet's house, which was at the far side of the estuary, on a road that led out of town.

'Just us and Violet, as far as I know,' replied Inez airily. 'Oh, and her maid of course, but Linda will only be serving the drinks and the dinner.'

Polly looked around sharply at her companion. Was Inez suppressing the giggles? What was so funny about her friend Violet having a maid? Admittedly keeping domestic servants was an incredibly old-fashioned and élitist practice, but it wasn't particularly funny, just a little bit quaint and sad.

'Intimate then?' said Polly, knowing she was being provocative, but feeling almost hysterically light-hearted now she'd made the decision about her strategy. She'd decided to enjoy herself and take anything that Chandler's Haven, the Enclave and Emperadora had to offer her. And she had a sneaky feeling that the mysterious matriarch would put in an appearance tonight, regardless of what Inez said. Polly couldn't wait to see Ellen again, even though it was only a few hours since they'd parted. Her thighs had almost stopped aching now, and she was ready to start again . . .

'Oh yes,' said Inez enthusiastically. 'It will certainly be that,' she added, then seemed to focus on her driving.

It took them about ten minutes to get to Violet's house, which was another of the strange, somehow out of place, brownstone structures that the eccentrics who'd built Chandler's Haven seemed to have favoured. It was softened, however, by trailing ivy growing all up the frontage, and a little front garden surrounded by a low wall and black-painted railings.

'Nice house,' she murmured to Inez as they walked up the short path to the house. As the car alarm beeped, Polly experienced a fleeting pang of worry for her security arrangements, back at Ash House, but then, with an almost giddy turn of abandon, she dismissed her qualms entirely. Her spirits rose. Who knew what the evening ahead would bring?

Inez pressed the doorbell, and a rather pleasant chime sounded somewhere inside the house. Polly tried to look in, discreetly, through the front window, but heavy velvet curtains were drawn, even though it was only early evening. Thwarted, she looked around, then shivered. A cool breeze had come up and she wasn't really dressed to defend against its onslaughts.

Although her thighs weren't really sore at all now, and there was barely a mark of her ordeal at the hands of Ellen, Polly's skin was still slightly sensitive, and so trousers were out of the question. Furthermore, it was a dinner party she'd been invited to, so it seemed only polite to make an effort with her appearance. She'd put on one of the very few truly feminine garments she'd brought away with her: a light summer dress in a floaty, flower-printed cotton voile. It was a thin thing, and not a little see-through, even with its accompanying slip, but somehow it had felt good to put it on tonight – and make herself look feminine. Some irrational instinct had told her that 'feminine' was the appropriate persona to go with . . .

Violet's much-vaunted maid seemed to be taking a long time to open the door, so Polly took the opportunity to check her own shadowy reflection in the window. Weird, she thought, looking at the image of a pretty young woman in a summer frock, light sandals and wearing make-up.

I suppose I should consider myself as a 'femme' now, if anything, she thought, because this is such a soft, girlish look. But such roles were still new to her, and she felt awkward trying to categorise herself. She was still searching, and it would be easy to get things wrong.

'Nervous?' enquired Inez from beside her. The older woman's voice was arch again, and vibrant, and as Polly turned to her she could almost taste a sense of mischief.

'What's to be nervous about?' Polly countered, beginning to feel the emotion more strongly now that it had been named. 'It's just an ordinary dinner party, isn't it? I've been to those before.' Although admittedly not one in Chandler's Haven, she added silently, thinking that in this place there was barely anything that was 'ordinary'.

'I suppose so,' said Inez, swinging her small, chic shoulder bag with a sort of studied, school-girlish nonchalance that only made

Polly feel even more suspicious. 'It's just . . . you know . . . you never quite know what's going to happen sometimes, do you?'

Polly wanted to say 'You can say that again!' but refrained. She must remain cool, calm, unflappable and unshockable. It was clear that something was indeed going to happen tonight, and had been planned, probably to the very last detail, by Emperadora. At the thought of Ellen, Polly's heartbeat speeded up and her thighs felt suddenly sore again.

Just then the door opened, and the two women were face to face with someone who Polly could only assume was Violet's maid.

Linda was a tall, raw-boned, but not unattractive woman. She was wearing a very old-fashioned classical maid's uniform dress, which, although it was black, reminded Polly of the grey dress that Ellen had made her wear last night. The woman before them, however, wore hers with a frothy white pinafore, a matching cap, and sheer black stockings; and on her surprisingly large feet she wore a pair of high-heeled, button-strap shoes.

Bizarre, thought Polly in the split second before the apparition spoke.

'Oh hello, Miss Parker –' she nodded at Inez, then turned to Polly '– and Miss Sayers. It's lovely to see you both. Won't you come through. Mrs Blackwood's waiting on the patio for you. Do follow me.'

Polly tried to catch Inez's eye as they made their way along the short hall, with its beautifully polished parquet, and then followed in the wake of the maid through a homely but extremely elegant sitting room. But Inez wasn't having any, and it seemed as if she were, in fact, deliberately avoiding making eye contact with Polly. Which was so frustrating when Polly was bursting with a million questions.

The first of which was had Inez seen the amount of make-up the maid was wearing? And had she noticed how deep Linda's voice was? And was one supposed to mention the fact that the prim, punctilious, beautifully turned-out woman ahead of them was actually and fairly obviously really a man!

When they reached the patio, which was lit with soft, Japanese lanterns already even though it was still not yet fully night, a rather heavily built but nevertheless sweet-faced and handsome woman rose out of a peacock chair and darted forward to meet them.

'My dears! I'm so glad you could come,' she cried, then enveloped Inez in a huge hug and kissed her comprehensively on the lips.

For a few seconds the women clung to each other, and Polly watched in amazement as their tongues clearly duelled, then Violet pulled away, setting aside Inez like a well-loved niece before turning her attentions to Polly herself.

'And you must be Polly,' she said, beaming and launching herself forward before Polly had any time to react. 'You're even prettier than they told me!'

The next thing Polly knew was that she was receiving the same treatment that Inez had done – an enveloping embrace and open-mouthed kiss directly on the lips – and the strangest thing of all was that, after the initial shock was over, she discovered she liked it!

Violet Blackwood was a good deal stronger than her soft, matronly appearance might have suggested. Arms like iron bands secured Polly against her, a pair of broad, countrywoman's hips moved ever-so-slightly suggestively, and a tongue like an eel dived right into her mouth and began to explore and taste her. It was the most blatant greeting she'd experienced so far in Chandler's Haven, and if Violet greeted total strangers like this, Polly could hardly imagine what liberties she might take when she got to know them better!

'Oh yes,' said Violet as she broke away, her rounded cheeks pink with pleasure. 'You're a juicy young miss, and no mistake, Polly. I think we'll be good friends, you and I, before the night's out, you mark my words.' Catching Polly unawares again, she reached around behind her and gave her bottom a playful squeeze.

Polly could not think of a single thing to say, but fortunately this didn't seem to bother Violet in the slightest. 'Come along, my dears, let's all have a drink while Linda finishes preparing the dinner.' She turned to her 'maid'. 'Bring the punch, Linda, will you?' she said. 'Come along, girl! Look lively, my guests are thirsty. This really isn't good enough at all!'

Polly wanted to say there was no rush on her part – a clear head seemed like a good idea at the moment – but the tall, black-clad woman looked suddenly fearful and scurried away into the house.

'I'm having awful trouble with her today,' said Violet matter-of-factly as she ushered Inez and Polly to matching peacock chairs, then bustled about plumping the cushions and rearranging them before letting the two of them sit down. 'I've a feeling I shall have to take her in hand before the evening's over. She gets so lax if I'm not vigilant. It's really a problem . . .'

As far as Polly could see the male maid's performance as a domestic was exemplary, but she sensed that in the strange and sexually rarefied atmosphere of Chandler's Haven, the relationship between actual misdeeds and shortcomings, and the retribution that was dealt out to correct them, was not exactly reciprocal. Shifting in her seat, she suddenly realised to her horror – and delight – that she was really looking forward to seeing the *faux* maid 'taken in hand', and even the small fact that he was a man didn't seem to blunt her anticipation. If anything, it only made the prospect more spicy.

Too weird, Polly thought, trying to get her head straight and sort out what it was that was exciting her the most. The only thing she knew for certain now was that the punch they'd been promised couldn't arrive soon enough!

'So, how are you feeling now, Polly?' enquired Violet, her eyes suddenly looking rather piercing in her soft and friendly face. 'Inez told me that you were experiencing a little soreness . . . in the thigh area. Would you like me to take a look at it for you? I did used to be a nurse.' Without waiting for an answer she advanced, sweeping up the full skirts of her own rather old-fashioned floral dress, and knelt down on the patio flags in front

182

of Polly. 'Come along, my dear,' she went on, her voice sinking low and acquiring a sultry note that seemed at odds with medical solicitude. 'Let's have this pretty dress out of the way, shall we? So we can see what we're dealing with?'

I can stop this if I want to, thought Polly as Violet plucked at the layers of voile and crêpe that covered her and began to lift them. I can stop it whenever I feel like it . . . So why aren't I doing that?

With what seemed like great ceremony Violet lifted up Polly's skirts, bunching them very carefully at her waist and uncovering not only her thighs but her tiny panties and quite a lot of her waywardly escaping pubic hair too. Polly thought for a moment of the scene, earlier, with Inez, and wondered if this time the unveiling would go further. She thought it would, somehow, a very great deal further.

'May I touch you?' asked Violet softly, and as she spoke, Polly sensed a distinct quickening of interest on Inez's part. The other woman didn't visibly move in her chair, but Polly could almost feel her hungry psyche crane forward.

'Yes,' Polly said, then felt like a wimp her voice was so tiny. 'Yes, please do,' she repeated, much more strongly, straightening her spine a little and pushing forward her crotch.

Violet smiled, her round face looking impish all of a sudden, and even more attractive. 'Just your thighs for the moment, my sweet,' she whispered, her gaze flickering from Polly's face to the V of her groin and back again.

Mortified, Polly felt her face and throat begin to colour up in a bright pink blush. Why was it that these women all seemed to take great pleasure in wrong-footing her?

Fingertips like thistledown traced the site of Ellen's recent endeavours. The pain was virtually non-existent now, and all that remained in evidence was the faintest trace of colour − but Violet's touch was as light and exploratory as it would have been if there had been serious weals and bruising. She traced every inch of first the fronts, then the inner surfaces of Polly's thighs, clucking and tutting as she went, her smooth brow crumpled.

Polly couldn't see why such consternation was necessary, but after a moment or two she hardly seemed to notice it. The featherweight caress was turning her on, and she started wriggling.

'Well, I must say she did a marvellous job on you,' said Violet at length, her hand settling flat on Polly's inner thigh, fingertips less than a centimetre from the crotch of her panties. 'I've never known anyone who could hit so hard, yet leave so little sign of it afterwards.' She paused, and seemed to go dreamy for a moment, her eyelids, dusted with a powder-blue eye-shadow, drooping languorously. 'The last time she thrashed me, it felt like hell but there was hardly a mark on my great fat bottom the following day.'

The vision of Violet's naked buttocks was suddenly too much for Polly. She gave a little gasp and pushed herself forward again, shimmying shamelessly as Violet's fingers touched the gusset of her knickers. She closed her eyes, leaning into the minute pressure as she imagined the mighty and beautiful Ellen laying waste to Violet's wobbly flesh with her leather slipper.

'That's it, relax, my dear,' said a soft, coaxing voice as Polly felt her legs parting of their own volition and a single finger worming its way beneath the elastic of her pants – in search of treasure. 'You need to let yourself go, and forget all your troubles with computers and suchlike . . . Just open your legs and let me give you a little rub. You'll feel much better.'

The mention of computers was a cold shower, momentarily – how did Violet know about her problems? Polly tried to think, and to remember what she'd said about herself, and to whom in Chandler's Haven she'd said it, but almost immediately the plump woman's importunate fingertips dispelled the chill. When Polly opened her eyes, after barely realising she'd closed them, she looked down and she saw that half of Violet's hand was inside her panties. Even as she watched, the rude sight became dynamic, and Violet's fingers were moving and circling between her labia.

Polly grabbed the arms of the peacock chair as Violet masturbated her with the same light precision that she'd used on her thighs just a moment ago. The woman's thumb rolled intoxicatingly over her clitoris, while a couple of fingers inveigled their way into her wet vagina. Astonishingly, at the same time, Violet's little finger managed to stretch back and massage her anus.

'Would you like to come, my dear?' asked Violet quietly, her left hand sidling up to cup one of Polly's breasts as she spoke. 'Or would you just like me to excite you so it'll all be nicer later?'

Oh, now! Now! Polly wanted to scream, as the infernal little finger began to poke its way through the muscular portal of her anus – but just then, footsteps sounded and the erotic spell was broken. When her eyes flew open, she found that Linda was standing a couple of yards away. The maid was carrying a tray which held a jug of punch and glasses.

Humiliation flooded through Polly, and she tried to pull away. Oh God, that was a *man* looking at her! A man watching her being stimulated and played with. She had an immediate flash of a long, thick penis beginning to stiffen.

'Hush now,' said Violet, sounding unexpectedly steely. She released Polly's breast and took her firmly by the arm, even though her other hand remained exactly where it had been. 'Nothing to get het up about. It's just a little masturbation. Nothing that any of us hasn't seen before.' Between Polly's legs, her fingers moved with intelligence, covering all bases. Polly tried to struggle, but she was held with a grip like fury.

Inevitably, Polly climaxed, but it was against her will. Biting her lip, she tried to keep in her sobs of shame and pleasure as her vagina clenched and grabbed at Violet's fat finger. She felt her juices flowing out and coating her vanquisher's hand.

Polly turned away and stared down fixedly into the gathering twilight of the garden. She strained to see the outlines of what she guessed were scrupulously tended lawns and flowerbeds, and to make out the silhouette of a carved stone cupid that held up a bird table. Anything rather than face the scrutiny of the assembled company on the patio. She felt Violet remove her hand, and leave her still revealed by her pushed-up skirts, but she was just too exhausted and overwhelmed to move and cover herself. After a few moments, there was a tap on her arm, and she looked up to see the maid, Linda, holding out a well-filled glass of punch. Prompted by the look of sympathy and, against all logic, sisterhood in the maid's liquid hazel eyes, she took the glass, lifted it to her lips, and drank long and deep.

The punch was delicious, quite strong, and gave Polly just the revivifying kick she needed. She took another long pull from the glass, then flipped her skirts down defiantly to cover herself. It was time to take control of her own pleasure, and indulge in it only when *she* wanted to! Turning towards Violet, who was thoughtfully sniffing at the tips of her fingers, Polly gave the plump woman a long and challenging look.

The message was passed, and Violet even went so far as to nod slightly. Polly felt a rush of strength, took another sip of punch, then looked around, smiling.

Inez, too, had been entertaining herself it seemed. She was pink in the face, and her narrow, artistic hand was still pressed to her groin. Obviously, she'd been so aroused by what she'd seen that she'd had to masturbate, and Polly felt vaguely superior in the fact that while Inez was still dishevelled, and a little disorientated, she herself had quite suddenly regained her poise.

Way to go! I'm getting the hang of this, Polly thought smugly, as she watched the little party in its attempts to re-establish normality. Linda was bustling around, first refilling glasses, and then offering scented wipes to deal with fingers that now bore certain distinctive odours. Polly wanted to giggle at the sight of Inez's further discomfiture, but even so, she had to admire Violet's tact as she engaged the other woman in a froth of inconsequential conversation, effectively smoothing over a moment that would otherwise have been tense.

As the other two began to discuss one of Inez's latest art commissions, and Linda disappeared, presumably to tend the forthcoming meal, Polly took the opportunity to gaze out more purposefully at her idyllic surroundings.

The Blackwoods – Polly found herself assuming that Linda was actually Mr Blackwood – had a large and very beautiful garden that lent itself perfectly to the drama of nightfall and an array of carefully placed lanterns. The area around the patio itself and the dining table set up under a striped canvas pavilion were quite brightly illuminated, but the regions beyond that brilliance were moody and mysterious. Polly could almost imagine concealed watchers amongst the bushes and the shrubs; women, clandestine members of the Enclave, assembled to watch the performance, their combined breath bated and their hands sliding involuntarily into their knickers.

She pictured them caressing themselves helplessly, driven into a frenzy by the sight of her own ecstatic contortions at the hands of Violet. To them she had been an icon of feminine abandon and deliciously enforced lust. They had used her vulnerability to lever themselves towards their pleasure.

But not any more, girls! Polly told these notional voyeurs. Not unless I *choose* it. From now on, I don't come unless I want to. You'll have to wait and see whether I *choose* to reveal myself.

After a short while of mulling over her thoughts, sipping, and almost detachedly observing the scene around her, Polly was drawn back to reality by the return of a flustered-looking Linda. Each time Polly saw the *faux* woman, she found it easier to accept 'her', and she now found the maid's unusual appearance more attractive than unsettling.

'Madame Tourneur is here,' the maid said, clearly driven into a state of high agitation by the announcement. Polly wondered what the big problem was. Surely one more guest for dinner wouldn't be all that much of a disruption? That was unless the numbers were crucial for far more than just the food.

Almost before the maid had finished speaking, there came the sound of footsteps from somewhere just behind her, and she stepped out of the way to let the newcomer on to the patio.

Newcomers, thought Polly, experiencing a renewed twist of interest as two figures emerged from the low light of the house into the zone of brighter illumination around the seating area.

The first was a very straight-backed and very elegant woman of medium height, who was dressed far more formally than a casual summer dinner party seemed to demand of her. Madame

Tourneur was of the old school, obviously, even though her smooth-skinned face was that of a woman in the prime of middle age, and she wore a chic suit, complete with handbag, gloves and hat. Her jaunty little chapeau even sported a frothy swathe of veiling, which only served to highlight the silvery sheen of her stringently coiffeured hair which was a startling dense and premature pure white.

'My dear Violet,' said the newcomer warmly, gliding forward to air kiss Violet, who'd risen to her feet. 'I hope you do not mind me dropping in unannounced like this? But I was on my way back from the city, and I was passing, and I suddenly realised that it is too long since we saw each other.' She paused delicately, letting an acute and very patrician gaze drift across Polly and Inez. 'Of course, if it is inconvenient, you only have to speak and we'll be on our way.'

She's French, thought Polly, taking in the clothes, the poise, and the indefinable air of understated style that overlaid every gesture and nuance of the woman's appearance. If she'd have been forced to rely on accent alone, Polly might not have been so sure of her analysis, as the white-haired woman's voice was warm and smooth and barely inflected.

'Don't be so silly, Miriam!' cried Violet, looking almost ecstatic to see the Frenchwoman, and more than a little bit disappointed that she was only being allowed a gesture kiss, and not the full-on mouth tango she'd clearly so enjoyed with Polly and Inez. 'I'd love you to stay! *We'd* love you to stay! Wouldn't we?' She turned towards them, looking for affirmation.

'Er, yes,' muttered Polly, realising that her opinion was genuinely being sought. She got to her feet, wondering what sort of greeting she should offer to this woman she didn't know, but with whom she may well soon be intimate if the mores of Chandler's Haven were anything to go by.

As she approached Miriam Tourneur, the Frenchwoman fixed her with a gaze that was level and blue and penetrating. Polly answered again, but this time in silence, feeling exhilarated by her ability to meet such power.

Again came the air kiss. It should have been an empty gesture, a matter of form, and yet the physical closeness of Miriam, and her haunting fragrance, made Polly's sexual spirit rise all over again. As her lips passed within centimetres of Miriam's cheek, she imagined melting the coolness, shattering the poise, and dishevelling the immaculate fashion perfection, finding the heart of the primitive woman beneath the façade. It was an intoxicating prospect and she felt almost dizzy as they drew apart.

As Miriam moved on to greet Inez, Polly was distracted from all this feminine ritual by the sight of the Frenchwoman's companion. Standing a respectful few paces behind Miriam was her chauffeur; an almost laughably stereotypical figure dressed in peaked cap, uniform jacket, boots and jodhpurs. He wasn't all that tall for a man, but nevertheless looked imposing and well capable of doubling as a bodyguard if necessary. A pair of opaque shades, despite the time of day, completed an image of menace and toughness.

But as Polly was about to glance away, in the face of a veneer even more impenetrable than that of Miriam Tourneur, she hesitated, held her ground, and looked more closely.

And got another shock.

Oh God, it's another of them! Polly kept her face as cool and mask-like as the chauffeur's but, as she returned to the vicinity of her seat, inside she didn't know whether to laugh or shake her head. Instead, she looked across at Miriam and the Frenchwoman caught her eye, and seemed to detect the source of her interest.

'Oh, don't worry about Francis, Polly. He's rather stern, and he doesn't say much but he's a sweetheart really.' True to the description, the silent chauffeur stepped back towards the house wall, and just stood there, stonily at attention.

'Oh, I'm not worried, thank you,' said Polly airily, accepting more punch from the now-circulating Linda. 'I'm sure he's a treasure.'

Francis? Or is it 'Frances', more like, she thought as she returned to the table and picked up her glass again. She took another drink of her punch, but with some wariness, in respect of its strength. It was now obvious to her that the poker-faced chauffeur was playing the same game as Linda was, only in reverse this time. There was a tough-looking woman inside that dapper stylised uniform, one who took her cross-dressing more seriously than Polly had previously ever thought possible.

I wish I could stop myself looking at it, thought Polly, swirling her glass and trying to focus on the vortex that the motion made in its rosy contents. Then she looked at Inez and Violet and Miriam, and tried to tune in to their complicated body language, and after that she watched Linda tottering on her skyscraper heels. Anything to avoid staring in the direction that her gaze suddenly felt magnetised towards . . .

Which was the fly area of Francis's dapper grey jodhpurs.

What the hell has she got in there? Is it rolled-up socks or is it actually a false dick?

In her recent readings, Polly had encountered the concept of 'packing' – the dyke practice of wearing a dildo beneath clothing to simulate a penis – but somehow she'd never really expected to actually see it. Even Ellen – who was as hard and as dominant and as butch as any woman could ask for – didn't bother to feign the masculine appendage. But it seemed that Francis the chauffeur went the whole and phallic way.

What a blast! Polly thought, taking a cautious mouthful of punch. In the beginning, when Pat had first initiated her, she'd tried to analyse what she should and shouldn't be feeling about her new status, and about gender and preference and bias and all those heavy concepts. But here in Chandler's Haven, the Enclave was showing her that 'anything went'!

Was Francis watching her in return, she wondered, unable to tear her attention from the enigmatic grey-clad figure? It was impossible to tell, because those Wayfarer-style shades were impossible to see through. Francis could be scoping her out just as thoroughly as she was scoping him. Her! Whatever!

But just as Polly was on the point of doing something mad – like touching herself perhaps? – to see if she could get a response out of the stone-like Francis, a disturbance amongst her other companions commanded her attention.

At the sound of a slap, Polly turned towards the other group and saw that there had been a mishap with the brightly coloured punch. On Linda's tray, there was a glass overturned – and down the front of Inez's expensive summer dress, a stain was growing. A stigmata of purple on the pallid smoke grey crêpe.

'You clumsy little twit!' cried Violet, her attention turned on the hapless maid. Polly saw that Linda's perfectly made-up face bore its own mark; one cheek was crimson where a stinging blow had fallen.

'How could you be so careless?' the plump woman went on. 'You've ruined Inez's beautiful dress, you nincompoop! I suppose you realise that you're going to have to suffer for this?'

There was a moment of almost crystalline silence, during which the miserable maid clearly fought to retain her composure. Polly watched her for a second as she put aside the tray and its contents. There were real wet tears in her widened eyes, and she was suppressing her sobs . . .

But as intriguing, and as unexpectedly alluring as the ambiguous maid was, the rest of the company soon reclaimed Polly's close attention.

She saw no signs of vexation or dismay on their faces; not even on that of Inez, whose dress was from a hot designer, and had cost a fortune. No, all the women were smiling and wore expressions that ranged from contained glee to outright lasciviousness. Even the impassive Francis had a tiny quirk at the corners of his lips.

Oh my God, here comes the floorshow, thought Polly, her own lips parting and her groin beginning to quicken. She could only speculate on what the performance ahead might be . . .

TWELVE
Floorshow

The entertainment began straight away; at least the preamble to it did . . .

Watched by several pairs of eager eyes, Polly's included, Violet took Linda tightly by the arm and made her face Inez. 'Just look what you've done, you silly little dolt!' she said sharply, shaking the maid hard. 'Now don't just stand there, do something about it!'

Linda took the spotless white tea towel that was tucked into the belt of her apron and began dabbing ineffectually at the soiled front of Inez's dress. The action was pointless, that was obvious, as the damage was probably irreparable, but the impression Polly received was that the action was purely token anyway, a kind of ritual. And Inez herself didn't seem to be too bothered by it. In fact, she swayed towards the pressure, her body lightly undulating as Linda dabbed and patted. Twisting her hips she managed to inveigle the maid into pressing against her crotch.

'For pity's sake, what on earth are you doing, you filthy girl?' demanded Violet, on observing this development. 'How dare you touch Miss Parker like that? How dare you take such liberties? If I didn't know better I'd say you were trying to grope her!'

Linda flinched back, dropping her towel, then swooped down

192

to pick it up again. Her slapped cheek was still red, but the other was blushing now to match it.

'Stay where you are, you horrible wretch,' Violet went on, moving towards Inez, and then touching her reassuringly on the shoulder. 'Are you all right, my dear?' she enquired, then to Polly's amusement, she too allowed her fingers the opportunity to rove. 'I'm so sorry about your dress, Inez,' she said, squeezing Inez's breast quite shamelessly.

Again, Inez responded to the contact, shimmying blatantly this time, her eyes closing as Violet massaged her nipple. Her voice was breathy when she finally managed to reply.

'I'm fine, Vi,' she gasped, her own hand sneaking down to her pubic mound and pressing. 'But the dress is ruined. I do think Linda ought to pay somehow.' Polly watched astonished as Inez's fingers began to work, pushing the cloth of the dress deep into the groove of her crotch.

'I'm afraid Linda doesn't have an allowance, my dear,' said Violet, looking down, past her own groping hand to that of Inez.

'No matter,' panted Inez, her hips weaving now. 'I'm sure you'll think of another way she can pay.'

Oh Lord, this is wild! Polly thought, feeling her own fingers flex as her pussy seemed to cry to them. All of a sudden, in the space of a few seconds, the entire area of the patio was drenched in a high voltage sexuality. She was dying to masturbate; Miriam's pale face bore tiny coins of pink colour high on the cheekbones; and even the imperturbable Francis seemed to exude a subtle excitement. And as for Violet, Inez and Linda? It wouldn't have surprised Polly in the slightest if they'd all three sank to the flags and started tearing each other's clothes off. The maid was clearly terrified, but she had one big hand cupped frantically around her crotch.

After a few moments of slow grinding and heavy breathing, Violet asked, 'Inez, would you like Linda to fetch you a robe? You can't sit at the table and enjoy your dinner in that sopping dress.'

'Don't worry, I'll be OK,' said Inez lightly, knocking Violet's hand away from her breast. 'It's a such a gorgeous night, I don't think I'll bother with a dress at all!' With that, she swiftly peeled off the punch-stained dress and the half-slip she wore beneath it, and flung them aside. Wearing just her white lacy bra and panties, she reached for a fresh glass of punch from the maid's abandoned tray and took a drink.

'Are you sure?' persisted Violet, her fat pink tongue popping out to sweep around her lips. Her eyes were bulging as she devoured the pale beauty of Inez.

'Of course,' said Inez, staring levelly at Violet over the rim of her glass. 'How about you?' Her eyes were bright now, as liquid and brilliant as the punch.

'No problem here,' said Violet, her gaze visibly tracking from Inez's high, firm breasts down to her groin, where her dark pubic bush was clearly visible through the virginal lace. 'Do you ladies have any objections?' she enquired, turning first to Miriam and then to Polly.

Polly didn't see the Frenchwoman's response, but found herself shaking her own head before she'd hardly even considered the question. Inez's body was too sumptuous to cover up again now it was on show.

'Very well then, shall we have dinner?' enquired Violet blithely, as if it were the most normal thing in the world for one of their number to sit down to a meal in her underwear. 'Take your seats, ladies,' she said, gesturing to the table, already set, beneath its canopy. 'I just have a little matter to attend to and then I'll come and join you.'

Polly, Inez and Miriam moved to the table, although Francis remained at attention, as still as a guardsman. Without trying to seem too obvious, Polly took a seat where she could still see Violet, as she was curious about what the 'little matter' might be. She wasn't disappointed when the plump woman began to speak again.

'You! You careless dimwit,' she said to Linda, taking the maid's hand – the one with which she'd clutched herself – and slapping it hard. 'You disgust me with your slovenliness and your lack of control.' Violet's words were soft, yet ironclad, and made Polly think of Ellen's style – absolute power wielded with subtle understatement.

'Now I want you to serve this meal to the best of your ability, Linda,' Violet went on, looking up at the tall maid, yet still effortlessly holding her in the palm of her small, plump hand. 'You can't save yourself from what's to come. That's irrevocable, my sweet.' Her tone softened a little, and Polly saw just the faintest nuance of what was a clear and genuine affection. 'But you can make my guests think better of you by performing the rest of your duties superlatively. Do you understand? Do you think you can do that? Will you try?'

Linda hung her head, then nodded and gave a wan little smile. Curiouser and curiouser, thought Polly, beginning to wonder if the initial mishap had been deliberate and this was yet another game. There was a puppy-like devotion in the strange maid's painted eyes.

'Now, I think we have to make a token gesture, for starters, considering the trouble you've caused.' Violet's voice was gleeful as she glanced at Inez, a vision of womanhood, clad just in lace. 'Turn around,' she ordered Linda, taking the maid by the arm and manhandling her. 'Pull up your skirts at the back . . . Come on! Right up!' The maid obeyed. 'Now pass me some safety pins from the pocket of your apron.'

Polly watched the procedure with amazement, fascination, and not a little growing excitement. Violet pinned the maid's skirt and petticoats until the whole of her underwear-covered thighs and bottom were exposed. Polly had half-expected Linda to be clad in the kind of archaic bloomers that Ellen had forced *her* to wear, but not so, the tall maid's lingerie was ultra feminine. Her man/woman body was all decked out in sugar-pink silk and lace-topped stockings. It was a peculiar sight as Linda's thighs were long and brawny.

'Now, step out of your pants, my dear, and arrange them over the arm of my chair, where everyone can see them.'

As Linda obeyed, Polly found herself shifting in her own chair in order to get a better view of what was happening. She couldn't begin to understand the skewed urges that were operating within her; she only knew that she wanted to see Linda's naked bottom, and to imagine the shame and the thrill that such an ignominious exposure would cause her.

Looking distinctly tearful again, Linda completed her task, then hovered by the chair, primping and rearranging her silky pink panties. Her stance was awkward as she tried to conceal her naked bottom.

Violet moved close again, and whispered something in Linda's ear. Polly craned even further forward, not caring what the others might think of her, and tried to hear the softly murmured words.

Linda shook her head, but Violet whispered again, and the maid appeared to slump in acquiescence. Slowly, as if under extreme duress, the maid turned around.

Polly knew that as male backsides went, Linda's was quite a handsome one – strong and muscular, neat in shape, and not exceptionally hairy. The way the maid was standing meant that the genitalia were not quite visible, but it was unequivocally a man's bottom despite the suspenders.

Violet whispered again, and Linda quite clearly pleaded, 'No! Please no!'

'Just for a moment, my dear,' replied Violet, her voice kind but firm, her hand settling on Linda's back.

With obvious reluctance, the maid parted her – his? – thighs, then dipped at the waist, bending over and tipping forward. At a further whispered urging, she reached around behind herself and parted the pale cheeks of her bottom with her fingers.

Feeling simultaneously repulsed and turned on, Polly squirmed in her seat and felt a strong urge to touch herself. It wasn't that the sight of a bare male backside and a pendant prick and balls filled her with any kind of sexual yearning, it was more the creature's predicament and state of vulnerability that made her blood surge. For a moment, she wished that she were the one bent over and showing her sex and her arse to the assembled dinner guests. That she was the one inviting them to come and do their worst to her.

'Come along, dear, do a little wiggle for the ladies,' said Violet, bending low, her lips near Linda's hidden face. There was another sound of protest, but after a second the maid began to move, rolling her hips in a slow, ungainly circle.

Beneath the cover of the tablecloth, Polly clasped her fingers to her crotch through her dress and petticoats – trying to imagine the depths of humiliation the maid must be feeling. She wondered if Linda was hardening, even as she moved, stirred as much by lubricity as she was by fear and shame.

The ugly, dance-like exhibition went on for just a few more moments, then Violet reached down beneath Linda, groped around slightly, and let out an almost theatrical squeak of outrage.

'Oh you wicked, wicked thing!' she cried playfully, and made a little jerking action. As she did so Linda groaned, but manfully held her pose.

'We'll have none of that, my girl!' Violet went on, mock-sternly, releasing Linda's penis, then giving her backside a swift, hard slap. 'You'd better pull yourself together, get into that kitchen and finish preparing the dinner . . . or it'll be the worse for you! I can't have my guests going hungry while you stand here getting excited!'

As Linda scuttled away, still bare-arsed, Polly didn't know whether she wanted to laugh out loud or put her hand in her knickers and masturbate. This really was the most mad, bizarre, and melodramatic ritual she'd ever seen in her life. Even by Chandler's Haven standards it was exaggerated, and yet every instinct told her that so far all she'd seen was the prologue. What the evening's main act would turn out to be, she could hardly contemplate.

She wasn't disappointed.

As the meal was served and eaten, it gradually became obvious to Polly that what constituted acceptable dinner behaviour at one of Violet's little gatherings bore no relation to that which was practised elsewhere. Linda was fondled and examined as she served first the soup, the entrée, then the fruit and cheese, and when the two other guests, and Violet, weren't touching up the maid, their hands were on themselves or others.

While Miriam was describing a recent trip to Paris, and her stay with an old friend, a legendary, almost iconic French film star, Polly suddenly noticed that Violet was squirming around and gasping. A closer inspection disclosed that both the hostess's hands were hidden from view and that her pale, plump cheeks were blushing as bright as peonies. Polly caught Inez's eye, but the other woman merely smiled and shrugged.

'Violet has something of a crush on "La Diva",' said Miriam, catching the look and turning to Polly with a glowing smile of her own. 'Whenever we discuss her, I'm afraid our dear hostess always feels compelled to masturbate . . . Do you feel that too, my dear?' she added. Her voice was accentless but nonetheless filled with delicate humour.

Caught on the hop, Polly blurted out the first thing that came into her head. 'Er, yes, sort of . . . I've never actually done it for her, but I've thought about it. She's very beautiful . . .'

It was true too. In recent months, as she'd begun to learn and experiment with her new worldview, Polly had looked at famous and glamorous women and opened her heart and mind to feelings. And when she'd considered La Diva's pure, icy beauty – which incidentally was not unlike Miriam's own – she had experienced a jolt of yearning, physical reaction.

'Then why not do so now?' the Frenchwoman suggested. 'There are no inhibitions here . . . Look at Violet, she's having an orgasm.' She gestured with a hand that was still primly gloved – indeed, she was still immaculately buttoned into her chic suit, her hat and veil still in place – to Violet who was bright puce in the face, grunting like an animal, and cursing roundly in time to the spasms of her hidden cunt.

Polly was tempted, oh-so tempted, but she thought of her earlier silent pledge that she would make her own choices. If she wanted to expose herself, to make herself come, she would do so not at the instigation of some Frenchwoman she'd met just less than an hour ago, but at a time of her own designation, exactly when she wanted.

'When I'm ready,' she said, feeling a rush of excitement at the surprise in the Frenchwoman's eyes, and the sudden respect. 'I've put on a show once already tonight . . . It's not my fault you missed it.' She held Miriam's gaze, flirted with her, drank in her disappointment, her silent hunger and her real desire. 'I feel like just watching the others for a while, and enjoying the entertainment.'

'Bravo,' said Miriam, so softly that Polly could have sworn she was the only woman to hear it. An unspoken communication passed between them, a delicious promise.

'And so you shall do!' announced Violet, who had clearly been listening and whose powers of recovery were apparently prodigious. The high colour was already fading in the woman's smooth, rounded cheeks, but her eyes were still brilliant and happily sparkling. 'Our little culprit has got away with things quite long enough, I think,' she said, throwing a significant look at Linda, who was at the table now, serving coffee and petits fours.

The maid trembled, and coffee slopped as the punch before it had done. Happily this time, though, the spill went on the tablecloth.

'Leave that,' said Violet abruptly. 'Go to the big chair. You know the drill. Take up the position.'

Linda walked slowly across the patio, her bare bottom gleaming in the gathering twilight. She looked back beseechingly over her shoulder, her eyes confused and liquid, yet excited as she locked gazes with Violet. The hostess was resolute, though, and nodded towards the chair.

Is it going to be a spanking, thought Polly, recalling the pain she'd experienced at Ellen's hands, and the libidinous effects it had produced in her. She wondered if just to see a thrashing would make her as horny as getting one. Probably yes, she realised, feeling her clitoris twitch and tingle.

Linda went over, kneeling in the big armchair in the corner of the covered end of the patio, rather than in one of the flimsier basket chairs. Bottom thrust outwards, she parted her legs and appeared to brace herself. Once again, her mismatched genitalia were clearly displayed.

'Come along, ladies, gather round,' encouraged Violet, leading them forward to get a better view. 'You wouldn't want to miss anything, would you?'

Polly and the others followed, Polly herself acutely aware of both Inez's near nakedness, and the extreme formality of Miriam's precision chic. Both women excited her, but according to entirely different parameters. Inez represented luscious sexuality, freely offered; Miriam was the mystique of what was hidden. As they all drew close to Linda Polly felt both of the other women reach out for her and, by the time they'd taken up their positions, she felt the touch of two pairs of hands.

'You'll enjoy this,' murmured Inez in Polly's ear, while long artist's fingers took hold of Polly's breast and squeezed it.

'Let us help you to enjoy it more,' echoed Miriam, her gloved hand cupping Polly's bottom cheek, her fingertips brushing her anal cleft.

Polly tried to protest, but Inez kissed her hard on the mouth and, by the time she was released, the sight of Violet massaging Linda's buttocks distracted her attention. The plump woman was circling the twin mounds of pale bare flesh with enormous gusto, stretching and closing the aperture between them as she worked.

'Oh!' gasped Polly, as Miriam's finger, encased in fine kid leather, began probing her. Somehow, the Frenchwoman had sneaked Polly's skirt up, and her hand was already inside her pants, attacking from behind. The insistent finger began to push against her anus, the touch of leather instead of skin feeling infinitely indecent.

'Relax, Polly,' said Inez, as if she knew exactly what Miriam was doing. Maybe she did? Her own hand still cradled Polly's breast, vigorously massaging.

'Come along, it's time,' said Violet briskly, abandoning her manipulation of Linda with a final playful slap. A look of voluptuous anticipation on her face, she turned, unexpectedly, to Francis the chauffeur, and went on, 'Are you ready to do the honours, Francis? I think you'll find that everything you need is in the usual place.'

Impassive behind the dark mask of his shades, the uniformed servant nodded slightly then left his self-appointed sentry post and walked smartly across to a weathered sideboard that stood on the covered portion of the patio. From a cupboard in it, he took a heavy glass jar – of the substantial type in which preserves and bottled fruit were kept – whose lid was fastened with an ingenious metal clip. This he unhitched, then peeling off his black leather driving gloves he dipped a finger into the jar. As he brought it out glistening, to Polly's astonishment, he suddenly smiled. Rubbing his fingertips together he seemed to savour the slickness that coated them.

'You'll need more than that,' observed Violet, watching the chauffeur closely as he wiped the stickiness casually over Linda's left bottom cheek, then he smiled again, his expression even more demonic this time.

A picture of what was going to happen began to take shape in Polly's imagination. It was a little blurred and smeared by the sensations that were beginning to build up in her breasts and her crotch, but even so, she could see the gist of things, the unspeakable symmetry. As Miriam pushed at her bottom, she groaned in sympathy with the waiting Linda.

Francis turned away for a moment, presenting his straight unyielding back to the watching assembly, but from certain small movements, and the sound of a zip, it was clear what he was doing.

I suppose it doesn't happen the way it does with a real one, thought Polly dreamily as she tilted her pelvis to give Miriam better access to her. The first joint of a finger was right inside her now, and her whole groin felt both energised and precarious. She imagined that Francis was going to approach *her*, instead of Linda, and her innards surged in a way that made her legs go weak and trembling.

'It could be you, if you want it,' suggested Miriam in her ear, whilst pushing yet more firmly down below. 'You have only to say the word.'

Polly couldn't speak. She felt as if she was going to choke as, at the same time, the finger in her anus swivelled and advanced a little; and across the patio, Francis turned around to reveal the protruding strap-on dildo.

The thing was huge, lifelike in shape and colour, and already well lubricated with plenty of gel from the large glass jar. The false penis swayed as the chauffeur moved forwards, brushing against Linda's bottom as the false man took up his position.

'Wait a minute,' said Violet. She darted forward and pressed a handful of the gel to the whimpering Linda's bottom crease, then worked it in deeper, her plump fingers moving graphically.

'Mmm, now doesn't that look good,' said Inez in Polly's ear as she took up the litany begun by Miriam. 'And look how the little slut's getting off on it. Look at her pumping her hips in time to the action of Violet's finger.'

It was true. Linda was groaning, but they were unmistakably groans of lust and excitement now, not fear or discomfort. The maid was eager to be fucked, it suddenly seemed.

Fucked? Buggered? Sodomised? What the hell did one call it in such a situation? Was there a special terminology that covered a man being fucked by a woman? Because that was what it was, when shorn of the dramatic masks of fantasy.

At that instant, though, Polly forgot all about semantics. Miriam's gloved finger was boring deep into her rectum. 'We need to get deeper, don't we, *ma petite*?' she whispered, the digit already in so deep that Polly was gasping. 'Perhaps if I remove my glove, and we employ some gel, I can properly possess you?'

Polly whimpered, feeling an overpowering urge to bend forward from the waist, just like Linda, and more freely offer herself. She parted her legs, and pulled up her own skirt, almost mindlessly preparing herself for Miriam.

'Good girl,' whispered Inez, one hand still kneading Polly's breast while the other stole downwards to her crotch. Polly felt cold air on her buttocks and then the touch of naked skin on skin as Miriam's now gloveless hand explored first her cheeks, then her folds and her entrances.

Torn between watching and simply feeling, Polly could not ignore what was happening between the couple who were the main part of the floorshow. Linda's bottom and genitalia were slick and plastered with the clear gel now, and Francis was massaging his plastic prick with all the relish that a man would employ when massaging his own, living flesh. The chauffeur's narrow hips rocked and swayed as if the masturbation were real . . .

Then, all of a sudden, the process of 'feeling' began to predominate, or at least acquire equal status. The fingers between her bottom cheeks were wet now, slippery with the same gel with which Francis had anointed himself, and with which Violet had anointed Linda. I'm being prepared, thought Polly, prepared for violation. They're going to take my arse, just as Francis takes Linda's. Like a mare on heat, she presented her buttocks, pushing backwards.

'That's it, sweetheart,' said Inez, her fingers sliding between Polly's labia as Miriam's took position round at her rear. Over at the armchair, Francis stepped forward, positioning the dildo. Linda sobbed as Violet reached beneath her, clasping her cock.

Then it all happened. In a series of syncopated jerks, thrusts, squeaks, squelches and long, heartfelt groans, the deliciously vulnerable yielded their all to their conquering vanquishers.

Through a red mist of breath-catching, almost horrifying pleasure, Polly watched Francis sink in deep as Linda shouted loudly, clearly climaxing; whilst at the same time, she felt not one but two fingers plunge unrelentingly into her bottom.

'Oh dear God,' she cried as Inez pinched her clitoris.

Polly woke in the middle of the night, her dreams a mad debauch of outrageous pictures and sensations. Snapping on the bedside light she saw after-images of buttocks, fingers, penises – false and otherwise – all combining and recombining in infinite patterns.

In the dreams she'd been a part of everything happening. She'd been perpetrator and recipient, both pleasure-giver and a willing, helpless, orgasming body. She'd been the vulnerable vessel, and a rampant penetrator with fingers and tongue and dildoes . . .

'Bloody hell,' she muttered, looking out across her bedroom and seeing her dress and slip flung across the floor, shoes lying askew, but no sign whatsoever of her panties.

She snapped off the light again, and buried her head in the pillow.

It had all been real.

I am not going to think about all that, Polly told herself as she took a shower the next morning, and looked for signs on her body of the previous night's orgy.

Her skin looked perfectly clear, however, and her flesh felt firm and resilient. If anything, she felt fitter and livelier than she usually did, as if those mad hours on Violet Blackwood's patio had energised her rather than been a drain on her physical resources.

But she still didn't think that she wanted to think about, or talk about, or analyse those events in any way. It had been a time out of time, and yet, as she'd gathered afterwards, not something that was particularly unusual for the Enclave of Chandler's Haven. The formidable Francis had driven them home from the Black-woods – Miriam having still been asleep somewhere, in one of Violet's unseen bedrooms – and though the chauffeur hadn't said a single word other than the most basic of required responses, Inez had chatted during the journey on the most inconsequential of topics. It really did seem as if what had happened was in no way an out of the ordinary occurrence.

I'll be just as blasé as they are then, Polly decided. Dressing in jeans and a T-shirt, she went down to the kitchen in search of some breakfast.

Inez was nowhere to be seen, but there was a note waiting for Polly smack in the centre of her place setting.

It was brief and unrevealing.

Severn called to deliver some fruit and veg, so I've hitched a lift with her to Violet's to collect the car. See you later. Enjoy your breakfast. There's some post for you. Love, Inez.

Polly felt vaguely annoyed at having missed Severn. The thought of the beautiful blonde gardener was like a breath of fresh air wafting through the veils of licentiousness that still lingered from last night. Although if Severn had been there, Polly supposed, she would have joined in just as enthusiastically as everyone else . . .

As usual, Inez had left all the components of breakfast immaculately assembled, and all Polly had to do was put heat under the coffee and slip some bread into the toaster. While she did these tasks, she kept trying to formulate some plan of positive action for the day, and to think about ways she could find out about E-Tech and the progress of the patent on Sanspareil, but all the while stray thoughts of eroticism constantly claimed her. She could still almost feel the sensation of fingers stealing over her body, and sneaking into all her indentations and orifices.

Especially the orifices. And especially her anus.

It was an erogenous zone she'd somehow always fought shy of before – probably not through fear, she sensed now, but through quite the opposite. What she'd been afraid of was liking her bottom played with far too much!

She had to wriggle in her seat as she remembered an instance of Violet possessing her. She could almost feel the life-size dildo still in her back passage . . .

For crying out loud, Polly, leave it, she told herself as she felt the slow, dark stir of lust deep in her belly. There was a real world to be dealt with now. And serious issues. There was lot at stake, yet all she could think of was being fingered and abused.

Post! Inez said I have post, she thought suddenly, in a serious, straw-clutching attempt to break free of the all-powerful grip of her own libido.

At first she couldn't see any post, but shoving aside the newspaper and a shrink-wrapped art magazine, Polly discovered some letters. All but one were for Inez, but the one that remained was decidedly ominous. Polly felt physically sick when she saw the stark but elegant logo – the crest of E-Tech.

Too wound up to pay any respect to the beautiful cream wove envelope, Polly ripped it open and unfolded the single sheet letter. Her eyes skipped and danced over fragments of the message it imparted, but she felt initially too scared to make herself read it as one piece. Truncated phrases seemed to dance and leap from the page and taunt her.

'Further to our recent communication', 'discuss terms', 'a generous offer' and 'meet formally with a panel'. Nothing seemed to make sense, and her feeling of nausea began to escalate. She took a sip of coffee, felt slightly worse for a moment, then managed to centre herself again. Taking a deep breath she picked up the letter and began to read it methodically.

They – E-Tech – wanted to have a formal meeting with her to discuss her joining their organisation with a view to developing and marketing Sanspareil. They were prepared to offer what seemed like an obscene amount of money, with the prospect of more to come if she went on to produce more 'product'. She would have to face a panel and make a detailed presentation. On reading the date, her shakiness surged again. All she had was two short days . . .

The letter was signed 'Jane Smith' who styled herself 'Assistant to the Chief Executive Officer'.

'Made-up name, or what?' Polly muttered as she studied the letter in more detail, and tried to work out how much or how little it really told her. She still knew nothing whatsoever of E-Tech's background, even though the letterhead impressively stated that they had offices in London, New York, Geneva and Tokyo. But there were no phone numbers given, no contact names and, most irritating of all to her, no addresses for either e-mail or web-sites. Which seemed downright peculiar for a company whose business was software. In fact, the whole approach was unlike that of any business organisation she'd ever had dealings with. It was almost unknown not to make the initial contact by telephone these days . . .

The only thing that could be pinned down in the letter at all was the date, time and place of the meeting. Which was the day after tomorrow, at eight in the evening, at a central London address which Polly recognised as being in one of the city's most exclusive and sought-after areas. Whoever E-Tech were, they were making so much money they were already as rich as Croesus.

This is so dodgy, thought Polly, turning the thick sheet of paper over and over again as if there might be further illumination somehow concealed on the reverse of the page. I know nothing of them, and they offer no information about themselves, and they summon me to an interview at a really suspect time of the day. It might be some kind of set-up; it might even be a scam by F&X, to entrap me. I'm not going to go. I'll just ignore them . . . I won't let myself be fooled.

Light footsteps in the hall shook Polly from her deliberations and, a second later, Inez appeared in the kitchen doorway.

'Good morning, Polly. Did you get my note? I've just been for the car.'

Polly had never seen Inez look more fresh and pristine. She projected an aura that was as pure as the driven snow, and as chaste as that of a reverend mother. It was difficult to believe what her cool, collected hostess had been up to the night before.

Inez was wearing a crisp white shirt, well-cut trousers and a pair of driving shoes; her hair was neat and glossy and her face already made up. Polly just could not equate her with the insatiable maenad who'd cavorted naked on Violet Blackwood's patio.

'Are you all right, Polly?' Inez enquired, tossing her car keys on the table and then pouring herself a cup of coffee. 'You look as if you've had a bit of a shock. Is it anything I can help with?'

'Um, no, I don't think so,' Polly said, almost automatically, but even as she spoke, she realised there was a possible way. 'Unless, of course, you'd mind me using your computer to log on to the Internet to do a bit of background research. There's this company I want to look up . . . I'd do it using my mobile and my laptop, but that's such a slow connection it'd take forever and a day.'

As soon as she'd asked, she realised the possibility of Inez agreeing was remote. After all the secrecy and evasion regarding the members of the Enclave, and the identity of Emperadora, it was hardly likely that Inez would blithely agree to let Polly loose with any possible access to Chandler's Haven's hidden intranet.

'Why, of course, Polly,' said Inez immediately, her smile as open and as genuine as Polly could have wished for. 'I should have offered before. I should have realised that you'd need to look things up.'

Polly took a long swallow of coffee, and almost choked, before she could reply. 'Why thanks, Inez, that would be wonderful,' she said, still trying not to see an overlaid image of her companion with her legs akimbo and masturbating every time she looked at her. 'I can run a little program to check how long I'm on-line and work out how much it'll cost. You needn't be out of pocket.'

'Now don't be so silly, I can afford it,' said Inez, reaching for a croissant. 'What's this firm you want to look up? Will I have heard of them?'

Polly showed Inez the letter, and gave her an edited version of the circumstances leading up to it. She didn't think the older woman would have any high moral scruples about the issues of software ownership and theft involved, but Polly had come to know, in the last few days, that it was deeply foolhardy to make any sweeping and obvious assumptions. In Chandler's Haven, things – and people – were rarely what they seemed.

'Well, it sounds to me like a wonderful opportunity for you, Polly,' said Inez eventually. 'I think you should go up to town and knock their socks off. You never know what a meeting like that might eventually lead to.'

Polly looked up sharply at Inez, but her companion was calmly nibbling a bit of croissant, an expression of total innocence upon her lovely face. The nuance of archness Polly fancied she'd heard a moment ago must have been imaginary.

'Yes, I think I'll go . . . In fact, I definitely will,' replied Polly.

'Which is why I need to do a bit of checking up on E-Tech. As research.'

'I've heard of them before, I think,' said Inez suddenly.

Polly shot another quick glance at her. This was an astonishing development. How come Inez, the artist and self-confessed computer novice, had heard of E-Tech, and she herself, who was in the business, hadn't?

'They sponsored an exhibition I once showed in. Or at least they were *one* of the sponsors –' she grinned, triumphantly '– which must mean that they're totally bona fide!'

Yet bona fide or not, when Polly later came to search for Internet references to the mysterious E-Tech, she found herself thwarted at every turn in her enquiries.

First, and somehow very suspiciously, the modem on Inez's computer had suddenly stopped working. Polly was tempted to pull open the casing and fiddle about a bit, to see if she could fix it, but before she could do so Inez began muttering about guarantees and service contracts. Polly urged Inez to get the machine mended immediately, but in spite of a phone call, a computer engineer was not forthcoming.

Then Polly had difficulties with her own comms equipment too. First her batteries were dead, when she could have sworn she'd charged them; then, when she attempted to use Inez's land line, that went dead as well.

'It does that sometimes, I'm afraid,' her hostess said, her face a picture of remorse. 'We're supposed to be having new cables laid soon, but so far, they just never seem to get round to it.'

There were ways to deal with all these obstacles, but each and every one seemed long-winded and fraught with potential disclosure. Weighing up possible courses of action, Polly felt as if she were swimming against a heavy current, her limbs bound with seaweed. She could do what she wanted to do; there was nothing that wasn't unachievable, and yet the simple effort of making the moves seemed suddenly wearying. There was a choice to be made; she could thrash around madly after the information she wanted, or she could focus her energies on more practical preparations. In the end, Polly gave up and concentrated on preparing her presentation. She still had the deepest of misgivings about E-Tech and their supposedly irresistible offer, yet somehow it seemed she was being inexorably swept towards them by a force far greater than she was. And it only added to her gathering disquiet that Inez seemed bent on 'helping' her.

'I'll drive you up to London,' the older woman suggested, then paused, thinking. 'No, better than that, I'll get Miriam to lend us her Bentley and Francis for a couple of days. That way you'll be able to arrive in style after a comfortable journey and be right on the top of your game!'

Polly tried to gracefully refuse, but again it felt as if she were strapped in place on a down-stream log ride. She nodded to the inevitable when Inez offered to lend her a smart suit to wear to the interview.

There seemed to be no way out now of facing up to E-Tech and a reluctant return to London – so she might as well look as fabulous as she could when the confrontation came . . .

THIRTEEN

The Usual Suspects

Despite Inez's best efforts, perhaps even because of them in some ways, Polly's journey to London, to meet E-Tech, was fraught with tension. Even the quiet luxury of Miriam's spacious Bentley only served as a further goad to overwrought senses . . .

I should be preparing myself, going over my notes, answering every possible question in my mind, thought Polly fractiously. And what am I doing? I'm weaving fantasies about Inez!

The older woman was dozing beside her on the wide back seat, the neckline of her jersey blouse gaping open to reveal the promise of her cleavage, and her long legs were stretched out in front of her, slightly parted, the cloth of her loose trousers moulding their toned and elegant shape. In an effort to squelch the images such relaxation and vulnerability inspired, Polly stared outside at passing streets, which were wet and moodily reflective, due to rain. It had been a strange stormy day, heavy since first thing that morning with low grey cloud, and now that it was early evening the skies above were already dark.

Glancing at her watch, Polly saw that it was just after half past seven, but they were well on time and already within the city's sprawling periphery. Traffic seemed light, and Francis was clearly a navigator second to none. They seemed to find their way around hold-ups as if the Bentley were running under a charm. Like a carriage propelled by magic through a wild, hostile landscape . . .

Considering the looming, glistening angles of the buildings that seemed to flank the road as they sped along it, Polly had never seen London look so strange and unknown to her. It was hard to believe she'd only been away from it for little more than a week; but then Chandler's Haven was such an experiential overload that it was no wonder she could hardly remember being anywhere else . . .

The last couple of days had been quiet, though, extremely quiet. Thwarted in her attempts to find information about E-Tech, she'd worked steadily on polishing the presentation she would make to them. She'd seen no one but Inez during all this time, and even her hostess had behaved with perfect decorum and chastity. There had been no overtures, no invitations to sex – not even a sniff of it. Which, after such a feast in the preceding few days, was unpleasantly frustrating!

Unable to help herself, Polly glanced back towards Inez.

The neckline of the shirt had drawn apart even further now and, either artlessly or deliberately, the long, tapered fingers of Inez's left hand were resting against her throat, just dipping slightly beneath the fabric. Was she going to reach in and cup her own breast, Polly wondered, knowing now that such an act was far from impossible, as Inez's inhibitions, within the Enclave, were unbelievably lax. It seemed impossible now to believe that she'd once thought her old family friend to be prim and uptight. Inez was like every single other woman in the Enclave of Chandler's Haven, she'd discovered; which meant ready for pleasure whenever, and wherever, she had a whim for it.

As Polly watched, Inez adjusted her position, scissoring her long thighs as if she were restless, and casually, oh so casually, letting her other hand drop to the valley between them. Her fingers flexed, curved, and then shaped inwards to cradle her pubic mound.

Oh my Lord, here we go again, thought Polly, snatching a quick look towards the front of the car, to see if Francis too was observing the scene, via the rear-view mirror. It seemed not, however. The ambiguous chauffeur was paying full attention to his driving.

Inez began to shuffle a little in her seat, her head moving against the deeply upholstered rest, her tongue flicking out to lick her raspberry pink lips. She was gripping her crotch now, squeezing quite hard, and Polly felt her own sex grow heavy as if speaking to her in answer.

I can't be thinking like this now, she told herself as her fingers began to itch with the drive to follow Inez's example. And I can't start *doing* anything either!

But as with any case of 'mustn't' and 'can't', the temptation to transgress only strengthened as Polly tried to resist it. The slim, dark suit that Inez had provided her with felt as if it were enclosing her like a cage of iron pressing down on the surface of her body. Her crisp poplin blouse seemed to chafe her chest, her throat and her arms, and her fine silk underwear felt strangely prickly and oppressive. All of a sudden she wanted to undress, to be free and naked.

Polly imagined stripping off all her clothes then presenting herself to Inez. Better than that, she could jostle her bare body against her friend as she 'slept', surprising her with a delicious erotic gift. She could rub herself against Inez, take those long artist's fingers from where they nestled now – against the seam of Inez's loose jersey pants – and lodge them against her own groin, pressing them in deeply between the fleshy moistening folds.

Glancing down quickly, as if she were afraid of giving away her urges to an unseen watcher, Polly wondered if she dare slide up the narrow skirt of her borrowed black suit and briefly touch her aching vulva through her panties. There might just be time for a quick rub; an orgasm even, stolen at speed from between the teeth of the night itself.

She was just on the point of making notion into action, and pulling up her skirt so she could masturbate, when she realised to her horror that the Bentley was decelerating. Looking out of the window, she was astonished to discover that they'd apparently reached their destination.

They were in the centre of London, at E-Tech's exclusive address, and the first thing Polly could think of was how different it was from the headquarters of F&X, the firm she'd so abruptly abandoned. Her former employers had operated from an anonymous-looking modern building; a square grey lump that was singularly unappealing and characterless, and adorned garishly by the company's logo, which was already shabby after only being up a year. E-Tech, on the other hand, resided in a beautiful Regency town house, large and spacious with an exquisitely maintained and discreetly anonymous façade. It could have been the London home of a duchess, or a rock star, or someone with American, Japanese, or Arab millions. No one would have pegged it for the HQ of a computer company.

Polly had but a few seconds to prepare herself, before Francis was opening the door and standing ready to hand her out of the car. She felt dithery and flustered and, as she fumbled for her briefcase and her laptop bag, she felt her slim skirt rise up her thighs, and sensed the eyes of the chauffeur fix upon her with understated lasciviousness. He was wearing his shades, but his unseen gaze bored through them. Polly had a sudden mad notion that if his *faux* penis had been real it would've been hardening.

'Are we here?' enquired a slightly sleepy voice from beside her, and she turned to see that Inez was awake now and, within the space of seconds, had righted the abandonment of her clothing. There was no sign now of the dreamy languorousness that had captivated Polly just a few moments ago, and now Polly herself felt as if she'd been caught in the first throes of something.

'Yes, this appears to be it,' Polly answered, in clipped tones, wishing suddenly that she'd never kowtowed to the mysterious summons of E-Tech, and that she was back once more in the dubious safety of Chandler's Haven. Was it worth pulling out, at this late stage, and asking Francis to drive on, and whisk her away?

'Don't be nervous, Polly,' said Inez, placing her warm hand on Polly's thigh below the hem of her skirt. 'You'll do marvellously, I just know it. This is an incredible chance for you.'

'I hope so,' muttered Polly, astonished and angry with herself that she was responding already to the slight contact of Inez's fingers. This was no time to be getting horny or distracted.

'Have you got the card with Francis's number on it?' enquired Inez, more businesslike now. She looked as fresh and on the ball as Polly would have liked to have felt herself, and Polly wished for a moment she could have passed the responsibility for the coming interview to her.

'It's OK. H– he needn't bother . . . I can get a taxi,' Polly protested, aware that she was half stammering with nerves and her stomach felt fluttery.

'Nonsense,' replied Inez. 'He doesn't mind at all, do you, Francis?' The chauffeur shook his head, ever so slightly. 'Just call that number when your meeting's over and he'll come and collect you. Then we'll go back to my flat and we can celebrate your famous success!' Inez smiled encouragingly and gave Polly's thigh one last squeeze. 'Now go get 'em, tiger!' she said, then leant over and gave Polly an encouraging kiss on the cheek.

In a stark, clear instant, Polly saw a sudden picture of herself in bed with Inez, their bodies entwined and writhing, the sheets soaked with sweat. It seemed that Inez had somehow picked up on the vision too, because when Polly drew away, she said, 'We'll finish that later, my sweet, and with champagne to toast your future.'

And then the car was pulling away into the night, and Polly was alone on the pavement with her briefcase, her laptop and her terrors.

She didn't have long to endure them, however, as before she could move her feet – which felt as if they were glued to the concrete – the glossily painted front door of the E-Tech building swung open and a figure emerged, then trotted down the steps to meet her. It was a man, tall and slender, and perfectly and anonymously dressed in a black suit, white shirt and black tie.

'Hello, Miss Sayers, welcome to E-Tech,' he said, holding out a graceful, long-fingered hand to greet her. There was a strange familiarity about the way he moved somehow and, in the simple gesture of politeness, and as she shook hands, the hairs on the back of Polly's neck rose suddenly.

'I'm Liam. I'll show you to the meeting,' the man said, his eyes twinkling as he looked at her. He was very handsome, Polly had to admit, but any confusion in her feelings was instantly submerged in the renewal of that bizarre sense of a prior acquaintanceship.

Where the hell have I met him before? she thought as her greeter led her through the porch and into a sumptuous foyer that, again, looked nothing like the corporate premises of a computer company. The quiet sense of luxury was much more like that of the lovingly maintained residence of a wealthy private citizen, or perhaps the ambience of an exclusive private club. Under other circumstances, Polly would have been helplessly rubbernecking, taking in the glorious but understated décor and the so-obviously real antiques and pictures, but her nerves and the puzzling nature of her companion swamped her appreciation of the beauty of her surroundings.

Slickly taking her briefcase from her, Liam indicated that she follow him up a wide, carpeted staircase to the next floor and, as she watched him precede her, a germ of recognition began to flower in Polly's consciousness. She *had* seen him before and not all that long ago, and though she was right on the point of pinning down his identity, the last shaft of illumination just wouldn't come to her. When they reached the landing, and he turned to her again, she sensed she was right on the very edge of knowing him.

'You're a little early, so if you need a moment to freshen up, there's a cloakroom just over there, through the door in the corner –' he made a rather slow, mannered gesture towards the end of the landing '– and when you're ready, the meeting is through there.' In a similar movement he indicated a larger door, slightly ajar, just ahead of them.

216

Holy shit! Oh, shit shit shit!

Suddenly Polly had to get away for a minute, so, without answering, she grabbed her case and turned and dashed into the bathroom Liam had pointed to. She was glad to have her back to him, to hide her shock, because now she did know him!

Once in the bathroom – beautifully appointed, but she'd expected nothing less – Polly had to sit down on the velvet-covered chaise longue that stood against one wall. She was shaking and beginning to see white splodges before her eyes; all the symptoms of an incipient faint. Tipping forward she stuck her head between her knees and hoped for the best. She couldn't remember how many years it had been since she'd passed out from illness or lack of food or from shock, but she sure as hell wasn't going to lose it now when she needed all her wits about her!

Polly wasn't sure how long she stayed in that position, trying to get the blood to circulate fully in the numbed and befuddled halls of her overtaxed and disbelieving brain. She tried not to think, not to analyse, not to speculate.

What could have been two minutes, or twenty, later, she heard noises out on the landing and, feeling it was safe to, she sat up and shook her head slightly to clear it. There were the sounds of running footsteps, then a creaking door, and then someone laughing and murmuring indistinct sounds of apology. It was a woman's voice, and so familiar that Polly could barely believe she'd heard it.

What's happening here? she finally asked herself as she washed her hands after having a pee, and ran cold water over her wrists to cool her fever and calm her raging nerves. What the hell is happening here, and why is Violet's maid here, answering the door, in his male persona?

It was as if someone had moved one piece in a puzzle and the entire picture of it had started clicking into view. The smooth, handsome and only very slightly effeminate Liam was the same person who had answered the door to her at Violet Blackwood's house. He was 'Linda', the transvestite maid, and Violet's husband who liked to be fucked as a woman by a woman dressed as a man.

Smoothing her hair and checking her face, Polly wondered if she'd stumbled into one of her favourite television programmes all about plots and conspiracy theories. If Liam Blackwood was here, who else was here? What other familiar faces would she find behind the door, in the conference room? She hardly dared speculate, and yet she couldn't help but experience a bubbling, almost visceral rush of excitement. What other issues besides Sanspareil would be explored in that room beyond the door that had stood tantalisingly ajar? What new boundaries would she have to cross, and how much greater and more stringent would they be than those she'd already breached back in Chandler's Haven?

As she took up her briefcase and her laptop case, she experienced one brief, heartbeat-length moment when she considered turning tail and running from the building. Making the fastest getaway she could and leaving all the threats and the games and the shadows far behind her.

No. You've run before, Polly. Don't let it get to be a habit. Stay now. Face your demons. Face your destiny. She chuckled softly at her own sense of melodrama, then opened the door out to the landing and walked across to the other door – the portentous one – before she could stop herself. Without knocking, she threw it open and walked inside.

The room was long and softly lit, the night outside excluded by the type of heavy, floor-length velvet curtains she had seen in various other rooms recently. A gleaming conference table stretched away from Polly like a polished, highly hazardous runway, and at its far end were clustered the assembled company who awaited her.

And there they were, the usual suspects, all clad in black suits and white shirts that were almost identical to the outfit that she had borrowed from Inez. Like the Reservoir Dogs, however, those who waited all wore thin black ties with their dour yet sartorial ensembles – although one of their number, presumably the late arrival who'd just run in, was still knotting hers as Polly drew a breath and approached.

What could she say? she wondered as she scanned their faces as boldly as she could under the circumstances, wondering how much she really had to fear from this so familiar group. It made a weird kind of sense, she supposed, wondering why she had ignored all the connections and coincidences that were really so blatant. She glanced momentarily at the screen of a computer that stood on a portable side table, a single brilliant letter revolving slowly in the centre of a field of purplish-blue.

E.

E for E-Tech. E for the Enclave. E for Emperadora.

So which of you is it? Polly thought, scanning the five faces she now knew so intimately. The faces of women with whom she'd recently made love, in one way or another.

Severn, city girl through and through; Ellen, primally feminine in her tight skirt and make-up; Violet, a perfect, powerful businesswoman; Miriam, wearing the same clothes as everyone else, but still looking French to her fingertips; and finally Inez, who looked cool and unflustered despite the fact that she might well have thrown herself into that black suit just moments ago, in the back seat of the limousine.

'Why am I here?' demanded Polly, biting the bullet. She raised her chin defiantly as she faced them, even though her guts felt as if they were full of butterflies and elephants. 'Why have you brought me here and what do you want from me?'

Inez detached herself from the group and came forward. For a moment Polly thought the dark-haired woman was going to attempt to shake hands with her – which was ludicrous, considering how recently they'd kissed – but instead, she simply led Polly to a seat next to the head of the table, and close to the computer. As she did so, the others took their places: Ellen and Severn beside her, Miriam and Violet on the opposite side of the table. Inez herself took the seat directly opposite Polly, but the chair at the end of the table, which was bigger, more imposing and had a higher back, remained empty.

Emperadora's throne, thought Polly, almost dreamily. She wondered which of the assembled women would soon assume it. There was no doubt in her mind that the Enclave's matriarch was already in the room with them.

'We want you to tell us about Sanspareil, Polly,' said Inez gently. 'You've gone to such trouble to keep it secret and secure that, clearly, it must be very special indeed.'

'What do you know about Sanspareil, other than what I've told you?' demanded Polly, trying to rise to her feet but being effortlessly restrained by Ellen, beside her.

'In detailed terms, very little,' Inez went on, unperturbed. 'But as far as the big picture goes, I – or should I say we –' she glanced around smilingly at her companions '– know that it has all the great and the good in Silicon Valley gnashing their teeth that they weren't the ones to develop it.'

'But why should I give it to you? To E-Tech?' Polly persisted, looking at Inez, and wondering again if she was Emperadora. And that she'd been quietly playing a waiting game all along. 'It's my software, I can sell it to whomsoever I please! I can even set up my own company if I want!'

'I think you'll find that if you try to do that,' said Violet, seamlessly taking up the confrontation, 'that certain details of your resignation from F&X Developments will quickly come to light . . . and to the attention of the Metropolitan Police's Computer Crime Division.' She paused, steepling her plump fingers like the villain in a classic James Bond movie. 'And then, alas, Sanspareil will belong to F&X . . . again.'

Polly went cold, then hot. There wasn't a lot she could answer that gambit with. She was caught, here in the firing line, without options. There was no alternative but to give her presentation, just as if the circumstances had been entirely normal and she hadn't been facing a cadre of manipulative, sexually voracious women who had her exactly where they wanted her . . . for the umpteenth goddamn time!

But there was one thing she had to ask, even if the likelihood of an answer was small.

'OK, I'm ready to give my presentation, but one thing first . . . Which of you is the one called Emperadora?'

Five pairs of eyes exchanged arch, knowing glances.

'She isn't here,' said Miriam softly, her expression guileless as the lamplight glistened on her preternaturally white hair.

'Not physically, that is,' chimed in Severn, before Polly could dispute the fact.

'But she is aware of this meeting. And she can see you,' finished Ellen, from her place at Polly's side. When Polly turned to her, the dominatrix nodded to a fixture on the top of the computer, a small grey plastic globe with a lens on the front of it.

A webcam, thought Polly, and quite a sophisticated one too, given the less than ideal lighting conditions. As all the women watched, Ellen removed the thronelike chair, and Inez wheeled the computer stand around to the head of the table, so that the position of the camera was optimum for both observing Polly and for her to see the computer itself. The tiny active light was glowing in the base of the camera, and as the lens seemed to balefully observe them all, like the mad computer HAL from *2001*, Inez placed the infra-red keyboard on the desk in front of Polly.

'She can see both the room and the contents of the screen. So if you'd like to begin, Polly, it only remains to load your marvellous Sanspareil . . .'

Polly had planned to display Sanspareil on her own laptop, using a mocked-up demo of how it would operate both on a PC and out 'in the wild' on the World Wide Web. She knew that would not be enough to clinch a done deal with a prospective client or backer, but it would certainly be enough to get them interested.

But now it seemed as if she would have to compromise her own security measures or lose everything she'd worked for. The Board of E-Tech – or the members of the Enclave or whatever they really called themselves – had got her squeezed right into a corner.

'I was planning to run my demo first,' she said, although with some diffidence, knowing the women around wouldn't accept half measures or any kind of fudging.

'Oh, I think we'd like the real thing, if you don't mind,' said Inez lightly. She gave Polly a square-on look, then reached into a small equipment hopper that was slung beneath the computer table. From this she took a lightweight ear-piece which, sweeping her glossy hair aside, she clipped it deftly into place behind her ear. After a moment when she appeared to be listening to some unheard instructions, she spoke again, a smile of glee upon her face. 'Emperadora is waiting, Polly. She'd really like you to load the program now.'

Polly assimilated the implications. There was a webcam; presumably the table was miked somehow; and now Inez was taking directions from the unseen Emperadora. It seemed that the mistress of the Enclave was all but in their presence.

Or this could still all be a put-up job, and she's one of this lot, thought Polly, sliding the high capacity disk from its case and hesitating with it just a few centimetres from the appropriate drive. That would be a very effective mind game to throw her further off her stride.

There was no way back now though. No way out of this jam, and she wasn't even sure that she wanted one. Inserting the disk into the drive was like taking a massive jolt of adrenalin to her system.

'Sanspareil, ladies,' she began, slipping quite easily into her 'presentation' mode, despite everything, 'the ultimate integrated software solution. One program gives you access to the Internet, to your own intranet, to your own discrete desktop. As its name suggests, Sanspareil is without equal in flexibility, ease of use, and stability. It's forgiving and friendly, light on system requirements and long on adaptions . . . It won't crash and it'll do exactly what you want it to!' Turning away from her watchers, she executed the command to run the program, aware that once it was in a 'foreign' machine she no longer had total control of it. Just like me, she thought, in a strange land and open to the wills and whims of others.

The demonstration ran with perfect smoothness, and there was a part of Polly that recognised that she had indeed created something impressive. Something that had a true value that would shine right through all her presentational bullshit. If E-Tech was a real company they would be damned glad they'd got this.

But there was another aspect of Polly that felt completely detached from her program, and all the implications that surrounded it. She was being played with, toyed with, completely manipulated. She wasn't even sure that any of the women around this table had any interest whatsoever in computer software or its utilisation – even though they were clearly following her discourse and seemed to understand it all. Which was part of their game, she knew, because she herself was the thing they were intent on taking possession of . . . It was just a matter of time before they, and Emperadora, made a move.

'Impressive,' murmured Inez, after Polly had just illustrated one of the program's special tricks. 'But don't you feel rather hot just now. Being the centre of attention, and wearing that heavy suit on a mild night like this?'

Oh God, here we go, thought Polly, turning her attention from the screen for a moment, and looking first up into the webcam, and then directly at Inez.

The older woman was watching her closely, but there was a minutely distracted quality to her. It was suddenly clear to Polly that she *was* listening to instructions. Either that, or she was a damn good actress and was faking the appearance of hearing her mistress's sovereign voice.

'I'm all right,' said Polly stoutly, preparing to move quickly on to the next feature of the program.

'I don't think so,' said Inez, her eyes suddenly steely. 'I think you should undress immediately, before you proceed any further.'

'What on earth are you talking about?' demanded Polly, aware somehow that she was expected to make a last stand, and that Emperadora would value her more highly for a little show of defiance. 'This is ridiculous! It's bullshit! What has taking my clothes off to do with selling you a computer program?'

Again, Inez appeared to listen. 'It's about co-operation, Polly,' she said after a second. 'And if you fail to co-operate and follow a few simple instructions now, that would tend to predicate a general lack of co-operation, wouldn't it? A lack of commitment to our future business venture?'

Polly looked around her. The eyes of all the women were upon her. They looked hungry. Like a band of she wolves eyeing up a juicy piece of prey. She'd never felt more like a sex object in her life, not even with the most chauvinistic of men.

'And if you can't commit to E-Tech . . .' Inez paused delicately. 'Well, I think we're all aware of what the consequences of that might be.' Her lips curved into a small smile, and she glanced quickly from face to face. Each one seemed to bear a strong glow of triumph, and Polly sensed that Emperadora, whoever she was, was triumphant too.

And so am I, Polly thought in wonder, as she moved away from the monitor, her fingers drifting to the buttons of her suit jacket. I'm here, the centre of attention, with five beautiful women who all desire me, and a hidden mistress who's enthralled by me, and they're all hanging on to my every move. It's not Emperadora who has the power here, it's *me*!

Slowly she unbuttoned the jacket then shucked out of it, with a flourish, and hung it over her chair back. She was very aware of the brilliance of her white poplin shirt in the low light, and ran her fingertips over its lapels, before unfastening it. As the front panels flapped open, she sensed a sharpening of interest, a collective breath being drawn by the women in the room.

Thrusting forward her chest, so her lace bra was revealed by her opened shirt, Polly made much of undoing her cuffs, then unhooking the fastener of her skirt. She looked towards the webcam, lightly touching her breast through the pretty bra, then towards Inez for Emperadora's instructions. They would always come from that source, even if their suprema was already in the room. This scene was choreographed, Polly was sure, but that didn't bother her. She rather liked the idea. It was like being in a film somehow; a movie that was arty, continental, and very erotic.

'Remove your shirt, Polly, if you please,' said Inez conversationally, even though her eyes were bright, yet dark with lust. 'And then your skirt, and your slip, if you're wearing one.'

Polly pushed back her shoulders and let the shirt slip off her arms. She was about to let it fall, but then Ellen retrieved it. The tall dominatrix sniffed the garment briefly, then folded it and set it neatly aside.

When her skirt and slip had followed, Polly paused again, awaiting direction. She faced the webcam. She threw back her shoulders again, flaunting her breasts, aware that her nipples were dark and prominent through the fine weave of the lace.

'Oh yes, yes . . .' murmured Inez, chuckling softly at Emperadora's latest mandate. She turned to Polly, her eyes challenging and mischievous. 'Now take off your knickers, but leave the bra, the stockings and the suspender belt on. She rather likes those.'

Polly felt a moment of uncertainty, and an illogical embarrassment. Somehow the fact that she couldn't be totally naked felt like a greater degree of exposure. Her breasts and legs would be covered to some degree, and yet her crotch would be naked and openly available. The sense of indignity turned her on, though, more than ever. She felt her sex begin to gape even before it saw the light of day.

Sliding her thumbs into the waistband of her panties, she hesitated. The moment of truth had come – one of many, it seemed, just lately – and yet in spite of everything there was a sweet thrill in showing her pubis. With as much grace as she could muster, she stepped out of her lace knickers and in a moment of bravado handed them to Ellen to see if she'd do the same thing she'd done with the poplin shirt.

Ellen didn't disappoint her. She held the scrap of lace and silk to her face and inhaled deeply. Then when she put the panties aside, she smiled at Polly and made a salute.

'Perhaps we could continue with the demonstration now,' suggested Inez as if it were quite usual for the presenter to be clad only in brassière, suspender belt and stockings, and high heels. Polly tried to oblige as best she could, under the circumstances.

It was difficult though. Exposed as she was, she felt fundamentally eroticised. She couldn't concentrate on Sanspareil and its features; no matter how critical it was that she do so. All she could think of was her body, and how best to display it. All she could think of was having sex, in all its forms, and having a lot of it. Her voice kept wavering, and she felt in danger of fumbling the mouse, or hitting the wrong keystrokes. Her fingers seemed incapable of doing anything that wasn't stroking her own body or touching it. They jumped and tingled with the need to contact flesh.

The women asked questions, surprisingly cogent ones, given the distractions and the fact that Polly had previously dismissed most of them as being computer novices. It was clear now that they knew far more than she had ever given any one of them credit for. In her current state of mind, it almost seemed they were more knowledgeable than she was.

'Yes, this is all satisfactory,' said Inez eventually, when Polly had completed her discourse and was standing at a loss, and burning inside, her body in ferment. Inez's head was a little on one side – the sure sign that she was listening to Emperadora, or that she was determined to continue her façade. 'But now we must move on to the next part of the demonstration.'

'But that's it. I've been through everything,' Polly said, fighting an intense urge to part her thighs, jerk her hips, do anything to relieve her growing arousal. 'All that remains is for me to answer your questions.'

Inez laughed. 'The demonstration's only just begun, Polly,' she said gently. 'But if you wish, we can have some questions, if you'd like some?'

Polly nodded. Aching . . .

'So, any questions, ladies?' prompted Inez brightly, looking around the avid faces of the group. Polly felt a terrible dread of what questions might be asked of her, and yet at the same time she longed for them. For borders to be breached, inhibitions smashed, new, virgin territories explored. She felt like shouting, 'Come on! Do your worst! I can take it!'

Severn spoke up first. 'I want to ask Polly to do something, if I may?' She hesitated, seeming to think, almost as if she too were hearing the commands of Emperadora, even though she wore no ear-piece. Maybe it was she who was the matriarch, now taking control and putting an end to the charade.

'Polly, will you put your foot up on a chair, push forward your hips, and open yourself up for us?' She paused, then added, 'Please?' It was, after all, supposed to be a question.

Polly nodded again, and prepared to comply. Ellen obligingly adjusted the position of the chair and offered a strong arm to help Polly keep her balance.

Oh God, oh God, oh God, thought Polly as she tilted her pelvis and reached down to open herself. She felt Ellen's supporting hand on her back, unexpectedly reassuring and kindly.

Peeling apart her labia, Polly was astonished by her own juiciness. She'd known that moisture had been gathering, but as she opened herself to the air, and to multiple scrutiny, she felt her own lubrication drip and dribble down her thighs. Her slit was awash; she was a river of excitement.

'Dirty little girl,' murmured Ellen, in her ear, as Polly lifted her hand from her crotch, her fingers glistening.

'Push forward more. I can't see,' ordered Miriam, and Polly knew that all pretence of asking her to do things was over. She was their creature now, their plaything, their living fantasy.

Polly did her best to obey instructions, angling her body to accommodate her audience, and once again holding the swollen lips of her vulva apart so they could see her better.

'Delightful,' commented the Frenchwoman, apparently satisfied.

'How much do you masturbate, Polly?' enquired Violet. 'Once a day? Twice a day? Every hour?'

Not 'do you masturbate?', Polly noticed. These women assumed a degree of libidinousness that matched their own, an appetite that demanded constant assuagement.

'I – I don't know,' she answered. Should she be honest, or fabricate an answer that might please them more? 'Once a day, sometimes . . . Sometimes I don't do it at all. More often lately, though . . .'

'It's not compulsory, you know,' observed Inez, with a grin, dragging up a chair and affording Polly's vulva a close, almost surgical scrutiny.

Why don't you shine a light on it? Polly thought, momentarily petulant.

A second later, to her horror, Inez snapped her fingers and Severn sped away to a cabinet at the side of the room and came back with a Maglite. As soon as Inez had clicked it on, and carefully aimed it, the others clustered behind her, staring and wide-eyed.

'Touch yourself now, Polly,' she said, running her tongue over her elegant red lips. 'Show us what you do.'

Funk washed through Polly. She felt her mad, bad confidence leaching away, and her old fearfulness regaining its hold on her. How had she got herself into this? What had happened to her? To the old, sensible Polly who had lived such a normal life until . . . until . . .

Until a woman called Patricia Keyser had marched boldly into her life and changed her every preconception about her own sexuality.

Strange she should think of Pat now, when she was surrounded by the beautiful faces of her bizarre new friends. And yet, in truth, it was Pat who'd started all this . . .

'Touch yourself, Polly,' reiterated Inez.

'Yes, Polly, do it!' urged another voice.

'Go on, Polly, rub yourself! Give us a show!' encouraged another.

Polly quailed. Shook her head. She felt her nerve weaken, almost physically retreat.

'I can't!' she blurted out, feeling herself sweat, blush, almost begin to cry.

228

Inez seemed to look inward for a moment, then said, 'Blindfold, please, Severn.'

The blonde young woman sped away back to the cabinet and, when she returned, she bore a black velvet blindfold in her hand. Violet took it from her and fitted it gently over Polly's eyes.

Blessed darkness brought freedom and, paradoxically, a lightening of Polly's spirit. In the sheltering blackness, she could do anything. Dare anything. If she couldn't see the lewd act she was performing, it had no power to frighten or disgust her. If she couldn't see the ravenous eyes devouring her nakedness and her vulnerability, they weren't there. They weren't looking. It was all her secret.

Answering the call, the call of her own flesh, she greedily applied her fingers to her sex . . .

FOURTEEN
Emperadora

It was easier in the dark, but Polly's first efforts were still a little tentative. Her vulva was sensitised, yet she found it difficult to let go and give herself over to the joys of touch.

The women, however, helped her. Other hands stroked her body; other hands supported her, in position, so that she could concentrate. After a few moments, she was slicking her clitoris, finding her rhythm. And as she found it, all her qualms began to fade.

Massaging and circling the tiny organ, she felt pressure build in her and inspire the urge to move. Secure in the hold of many caring hands, she twisted her hips and thrust in time to her caresses, her feet waving as she felt herself lifted off the floor. She heard the rustle of papers, and the shifting of chairs and equipment; and realised that the women were rearranging the room, the furniture, and themselves. They were reconfiguring the environment to suit the needs of sex, not business.

Throughout the changes, Polly continued to finger herself. She could feel the distinct texture of leather under her naked bottom, and knew that she was dripping on the burgundy-covered hide that covered the table. There was a little puddle of stickiness gathering beneath her, and as she jerked and wriggled the sound of her squelching was grotesquely loud.

There were other sounds too. Freed by the blindfold, she felt at liberty to gasp and groan as the pleasure increased, and she could also hear the women moving about, whispering amongst themselves, and making unknown preparations about which she didn't care to speculate. A door opened, but she couldn't tell if anyone had left the room or whether someone new had entered it. As her vagina clenched in orgasm, she found she really didn't care.

'Enough of that,' said Inez softly, grasping Polly's hand and drawing it away from her pussy. 'We don't want you to peak too soon, Polly. The night is young, and there's a long, long way to go.' Polly felt her sticky fingers being sucked into the cavern of a warm, wet mouth, but for the life of her she didn't know if it was Inez's or not. Then the mouth was gone and her arms were held back against the table at either side of her, while more strong hands made her bend her knees and part her thighs.

And still the voices murmured in the background. Exposed and exhibited, Polly sensed they were discussing all the things they might do with her. Or *to* her. She was just their love toy now, a piece of art, her genitals accessible.

A few moments passed, and then she felt a blade passed beneath first one shoulder strap of her bra, and then the other. The cups were peeled downwards and then her breasts were naked too. A similar procedure dealt with her suspender belt, leaving it in tatters around her waist, her stockings sagging.

'What's going on? What are you doing to me?' she demanded, not feeling diminished by what was happening, but empowered by it. These women were worshipping her like a goddess on an altar. Her body was their talisman, the object of pleasure they all adored.

Someone craned across the table, and then a mouth possessed hers, the hot tongue ravaging. Simultaneously, between her legs she felt a great sense of pressure, and the advance of something hard and slippery against her vulva. While she was being kissed, an enormous dildo was being put into her. She tried to groan, but the woman who was kissing her simply redoubled her efforts and suppressed the sound of Polly's cries. All that managed to get out of her was a wet and muffled gobble.

It's going to split me, thought Polly as her vagina clung to the monster, and whoever was kissing her continued to rape her mouth with their tongue. Her legs were being held, and so was her face, yet she could tell that the woman who was kissing her was not the one who was holding her. The whole of the Enclave seemed to be involved in enjoying and subduing her. Indeed she could smell them all, smell a bouquet of their different perfumes; and not only the cosmetic ones, she could smell their bodies too.

There was also a strong smell of leather all of a sudden, but whether that was from the surface of the desk, or some other source, Polly couldn't tell. It was comfortingly familiar though, and somehow seemed to fuse harmoniously with the overpowering smell of cunt.

Another mouth replaced the one that had begun the kiss, but down below the huge intrusion remained inside her. Someone was beginning to move it now, rock it in and out of her, in a long slow rhythm, dragging on her clitoris. The tiny bump of flesh began to delicately pulse, demanding some attention of its own, but it was ignored in favour of her mouth and her overstretched channel.

And soon that wasn't all. Polly tried to protest, but still couldn't, when other hands began to play with her breasts and her anus. Her nipples were pinched and tugged, and she felt something narrow, hard and bumpy probing its way into her bottom. It felt like a series of beads threaded on a kind of stiffened string, and it was being fed inside her in a steady insistent push.

No! she tried to shout as more and more of the beads were insinuated into her rectum and the fingers that were playing with her nipples became more and more severe. She was being pinched hard now, very hard, and after a few moments the manual attentions were replaced by that of clips.

Polly bounced against the table, excited by the fiery clamping pressure that seemed to bite at the tips of her breasts. Half of her wanted to plead, piteously, for them to be removed, while another part of her, her heart of darkness, wanted them tightened and tugged and jiggled. Almost sinking into herself, she became aware of the same perverse element in her psyche longing for more clips to be applied, to the rest of her body. One each on her labia, and another, far more stringent, on her clitoris.

I must be going insane, she thought. I must be going crazy. There must be something wrong with me . . .

Yes! Yes! Yes, she cried out inside as she threw herself around in the many-handed hold of the women of the Enclave. The clips on her breasts dragged painfully with every squirm she made, the swaying dildo stretched her, and the beads jiggled and joggled subversively inside her bottom. She was being assaulted in every possible way, save having her clitoris tweaked, and her frantic body adored it. The happiest of supplicants, she sucked on the intruding tongue and invited it further down her throat.

The many-faceted stimulation went on for a while, and Polly felt herself become a part of it, as if she were dissolving in a bath of raw sensation. The more the women played and tantalised her, the more she seemed to want them to, and her clitoris felt as if it had swollen to four times its size. 'My clit! Please!' she managed to gasp, as one mouth replaced another in kissing her – but the only response she received was a soft and cryptic laugh.

As she squirmed harder, the one who'd laughed murmured, 'Patience . . .'

Then, as it had done before, the configuration began to change. The kisses ended, even though by now she was too breathless to protest, and between her legs she felt the dildo coming out of her. For an instant, just after it was gone, her cunt felt cavernous.

But just as she was about to gather her energies, and to start asking questions and making her own demands, she felt a rush of slippery coldness engulf her vulva. Someone was lubricating her, and really going overboard with it. What felt almost like litres of cool slick jelly was being poured between her legs.

'What is it? What's happening?' she gasped, then felt someone run their fingers over her mouth in a small soft circle. The hand that touched her was gloved this time, in fine grade latex, and she could smell the pungent odour of rubber quite distinctly.

Then, as she tried to suck the explorer, she caught the essence of another smell. It was leather again, the soft, fine hide of a well-worn garment.

'Emperadora,' she breathed, wondering if she knew her, then realising she did.

I *do* know you, she thought, smiling inside and suddenly deciding she would not disclose the knowledge. Her goddess would know she knew anyway, she realised happily. There was no need to speak; she could keep her joy inside her.

She was kissed again. A light, almost reverent kiss, a faint tracing of the echo of latex with the feather of a tongue. When the mouth had gone, Polly knew that the kiss, too, had been Emperadora's.

Almost immediately she was penetrated again, but this time by fingers, gloved fingers, in an unremitting wedge of three. The rubber-sheathed hand was fucking her, as strongly, if not more strongly than a man's dick ever would, yet the rhythm was slow and measured, almost stately. As Polly groaned, she knew in her mind that hand's intention . . .

Even though she was still being held secure against the table by the combined efforts of the Enclave, Polly pumped her hips to meet the thrusts of the gloved hand that possessed her. The sense of being stretched and expanded was glorious, better by far when created by living flesh than by the hard and mindless dildo.

Not even when four fingers went in, instead of three, did she protest.

'Oh please, yes,' she begged, wanting more, wanting all she could get, wanting the ultimate.

'Patience,' a voice in the darkness said again. It wasn't Inez, or any of the other dark-suited members of the panel, Polly realised. This time it was Emperadora herself who was doing the whispering, her low words an incantation of husky promise. 'This has to be done slowly, oh-so slowly, or I'll hurt you.'

And yet still Polly was impatient. She realised that there was a part of her that wanted the pain, that wanted the extremity and the completion of it. In essence, she simply wanted everything about this experience: good and bad. Bucking up wildly, she jammed her hips towards the hand.

'Go easy, young Polly, do as you're told,' said Emperadora firmly, stilling the hard phalanx of her fingers inside Polly. 'Keep still, and be a good girl and you'll enjoy it more.'

Polly stopped struggling and lay still, concentrating on the sensation of feeling the gloved fingers lodged inside her. Emperadora was experimenting now, flexing her hand, enlarging it, and expanding Polly's inner walls. She's making space, thought Polly dreamily, as her vagina yielded.

There was another period of inactivity, another plateau of preparation. Polly felt as if she had the sturdy branch of a strong young tree resting inside her, and though the penetration was still, the sensation also felt dynamic. Her opening seemed to caress the obstruction inside it.

'Do you want it, Polly?' the voice of Emperadora, her mistress, asked her softly. 'Do you want it all, Polly? Do you dare to try? Do you want it inside you?'

'Oh God, yes!' gasped Polly, craning up to kiss the mouth so close to hers. The woman allowed this and she was granted a small, delicious kiss.

The fingers inside her retreated a little, adjusting their angle slightly, and she felt again the cold slick shock of lubrication. Yet more of it was being poured over her cunt and the hand that immolated it. She was being slicked up; they were taking no chances: her sex was a river.

'Relax, my darling,' murmured Emperadora, and Polly sensed the woman gathering herself, and readying herself, both mentally and physically. Then the fingers swivelled somehow, and the whole hand folded, edging slowly inside her.

Oh sweet Jesus, it felt so huge! Panicking suddenly, Polly started to struggle. Surely she could not take the entirety of a fist inside her? She just wasn't big enough; she'd never had a child; she'd never really fucked all that much. Her legs began waving in the grip of the women holding her, and from her mouth came a series of agonised keening groans. Inside her head, the very fear itself screamed 'No!'

Once again, a mouth possessed hers in a voluptuous kiss; one that seemed to silence both of her voices, the inner and the outer. Unseen and unknown hands began stroking her body soothingly, while others firmly gripped her thighs, opening her beleaguered cunt wider.

'Relax,' said Emperadora again, more firmly this time, while between Polly's stretched labia, her relentless fist pushed forward, progressing. Polly still tried to fight, but at that moment a single finger touched her clitoris.

She did not know which of the women it was who was touching her. The finger was gloveless, and it was certainly not that of Emperadora, whose entire concentration, Polly sensed, was focused where their bodies met and melded. The stroking finger felt light as a feather, deliciously playful. It moved around in the smallest of circles, teasing and flicking.

In the velvet darkness, Polly experienced a shift of consciousness. Physical sensations seemed to blur and metamorphose. The extreme stretching – as a woman's entire hand began to move in and out of her – acquired a new, primal, almost sacred quality. It made her feel more than herself, more than just one woman; she was the entire female gender embracing and celebrating itself. She felt almost as if she had become both vagina and fist – and at the same time she was the assembled Enclave too, looking on and playing their parts.

And in the tip of her clitoris she experienced a pleasure of such intensity it felt like pain.

'Oh God! Oh God!' she chanted directly into the kissing mouth as the fist pistoned in and out of her now, and the finger that plagued her twitching clitoris continued to swerve and circle. In the blackness behind the mask, she could swear that she could see her orgasm approaching her like a great white wave; a front of flame whose progress seemed to strike off sparks.

And when the great wave reached her, Polly shrieked, her body convulsing . . .

'I didn't actually get away at all, did I?' observed Polly, sipping at the cup of tea, and finding it the most delicious thing she'd ever tasted.

They were in what she supposed was a hospitality suite, which lay behind one of the boardroom's mysterious doors, and the lights were low, the air was warm, and the furnishings luxurious. Polly was half sitting, half lying on a broad, cushion-strewn settee, and her bare legs, emerging from her robe, were partially entwined with those of the reclining Emperadora.

'No, of course not,' the matriarch said with a throaty laugh. 'You were, shall we say, directed to Chandler's Haven. It was no accident that you ran into Inez in the Tate.' She glanced across the room, and Polly followed her look into the shadows where Inez too sat sprawled on another settee, her body slowly writhing. Between her legs, Violet Blackwood's head bobbed and dived with enthusiastic energy. 'You were always intended to encounter the Enclave and join it.'

'I see,' said Polly, taking a thoughtful sip of her tea, then setting the cup aside on a low table next to where she was sitting. 'But wouldn't it have been simpler just for you to approach me in the normal way, back here in London? After all, we did work together, sort of, for a while.' She paused, looked across at her companion and, despite her curiosity and her need to know what had happened to bring her to this place and time and situation, a delicate plume of freshly born lust speared her belly and her clitoris. Her cunt felt as if it had recently had an argument with a hydraulic jackhammer, but somehow the sensation that she'd been pummelled was deeply pleasant. And with care, she felt that she could probably withstand another session . . .

Emperadora looked magnificent, as well befitted a woman of so many kinds of power. She wore only a leather shirt, unbuttoned and with the sleeves rolled up in a businesslike fashion, and her sleek thighs were flung blatantly apart as if to exhibit her blonde-furred vulva. From time to time, as she gazed levelly at Polly, she negligently touched herself.

'Now, Poll, you know that wouldn't have been nearly as much fun as doing it this way,' she said, adjusting her position and opening herself even more. 'The journey is equally as important as the destination itself . . . if not more so.'

Polly frowned, trying to make her sex-hazed brain make sense of what had happened to her.

'Do you still work for F&X then?' she asked, feeling her eyes bug as Emperadora casually began masturbating. It wasn't as if it was the first time she'd seen this, but each time the shock and thrill were just as new.

Emperadora chuckled again, a sound that seemed to play havoc with the pleasure receptors in Polly's breasts, clitoris and vagina. 'I never worked for F&X,' said Emperadora, inserting a finger into herself. 'I own that company, or at least I should say the Enclave does.' As she started pumping herself, a small, sharp gasp escaped her lips.

For a moment, Polly was immune to the erotic sight before her. 'But what about E-Tech? Where do they fit into the picture? Do you work for them?' It was all getting quite convoluted now, but she had a feeling she would soon be granted sight of the bigger picture. At least she would when Emperadora had had her fun.

'E-Tech *is* the Enclave,' said Emperadora, beginning to shift her bottom around as her fingers danced and played. 'And vice-versa. It . . . We own any number of companies. You've probably heard of most of them.'

As Emperadora continued to play with herself, and Polly continued to watch her, rapt, despite the astounding new developments, the matriarch reeled off a whole string of names of prominent companies. Polly's jaw fell open. E-Tech was behind so many of the major players in new technology and cutting edge science that it was almost mind-blowing, and their strongest bridgeheads were all in the arena of computing. Only one major name was missing, but it would not have surprised her in the slightest to hear it included.

'And what about, well, you know? The big Kahuna?' she asked, knowing that Emperadora would know precisely who she meant, despite the distractions of her own efficient fingers.

'Oh, that day will come,' the masturbatrix proclaimed, laughing and panting as she slicked noisily at her flesh. 'Believe me, Poll, we've got him in our sights!'

'I don't believe this!' exclaimed Polly, feeling her mind torn in two directions – the pull of lust and fascination of sheer astonishment. 'How can half a dozen women living in a small seaside town on the south coast of England launch an attempt at world domination of the computer industry? It just doesn't seem possible!'

'Oh, it's possible all right,' said Emperadora, still writhing. 'Although I think you're labouring under some misapprehensions about the nature of the Enclave.' At that moment she seemed to come, and her strong, beautiful face distorted wildly . . . There was an extended pause, then she resumed, her voice more airy. 'Tell her, Ellen,' she instructed the taller woman, who had sidled over.

Ellen sat down beside Polly, and as she did so Miriam and Severn joined them too. Inez and Violet were still deliciously engaged, but Polly had a feeling that they were peripherally following the proceedings.

'This group isn't all of the Enclave,' said Ellen, gesturing around the partially lit room. She was still wearing the skirt of her sharp business suit but from the waist up she was naked, and Polly experienced a sudden and powerful yearning to kiss her nipples. 'The Enclave is global, Polly. There are very, very many of us . . .'

'I – I didn't realise,' breathed Polly, struggling to take in the enormity of what she was hearing. She had run from one acquisitive corporation that threatened to exploit her, right into the hands, or should she say the arms, of yet another. As the implications whirled inside her mind, she barely noticed as a pair of gentle hands settled upon her.

'I must say that the women of Chandler's Haven are my special friends,' said Emperadora, recovered now and leaning back indolently against the cushions. 'They are the inner circle, aren't they, Ellen? The chosen elect . . .' She nodded at her dark-haired companion, who was even now pushing the protection of the robe from Polly's shaking shoulders. 'But beyond them are a legion of women, in many, many cities . . . And you of all people should know that communications aren't a problem, Polly. A simple e-mail or a video-conference, it's as easy as that.'

'What now? What happens now?' asked Polly, her voice tiny as Ellen took her by the shoulders and made her stand up, then forced her to her knees again. 'I suppose you want Sanspareil . . .'

'Eventually. Of course I want it, Poll. Although technically, and by right of law, it's mine already . . .' She parted her legs again and, as she did so, Ellen nudged Polly firmly forward. 'But right at this moment, my sweet, I want your mouth upon my cunt.'

As Ellen's strong hand pressed down on the back of Polly's neck, and the hands of Miriam and Severn began to roam her back and buttocks, Polly came to an instantaneous decision of simplicity and clarity.

She wanted to be part of the Enclave. She wanted what Emperadora wanted. And she wanted Emperadora. Right now.

She wanted this woman even more powerfully at this moment than she'd wanted her in the beginning – before she'd run, before she'd made her getaway from London and F&X.

'All right then,' she said, edging nearer to the fragrant sex that was the first one she'd ever tasted, the first one she'd ever loved and worshipped and hungered for. 'But after that, I want to talk terms. And I want to talk money. Because I'm not giving up Sanspareil for peanuts ... and ... and ... I want to be part of the inner circle myself!'

'You've got it, Poll! You always did have it. Now please, for the love of God, woman, get down there and lick me!'

'With the greatest of pleasure, Pat,' said Polly. After pausing only to smile, she plunged her face into Patricia Keyser's cunt.

SAPPHIRE NEW BOOKS

SWEET VIOLET

Published in September 1999   Ruby Vise

Violet is young, butch and new in town, looking for a way to get over her childhood sweetheart Katherine. And there are plenty of distractions in 1980s London, as the rarefied big-city dyke scene is both sexually and politically charged – full of everything from cosmic mother-earth worshippers to sexy girls in leather.

£6.99   ISBN 0 352 33458 4

GETAWAY

Published in October 1999   Suzanne Blaylock

Brilliantly talented Polly Sayers has had her first affair with a woman, stolen the code of an important new piece of software and done a runner all the way to a peaceful English coastal community. But things aren't as tranquil as they appear in this quiet haven, as Polly realises when she becomes immersed in an insular group of mysterious but very attractive women.

£6.99   ISBN 0 352 33443 6

NO ANGEL

Published in November 1999   Marian Malone

Leather. Fetishes. SM. The words conjure up a multitude of feelings for erotic fiction writer Sally Avery, for Sally has a secret. Despite her explicitly written prose, she is relatively inexperienced when it comes to forbidden pleasures. Frightened by the depth of her yearnings, she starts to explore her darker side with other women. Her journey of self-discovery begins in the sleazy, sexy fetish clubs of Brighton . . .

£6.99   ISBN 0 352 33462 2

PREVIOUSLY PUBLISHED

BIG DEAL

Published in May 1999   Helen Sandler

Lane and Carol have a deal that lets them play around with other partners. But things get out of hand when Lane takes to cruising gay men, while her femme girlfriend has secretly become the mistress of an ongoing all-girl student orgy. The fine print in the deal they've agreed on means things can only get hotter. It's time for a different set of rules – and forfeits.

£6.99   ISBN 0 352 33365 0

RIKA'S JEWEL

Published in June 1999   Astrid Fox

Norway, AD 1066. A group of female Viking warriors – Ingrid's Crew – have set sail to fight the Saxons in Britain, and Ingrid's young lover Rika is determined to follow them. But, urged on by dark-haired oarswoman Pia, Rika soon penetrates Ingrid's secret erotic cult back home in Norway. Will Rika overcome Ingrid's psychic hold, or will she succumb to the intoxicating rituals of the cult? Thrilling sword-and-sorcery in the style of Xena and Red Sonja!

£6.99   ISBN 0 352 33367 7

MILLENNIUM FEVER

Published in July 1999   Julia Wood

The millennium is approaching and so is Nikki's fortieth birthday. Married for twenty years, she is tired of playing the trophy wife in a small town where she can't adequately pursue her lofty career ambitions. In contrast, young writer Georgie has always been out and proud. But there's one thing they have in common – in the midst of millennial fever, they both want action and satisfaction. When they meet, the combination is explosive.

£6.99   ISBN 0 352 33368 5

ALL THAT GLITTERS

Published in August 1999   Franca Nera

Marta Broderick: beautiful, successful art dealer; London lesbian. Marta inherits an art empire from the man who managed to spirit her out of East Berlin in the 1960s, Manny Schweitz. She's intent on completing Manny's unfinished business: recovering pieces of art stolen by the Nazis. Meanwhile, she's met the gorgeous but mysterious Judith Compton, and Marta's dark sexual addiction to Judith – along with her quest to return the treasures to the rightful owners – is taking her to dangerous places.

£6.99   ISBN 0 352 33426 6

———————✂—————————————————

Please send me the books I have ticked above.

Name   ....

Address   ....

            ....

            ....

            .... Post Code ....

Send to: **Cash Sales, Sapphire Books, Thames Wharf Studios, Rainville Road, London W6 9HA.**

US customers: for prices and details of how to order books for delivery by mail, call 1-800-805-1083.

Please enclose a cheque or postal order, made payable to **Virgin Publishing Ltd**, to the value of the books you have ordered plus postage and packing costs as follows:

UK and BFPO – £1.00 for the first book, 50p for each subsequent book.

Overseas (including Republic of Ireland) – £2.00 for the first book, £1.00 for each subsequent book.

We accept all major credit cards, including VISA, ACCESS/MASTER-CARD, DINERS CLUB, AMEX and SWITCH.
Please write your card number and expiry date here:

....

Please allow up to 28 days for delivery.

Signature ....

———————✂—————————————————

WE NEED YOUR HELP . . .

to plan the future of Sapphire books –

Yours are the only opinions that matter. Sapphire is a new and exciting venture: the first British series of books devoted to lesbian erotic fiction written by and for women.

We're going to do our best to provide the sexiest books you can buy. And we'd like you to help in these early stages. Tell us what you want to read. There's a freepost address for your filled-in questionnaires, so you won't even need to buy a stamp.

THE SAPPHIRE QUESTIONNAIRE

SECTION ONE: ABOUT YOU

1.1 Sex (*we presume you are female, but just in case*)
     Are you?
          Female   ☐
          Male   ☐

1.2 Age
          under 21   ☐   21–30   ☐
          31–40   ☐   41–50   ☐
          51–60   ☐   over 60   ☐

1.3 At what age did you leave full-time education?
          still in education   ☐   16 or younger   ☐
          17–19   ☐   20 or older   ☐

1.4 Occupation _____

1.5 Annual household income _____

1.6 We are perfectly happy for you to remain anonymous; but if you would like us to send you a free booklist of Sapphire books, please insert your name and address

_____

_____

_____

_____

SECTION TWO: ABOUT BUYING SAPPHIRE BOOKS

2.1 Where did you get this copy of *Getaway*?
Bought at chain book shop ☐
Bought at independent book shop ☐
Bought at supermarket ☐
Bought at book exchange or used book shop ☐
I borrowed it/found it ☐
My partner bought it ☐

2.2 How did you find out about Sapphire books?
I saw them in a shop ☐
I saw them advertised in a magazine ☐
A friend told me about them ☐
I read about them in _____ ☐
Other _____

2.3 Please tick the following statements you agree with:
I would be less embarrassed about buying Sapphire
books if the cover pictures were less explicit ☐
I think that in general the pictures on Sapphire
books are about right ☐
I think Sapphire cover pictures should be as
explicit as possible ☐

2.4 Would you read a Sapphire book in a public place – on a train for instance?
Yes ☐ No ☐

SECTION THREE: ABOUT THIS SAPPHIRE BOOK

3.1 Do you think the sex content in this book is:
Too much ☐ About right ☐
Not enough ☐

3.2   Do you think the writing style in this book is:
      Too unreal/escapist   ☐   About right   ☐
      Too down to earth   ☐

3.3   Do you think the story in this book is:
      Too complicated   ☐   About right   ☐
      Too boring/simple   ☐

3.4   Do you think the cover of this book is:
      Too explicit   ☐   About right   ☐
      Not explicit enough   ☐

Here's a space for any other comments:

SECTION FOUR: ABOUT OTHER SAPPHIRE BOOKS

4.1   How many Sapphire books have you read?

4.2   If more than one, which one did you prefer?
      _____

4.3   Why?

SECTION FIVE: ABOUT YOUR IDEAL EROTIC NOVEL

We want to publish the books you want to read – so this is your chance to tell us exactly what your ideal erotic novel would be like.

5.1   Using a scale of 1 to 5 (1 = no interest at all, 5 = your ideal), please rate the following possible settings for an erotic novel:
      Roman/Ancient World   ☐
      Medieval/barbarian/sword 'n' sorcery   ☐
      Renaissance/Elizabethan/Restoration   ☐
      Victorian/Edwardian   ☐
      1920s & 1930s   ☐
      Present day   ☐
      Future/Science Fiction   ☐

5.2 Using the same scale of 1 to 5, please rate the following themes you may find in an erotic novel:

Bondage/fetishism ☐
Romantic love ☐
SM/corporal punishment ☐
Bisexuality ☐
Gay male sex ☐
Group sex ☐
Watersports ☐
Rent/sex for money ☐

5.3 Using the same scale of 1 to 5, please rate the following styles in which an erotic novel could be written:

Gritty realism, down to earth ☐
Set in real life but ignoring its more unpleasant aspects ☐
Escapist fantasy, but just about believable ☐
Complete escapism, totally unrealistic ☐

5.4 In a book that features power differentials or sexual initiation, would you prefer the writing to be from the viewpoint of the dominant/experienced or submissive/inexperienced characters:

Dominant/Experienced ☐
Submissive/Inexperienced ☐
Both ☐

5.5 We'd like to include characters close to your ideal lover. What characteristics would your ideal lover have? Tick as many as you want:

Dominant	☐	Cruel	☐
Slim	☐	Young	☐
Big	☐	Naïve	☐
Voluptuous	☐	Caring	☐
Extroverted	☐	Rugged	☐
Bisexual	☐	Romantic	☐
Working Class	☐	Old	☐
Introverted	☐	Intellectual	☐
Butch	☐	Professional	☐
Femme	☐	Pervy	☐
Androgynous	☐	Ordinary	☐
Submissive	☐	Muscular	☐

Anything else? _____

5.6 Is there one particular setting or subject matter that your ideal erotic novel would contain:

_____

_____

SECTION SIX: LAST WORDS

6.1 What do you like best about Sapphire books?

_____

6.2 What do you most dislike about Sapphire books?

_____

6.3 In what way, if any, would you like to change Sapphire covers?

_____

6.4 Here's a space for any other comments:

_____

_____

_____

_____

Thanks for completing this questionnaire. Now either tear it out, or photocopy it, then put it in an envelope and send it to:

> **Sapphire/Virgin Publishing**
> **FREEPOST LON3566**
> **London**
> **W6 9BR**

You don't need a stamp if you're in the UK, but you'll need one if you're posting from overseas.